"What's wrong?" she asked. "I just want to make sure you still want to get married. The nightmares might never go away. The flashbacks can happen anytime. I want to give you so much, Laura...."

The worried look faded and she wrapped her arms around his neck. "When you asked me to marry you, I said yes and I meant yes."

"I'm not the boy you met on the courthouse steps."

"No, you're not. And I'm not the girl you dragged away from trouble that day. We've both changed. I think that's what being married is all about—growing and changing together." She leaned back, worried again. "Now, if *you're* having doubts..."

"No doubts. From today on we're only going to talk about the future—not the past. Agreed?"

Dear Reader,

Every novelist writes a book at some point that is quintessentially "hers"—a book that reflects her life experiences in pure fiction yet pure feeling. I attended college in the late sixties and early seventies and was part of the Peace Moratorium Day that swept the country, especially on college campuses. As I wrote to a serviceman in Vietnam, I waited hopefully and fearfully for each letter from him. In 1969 my husband and I faced the draft lottery. My personal history led the plotline of this book so naturally that at times the emotional depth of the scenes and the memories that rushed back were overwhelming.

The Bracelet is a novel about how the Vietnam conflict affected Brady Malone's life. It is a novel about Laura, the woman who loved him deeply enough to be devoted to him for her lifetime in spite of what he experienced…in spite of the tears in their marriage… because of the bond with Brady that enveloped her heart the first day she met him at an antiwar demonstration on the town's courthouse steps.

This is a story about duty, honor and everlasting love that is quintessentially "mine." I hope you fall into it as deeply as I did when I was writing it.

Peace and love,

Karen Rose Smith

The Bracelet

Karen Rose Smith

TORONTO • NEW YORK • LONDON
AMSTERDAM • PARIS • SYDNEY • HAMBURG
STOCKHOLM • ATHENS • TOKYO • MILAN • MADRID
PRAGUE • WARSAW • BUDAPEST • AUCKLAND

ISBN-13: 978-0-373-65416-1
ISBN-10: 0-373-65416-2

THE BRACELET

This edition published by arrangement with Harlequin Books S.A.

www.eHarlequin.com

Printed in U.S.A.

ABOUT THE AUTHOR

Karen Rose Smith, award-winning author of more than fifty published novels, remembers the sixties well, along with the Flower Power signs, pop art and peace insignia on her college dorm walls. The spirit of those years is still with her today. She now lives with her husband of thirty-six years in Pennsylvania and often visits her hometown of York—the setting for this book.

Readers can e-mail Karen through her Web site at www.karenrosesmith.com or write to her at P.O. Box 1545, Hanover, PA 17331.

Books by Karen Rose Smith

SILHOUETTE ROMANCE

1348—THE NIGHT BEFORE BABY
1407—WISHES, WALTZES AND A STORYBOOK WEDDING
1434—JUST THE MAN SHE NEEDED
1455—JUST THE HUSBAND SHE CHOSE
1480—HER HONOR-BOUND LAWMAN
1492—BE MY BRIDE?
1506—TALL, DARK & TRUE
1523—HER TYCOON BOSS
1536—DOCTOR IN DEMAND
1577—A HUSBAND IN HER EYES
1591—THE MARRIAGE CLAUSE
1612—SEARCHING FOR HER PRINCE
1638—WITH ONE TOUCH
1692—THE MOST ELIGIBLE DOCTOR
1737—ONCE UPON A BABY...
1794—TWELFTH NIGHT PROPOSAL
1810—TO PROTECT AND CHERISH

SILHOUETTE SPECIAL EDITION

930—ABIGAIL AND MISTLETOE
1074—THE SHERIFF'S PROPOSAL
1426—HIS LITTLE GIRL'S LAUGHTER
1535—EXPECTING THE CEO'S BABY
1588—THEIR BABY BOND
1599—TAKE A CHANCE ON ME
1655—WHICH CHILD IS MINE?
1682—CABIN FEVER
1753—CUSTODY FOR TWO
1767—THE BABY TRAIL
1779—EXPECTING HIS BROTHER'S BABY
1797—THE SUPER MOM
1807—FALLING FOR THE TEXAS TYCOON

For those who serve.

For my husband—I remember our courtship as if it were yesterday…from our first kiss to the draft lottery to our wedding.

ACKNOWLEDGMENTS

With deepest appreciation to Vietnam veterans Richard Hoff and Clifford Gissell, whose input added reality to my research and my hero's experience.

With thanks to Philip Sweeting and patrolman Jeffery Leer, who helped me with research from autopsies to crime scenes.

With appreciation to Dee Wagner, for sharing her experience with open heart surgery.

With thanks to Edie Hanes, my critique partner and second set of eyes.

To Susan Meier, who realized what this book meant to me and understood my characters so well.

To Marilyn Puett, who gave this book that last critical look.

With gratitude to Paula Eykelhof and Beverley Sotolov, for the opportunity to write a story so close to my heart.

Prologue

"You've got to tell Sean and Kat what happened over there!" Laura Malone couldn't keep her voice calm, couldn't keep fear from beating against her chest, couldn't alleviate the turmoil in her husband's eyes.

After yanking off his tie, Brady tossed it on top of his desk. "Sean's going to believe what he wants anyway. He doesn't listen to anything I say. He hasn't for years."

Eighteen now, Sean admired his father. Yet in a way, that was the reason they disagreed as often as they did. Sean felt he couldn't live up to his dad's expectations. Kat? Kat adored her dad and would listen to any explanation he gave.

"If you don't talk to them, they'll hear the reporters spin the story. It might even make the eleven o'clock news. Sean could hear about it at baseball practice. Kat's been upstairs with her headphones on since she got home from school and is oblivious for the moment. But as soon as she comes down, she'll see the news vans and have questions." At fourteen, their daughter was always full of questions.

Anxiety and worry had arrived on the Malone doorstep with the evening paper. Laura couldn't believe the local reporter had dug into Brady's service records and then snooped until he'd found someone to talk to him. She couldn't believe he'd unearthed the details of what had happened to her husband thirty-seven years ago. Just because Brady would soon be honored with the York, Pennsylvania, Millennium Club's Man of the Year Award....

He was such a tall man, such a strong man, usually so full of energy, his blue eyes so intense and clear. As she studied her husband of thirty-three years, she realized he'd taken control of his emotions as he always had. He'd withdrawn and was hiding them from her.

He looked so tired. When he'd returned home from the office, he'd found the news vans outside and the newspaper article he didn't want to deal with.

Their phone rang insistently. More reporters. Probably Brady's sister. They'd had Easter dinner with her like a normal family yesterday. Today...

"The reporters can do what they want, say what they want, spin what they want." Apparently Brady wasn't able to check *all* of his anger. It edged every word. "The past is in the past."

That had been her husband's mantra for years. She'd never agreed. But she'd gone along because she loved him...because she wanted their marriage to be solid...because she understood why he wouldn't want to dig the past up. "I'm afraid that with all this Sean will start drinking again. We think he's stopped. But do we really know?"

Brady's angular face was tight with strain as he ran his hand through his black hair. "Sean's ready to live his own life. You worry too much about him."

Her voice rose in spite of her efforts to keep calm. "Maybe you don't worry enough! You think grounding him when he gets out of hand is all the attention he needs."

She hated fighting with Brady. Arguments during their marriage had been rare. But lately, they were at odds more often, especially over the kids.

"Sean needs to learn how to handle life on his own," Brady protested. "Once he goes to college—"

"Then you won't have to deal with him. Maybe if you did…if you faced the kids learning about what happened in Vietnam—"

As Brady turned away from her, she thought he was putting up his guard again. She thought he was going to shut down, walk away and—

Brady's palm went to his chest. One shoulder sagged and he collapsed onto the carpet.

"Brady! Brady," she called as if she expected him to lever himself off the floor and be fine. Then reality struck. She ran to him and fell on her knees beside him, shouting for their daughter.

But it wasn't Kat who appeared at the door. It was Sean, in his baseball uniform. His face was almost as pale as Brady's.

He rushed to his dad. "What's wrong with him?"

"I think he's having a heart attack." Shaking off her

panic, Laura felt light-headed. This man was her love… her life. She couldn't lose him. She *couldn't*.

Brady's face turned gray as sweat beaded his brow.

Strands of light brown hair escaped Laura's ponytail and brushed her cheeks as she laid her hand on her husband's chest. "Brady? Brady! Can you hear me?"

He wasn't breathing.

She almost panicked. Then she knew what she had to do. She directed Sean, "Help me—you know CPR."

She tilted Brady's head back and listened, desperate to hear breaths. She heard none. Checking for a pulse, she found none.

"I've never worked on a real person." Her son's voice shook.

Pinching Brady's nose, she covered his mouth with hers and blew until his chest rose, then checked for a pulse again. She still didn't feel one. "Start the compressions."

Sean knelt beside his father and did what he'd learned in a summer safety class.

After Laura administered two breaths, she stared at Brady, hoping for signs of life. Tears burned in her eyes as she thought about their argument.

"What's going on? I heard you yell—" Kat froze as she saw her father collapsed in front of the bookshelves.

"Call 911," Sean shouted at her. "Dad's having a heart attack. Call them *now!*"

She stood immobilized.

Watching Brady's chest rise and fall, monitoring Sean's compressions, ready to give measured breaths again, Laura fought for calm and said, "Kat, pick up the phone and call 911."

As Kat crossed to the desk, Laura breathed into her husband, knowing she loved him as much as life itself. She would do anything in her power to save him.

Chapter 1

Brady's heart attack was her fault. *Her* fault.

As guilt ate at Laura, she knew she had to be strong for Sean and Kat. She couldn't cry. But her abhorrence of hospitals had her trembling inside. This waiting room for the cardiac intensive care unit was supposed to be an oasis in the midst of mayhem. Outside of its walls there were shiny tile floors, glass cubicles, nurses clad in scrubs and patients the staff couldn't save.

Her first encounter with York General Hospital had come when she was twelve. Her parents had suffered a terrible automobile accident and they'd been brought here. They'd both died a few days apart. Early in her marriage to Brady, three miscarriages had been confirmed here. Their child who'd died of SIDS had been autopsied here.

She'd thought she'd learned to steel herself when she

walked into the bright atrium lobby, trying to wrap a protective layer around herself—some kind of barrier that would remove her from everything that was going on behind the doors, on upper floors, in operating rooms. But even as recently as last year, when she'd brought Kat to the E.R. after a skateboarding accident, she'd known she could never protect herself from what happened in this building. It had only taken her fifty-eight years to learn that.

Worried sick about Brady, waiting to hear from the cardiologist, she glanced at Sean and Kat, who were seated on the long sofa, still in shock and silent.

A white-coated doctor finally strode into the room. "Mrs. Malone?"

She realized so many of the doctors she saw in this time of her life were younger than she was. This one appeared to be in his forties. His brown hair, parted to one side, dipped boyishly over his brow. However, when she looked into his gray eyes, she saw the maturity he needed to do what he did.

"Yes, I'm Laura Malone." She extended her arm to Kat and Sean. "These are my children. Brady's children." She and Brady had gone to great lengths to make sure Sean and Kat never felt adopted, always understood they'd been specially chosen. Kat had believed them. Sean…

"Why don't we sit down," the doctor suggested as he extended his hand to her. "I'm your husband's cardiologist, Dominic Gregano."

Laura gave his hand a quick shake, then followed him to the love seat perpendicular to the sofa.

He waited until she was seated, then lowered himself on the cushion next to her. "Your husband had a myocardial infarction—a heart attack. We're going to do a catheterization at 7:00 a.m."

"To find out if there's blockage?"

His brow furrowed. "And how much damage. The cath will tell us."

He was watching her, and she wondered if he thought she might collapse. She couldn't with two children to think of, not with Brady and her kids depending on her.

There was only one thing she was concerned about now. "Is he conscious?"

"Your husband is on meds, but he's probably conscious enough to realize you're present when you talk to him."

"I want to see him."

"I know you do." His face reddened. "I mean, I imagine that you do. But I'm going to monitor him another half hour or so before you come in."

With Sean and Kat right beside her, she had to be careful with what she said and how she said it. "What if something happens in the meantime?"

"If it does, our staff needs to be with him, rather than you."

Regrets pushed at her. "I have to tell him I love him. I have to let him know we're here."

"It's amazing what our patients know without our telling them. Were you with him when this happened?"

"Yes, but—"

"Then I'm sure he knows you're here. A half hour seems like forever right now, but I'll be back for you as soon as I can." The kindness in this lean, tall doctor was evident, and she was grateful for it.

He was no sooner out the door than Kat turned to her mother and questions tumbled out. "Why did Daddy have a heart attack? And why were those vans in front of our house? I didn't see them until you yelled and I ran downstairs."

Laura was attempting to find the right words, when Sean responded first. "There was an article about him in the newspaper."

Kat focused on her mother again for an explanation.

How could she say *she* had caused Brady's heart attack? How could she explain the impetus behind their argument and the stress that had caught up to her husband after all these years?

"A reporter wrote an article about something that happened when your dad was in the service," Laura replied carefully.

"It said he killed people." Sean ran his hand through his spiked brown hair, looking miserable. "Women. And maybe even kids."

So Sean had read the article already. She couldn't talk about this without Brady. She simply couldn't. "We're not going to discuss the article or your dad's experiences now."

"Is it true?" Sean persisted in spite of what she'd said.

When she didn't answer immediately, deciding what to tell him, Sean asked, "Have you known all these years?"

She took a steadying breath. "I knew about what happened. But that article isn't the whole story."

That didn't seem to matter to Sean. He looked at her as if he didn't know her…as if she was some type of co-conspirator. Oh, to be eighteen again. To be full of idealism and passion and to be able to separate black from white. Yet she noticed something else on her son's face. Fear? Was he afraid his dad would die?

That was on Kat's mind, too. "Will Daddy be okay?"

Kat was beautiful, with her curly chestnut hair, her blue eyes, her heart-shaped face. There had never been any doubt that she was daddy's girl and would always be.

"This is a good hospital, with good doctors. We have to believe he'll be fine." Laura's fingers went to the charm bracelet on her arm, which she rarely removed. It represented her life and Brady's. It represented years of happiness as well as heartache.

Suddenly Kat jumped up from the sofa, as if she had too much energy trapped inside. "I can't stay sitting in here just waiting. I'm going to go get something to drink."

"This is a big place, Kat—"

"Mom, I'm fourteen, not four. I won't get lost. There are signs everywhere."

"We don't need to worry about where you are," Sean argued.

Kat went to the door anyway and said over her shoulder, "Then *don't*," and was gone.

A heavy silence settled over the room until Sean asked, "Do you want me to go with her?"

Her daughter was independent. Yet she *was* intelligent and usually acted with some degree of common sense. "She'll be okay. She has to let off a little steam. She doesn't understand everything that's going on."

"Neither do I," Sean mumbled.

"The article is something your dad has to discuss with you. If something happens to him—" She'd never intended to say that. It had just spilled out.

"If something happens to Dad, it'll be my fault. I heard you arguing about me."

How could he have— Then she remembered. He'd run in as soon as Brady collapsed. He must have returned home after baseball practice, seen the vans and heard them arguing. The most important thing was that he didn't blame himself. She knew what guilt did. Brady had taught her.

She moved closer to her son. "You are *not* to blame. The argument wasn't about you no matter what you think you heard. It was about the newspaper article. If anyone's to blame, I am. Vietnam is a touchy subject and I should have—" She stopped, not sure exactly what she should have done.

After a deep breath, she continued. "Sean, your dad had a medical condition we apparently didn't know about. That's what caused his heart attack. Okay?" If she repeated that often enough, maybe she'd believe it, too.

He stared back at her for a long time, then finally agreed, "Okay."

"The important thing now is to let the doctors do their job, then listen when they tell us what *we* can do."

She always felt better when there was something she could do. She'd always been like that.

Her fingers went to the bracelet again. *She* was the one at fault. She and Brady had made an agreement the day of their wedding not to talk about the past again. Yet when that past stood up and socked you in the face… Guilt gnawed at her anew. Why had she pushed so hard, when dealing with the article was her husband's decision to make?

Because the past still cast a shadow over him no matter how much he denied it.

Sean noticed her absently fingering a charm. Since he obviously preferred to change the subject, she let him when he remarked, "You've got a lot of charms on there. When did Dad buy you the last one?"

Her children knew the gold charms made her happier than any other gift. But they'd never shown much interest in their meaning.

She singled out a tiny ski. "The last one Dad gave me was two Valentine's Days ago. It was supposed to bring back all the memories from our winter trip to Vermont."

"The vacation I wanted to ditch?"

She nodded. It had been the vacation she'd proposed so they'd all have time to spend together as a family.

At first Brady had insisted, "I can't take a vacation now." As CEO of his own robotics firm, he could work twenty hours a day, get four hours of sleep and be perfectly happy. And more often than not, that was what he tried to do. But Sean had been having trouble in school because of his dyslexia. He'd become rebellious and needed reinforcement that they *were* a family. Kat had been entering her teenage years and Laura had known that soon Kat wouldn't want to spend time with her parents, either. Then to Laura's surprise, one day that January, Brady had come home early to celebrate winning a government contract and agreed they all deserved to get away for a few days.

She and Brady had slipped back to the chalet while the kids were taking a skiing lesson and made love in front of the fire.

"Which charm's the first one he ever gave you?" her son asked now.

Smiling, she pointed to two charms, both rife with symbolism of everything she and Brady had shared from the beginning. "He gave me the bracelet with the heart and the daisy before he went to basic training."

"You met Dad when he was home from college on spring break, didn't you?"

That had been their story all these years. And it was true. But it was a very small part of how they'd met. They'd never gone into it with the kids because their first encounter was connected to the memories Brady had of Vietnam. So they'd always kept their story simple. But now simple might not be enough. With Brady lying in intensive care, maybe it was time to break down barriers, even if she had to do it alone. Maybe it was time to let their children realize who she and Brady had been and possibly understand who they were now. They would only be able to do that with the truth.

Laura slipped back in time so easily that she could almost touch the daisy in her hair. Flower power at its finest. She could practically feel the wind whipping her long skirt around her knees as she'd stood with the antiwar protest line in front of the courthouse in York, in early April 1969—girls in everything from miniskirts and beads to guys with ponytails and beards taking advantage of their right to make their opinion count. Even more than that, they were rebelling against institutions they no longer believed in. All that passion paired with rebellion was scary, and Laura had shivered in spite of the warm day.

Although much of the protest against the war had originated on college campuses—she'd gone to business school for two years, then started working full-time—

everyone seemed to have an opinion. That day she'd worked until four at the Bon Ton department store, then had walked to the courthouse.

The underground newspapers at the coffeehouse along with the antiwar lyrics strummed on a guitar had touched deep chords inside her. Throwing off her fear of getting involved, she'd decided another voice might make a difference. This was her first demonstration and she was jittery about it. But she had high-school friends who were in Vietnam and she wanted them home. Why should they be fighting a war the U.S. could never win? Maybe didn't even *know* how to win.

She'd arrived at the courthouse steps, where about twenty-five other young people were gathered, holding signs, many wearing peace symbols. She had on a silver one on a leather thong around her neck. As she lifted her sign—it had taken hours to design it the night before, with its big blue peace letters and flowers around the borders in fluorescent shades of orange and green—someone started strumming a guitar, singing the Beatles' "All You Need Is Love." The song brought tears to her eyes. There was something rousing and deep-down wrenching about raising her sign, singing along, wishing and hoping she'd see friends again who hadn't been able to get college deferments and had gone to fight a war they didn't understand.

When she turned away from the musician toward the sidewalk at the base of the steps, she noticed *him.* She was on one of the lower steps, her gauzy sleeves laced with ribbons flapping around the handle of her sign. *He* was standing across the sidewalk, seemingly removed from all of it, observing, a bystander rather than a protester. Their gazes met. She felt a ripple of awareness dance through her.

His eyes were blue, his shaggy hair coal black and wavy. Her heart lurched. Her breath came faster. *He* stood a little straighter, gave her a wry smile as if to say, *It's a shame you're over there and I'm over here.* His stance was so optimally male. His gaze held hers as the protesters began chanting. Remembering why she was there, she joined in. Still he stood watching as she turned to face the courthouse. She listened to one of the protesters spout his views of the war, but she was still distracted by *him*.

When she slanted toward the street again, she'd half expected the man—and he did look like a man rather than a boy—to be gone. But he was still there, interested in all of it, with his focus returning to her.

She'd dated in high school. She'd attended her senior prom. She'd gone out a few times with guys from business school. But losing her parents and living with an aunt who pretended Laura didn't exist had made her yearn for self-sufficiency. In an era of girls learning that sex was fun, she wasn't so sure. Before she gave herself to anyone, she had to be certain they'd have more than one night, one date, one groping session to build on. Besides, she was Catholic and the teachings of her parochial-school days had stuck whether she liked it or not. Deep down, she'd believed in the idea of saving herself for the man she'd spend her life with.

Yet, one look at this man, one fall into his eyes and she felt all trembly.

The police had surrounded the gathering now, watching just as the wavy-haired man was watching.

Suddenly an old bus rattled to the curb. The front and back doors opened simultaneously and twenty-five to thirty more protesters filed out. The bus's arrival surprised everyone, including the police. The officers spread out. Laura heard one patrolman encouraging the new protesters to get back on the bus. But they were on a mission, even if they were late.

They shouted in unison, "Bring our boys home now!"

Then all at once, nothing was peaceful anymore.

As bedlam erupted, someone caught Laura's wrist. When she turned, she was standing toe-to-toe with…*him*.

"You've got to get out of here," he said, "or you'll be arrested. Or worse."

From demonstrations that had gone before at colleges and in other towns, she knew anything could happen.

He tugged on her arm. "This way."

Without a second thought, she followed him across the street as he somehow kept her safe from a station wagon that almost mowed them down. As they ran up the block, Mr. Blue-eyes slipped the sign from her hands and dumped it in an office doorway. They kept up their fast pace until he guided her around the corner where the public library stood.

Breathless, they stopped.

"Are you okay?" he asked, placing his hand protectively on her back, peering into her face.

"I guess." Her voice was shaky from everything that had happened—from running…from being so close to him. Yet underneath it all, she felt indignant. "We could have demonstrated peacefully." She added angrily, "If only everyone had just kept their cool."

"Have you demonstrated before?"

She shook her head. "No. That was my first."

"And your last?" His eyes looked a bit amused now.

"No! Absolutely not. I don't want to see anyone else sent over there."

"*I'm* going to be going over there."

She stared at him, dumbstruck.

He was six inches taller than she was, at least six-two. His shoulders were so broad. He was a stranger and she shouldn't have just followed him like that, but no one could tell her now what she should or shouldn't do. She was twenty and becoming liberated day by day.

Eager to know more about him, she asked, "When are you going?"

"I'll be called up as soon as I graduate."

"Graduate from where?"

"Lehigh Valley. I'm just home on break." He extended his hand to her. "Brady. Brady Malone."

His fingers felt so wonderfully warm engulfing hers. He didn't exactly shake her hand, but rather just held it.

"Laura. Laura Martinelli."

Ten more buses could have stopped at the curb and expelled demonstrators, but they wouldn't have noticed.

"I have a car," he said. "It's parked in the public lot. Would you like to go for a burger and shake?"

"That depends," she decided. "Will I be safe with you?"

"You'll be as safe as you want to be."

This Brady Malone was obviously a lot more experienced than she was. But instinct told her she had nothing to fear from him.

Nothing at all.

★ ★ ★

As Laura finished recounting the first time she'd met Brady, Sean studied her and asked thoughtfully, "So you just went off with him without knowing him?" His voice didn't hold reproach, rather surprise.

"Yes. But don't tell your sister. It's not something I ever want her to do."

"Don't want me to do what?" Kat asked, suddenly standing in the waiting room, a soda in her hand.

"I was telling Sean how I met your dad. It was at an antiwar protest."

Kat's eyes grew big.

But before her daughter could ask questions, Dr. Gregano appeared, a serious expression on his face.

Chapter 2

When Laura opened the glass door into Brady's CICU cubicle a few minutes later, she drew in a huge, bolstering breath. She felt so responsible for what was happening now...the condition he was in. The last thing she ever wanted was to hurt him.

Brady was hooked up to monitors, IVs, oxygen and a blood pressure cuff. The leads on his chest were producing the green lines—the hills and peaks on the largest monitor. He was so white, so lifeless, that she feared she'd lost him already. She was paralyzed for a moment, afraid to go forward. She'd been afraid so many times with Brady. But she'd covered it, and in acting strong she'd discovered strength—when he'd returned home from the army, when she'd tried to get pregnant, after they'd adopted Sean. Although when their baby had died of SIDS, *Brady* had been the strong one.

She only had ten minutes with him, so she dragged the orange vinyl chair to the bed. Nurses bustled in and out constantly. To have a few seconds alone with her husband, she'd have to talk to him now. Who knew what could happen next?

She covered his hand, the one without the IV line, with hers. He was cool to the touch, not at all like the man who always emanated heat. He could be hot in the dead of winter, when her hands and nose were usually cold.

"Brady," she whispered.

When there was no response, she cleared her throat and said his name again, louder.

His eyes fluttered but didn't open.

"Brady, it's Laura. I'm so sorry. I never should have pushed you—" Her voice broke. Regaining her composure, she said, "I love you. You have to fight. You can't let anything happen now. I want to be married to you for another thirty-three years."

She kept talking. "Soon the doctors will determine exactly what's wrong. You have to cooperate with them. You have to fight to get well. Kat and Sean and I need you."

"Sean," Brady mumbled, then drifted off again.

"Brady?"

He appeared oblivious to her presence. She understood his body needed rest, but *she* needed all the time with him she could get. With a lump in her throat, she stroked back her husband's hair. Although it had silvered at the temples over the years, it hadn't gotten any thinner. She loved running her fingers through it. She'd loved him from the moment she'd met him. Definitely from that first night when they'd gone to dinner and talked.

* * *

After Brady had rescued her from the protest demonstration, they'd walked to the public lot where his car had been parked. The blue Camaro was shiny and new.

"Wow!" she'd said, impressed. "Nice car."

"I just got it last week. The old one broke down when I was driving home from school."

He was dressed in bell-bottom jeans and a knit shirt, but from the way Brady Malone spoke and acted, she'd expected he'd come from a middle-class home. Now she knew he was probably upper middle class. "Did you buy the car yourself?"

"I work summers on my dad's construction sites. But I have to admit, he helped with this. Bottom line is, he and Mom don't want to drive me back and forth to school. And I'll need a car eventually. It'll sit in the garage when I'm away, but I think my dad wanted something tangible of mine that he could take care of. Sort of like he's doing something for me."

She hated the fact that this man was leaving the U.S. to risk his life in a war everyone was confused about, a war that took up so much of the news and caused controversy. "You might not go. More troops could be pulled out. You could get a medical deferment."

"Nothing's wrong with me," he told her over the hood of the car.

She saw the truth of it in his eyes. Her heart pounded every time she looked at him. How could that be when she'd known him such a short time?

"Where do you live?" he asked.

Now she went on alert. "Why do you need to know?"

"We could get something to eat near wherever you live, then I could drop you off at home." Studying her face, his gaze lingering on the daisy over her temple, he suggested almost casually, "On the other hand, if you're afraid to ride in the car with me, if you think I'm going to take advantage of you, I can walk you to the bus stop."

He seemed annoyed that she would even consider he wasn't a man with a fine reputation. That bit of arrogance wasn't unattractive. "Where do *you* live?" she asked.

"So you can seek vengeance if I don't behave?" Now he grinned and the annoyance was gone.

That smile. With it, he could become president of the United States. Or join a rock band. "I'm keeping my options open."

He laughed. "I live behind the hospital."

Those were nice homes, and reinforced her feeling that this man might be out of her league. "I live in Elmwood—Third Avenue. Half a house." She wanted to make it clear she didn't come from one of the large homes on the boulevard or even in the nicer single-family dwellings on Fourth Avenue.

"We can go to the Sportsman Diner."

The restaurant was close to Third Avenue. "They have more than burgers and fries."

He gave her another one of those long appraisals. "I think you could use more than burgers and fries."

"Hey, if you don't like the way I look—"

"I didn't say that." His voice had a sensual *I'm interested* quality to it.

She was skinny and her legs were long. That was why

she preferred skirts that fell below her calves. Her tummy tumbled as her gaze met his again. What *was* she doing?

Suddenly he came around to her side of the car and opened the door. The gesture was his personal invitation. She couldn't resist it. She couldn't resist him. She slid into the low, blue vinyl bucket seat, and when he closed her door, a happy feeling warmed her.

Over the next hour, they'd eaten and gotten to know each other. They'd stayed away from discussing the demonstration and the war, sensing they were on opposite sides, if not by belief then by circumstance. She loved listening to Brady's deep voice. She liked studying his interesting face with the slight bump on his nose, the scar along the right side of his mouth, the beard line growing darker on his jaw.

It distracted her so. She yearned to touch it. Instead she tried to focus her mind on the conversation.

"So your parents were killed when you were twelve?" he asked, finishing a slice of coconut cake.

When she nodded, an old weight filled her heart. The deep cavern of missing would never have a bottom no matter how many years passed. "Yes, and my aunt Marcia took me in. It wasn't a free choice. She was my only relative. She let me live with her because she knew I wouldn't give her any trouble."

"That's not a reason to take in a child who's lost her parents."

"It's been okay. I'm hoping by next year to be promoted to department manager. When I get that jump in salary, I can rent my own apartment."

He reached across the table, and she thought he was going to take her hand. But he backed off. "You've been through some tough times. I can't imagine only having an aunt for family. I have two younger brothers and a younger sister. I always have family around. Holidays at our house are wild."

"Holidays at my aunt's are quiet. In fact, she went away over Christmas and I spent it with a friend." Laura mentioned it as if it was no big deal. The truth was, she'd had a great time with her best high-school friend and her mother, better than she would have had with her aunt. But she longed for a family of her own. More than anything, she wanted to be a mother. But she couldn't tell Brady that. Not yet. Maybe someday.

They talked until the restaurant emptied, asking for refills on coffee to occupy the waitress. They had so much to say. All the while Brady had gazed at her with a focus she'd never felt from a man. They listened to much of the same music, and after dinner when "Aquarius" played on the car radio as he drove through Elmwood, they sang along—"Let the sunshine in."

Laura loved the unselfconscious way she felt around Brady. It was as if she'd known him for years instead of hours. Her sixth sense told her he wasn't leading her on.

After he drove down her street and she pointed out her house, he parked at the curb, then came around to the passenger side and opened the door for her. She was terrifically aware of him as they walked up the path to the three concrete steps.

"Is your aunt strict?" he asked. "I mean, does she expect you home at a certain time?"

Laura checked her watch. "My aunt spends Saturday nights with friends. She won't be home for a while."

A corner of his lips quirked up. "Does that mean you're going to invite me in?"

"I shouldn't."

"You shouldn't have been involved in an antiwar demonstration that could have landed you in jail," he muttered, obviously disappointed with her answer.

"I stand up for what I believe in," she replied quietly. He'd better understand that about her.

The porch light her aunt had left on backlit him. After a thoughtful pause and a frown, he stared into her eyes. "Do you believe we should get to know each other better?"

She was feeling too much already and realized she should be smart. "If you're going into the service, is there any point?"

Moving closer to her then—just a step, yet it seemed to cover a mile—he enveloped her hands with his. "It would be nice to have someone to write to, someone who mattered."

"You don't have anyone who matters?"

"I have my parents, sister and brothers. But family is one thing—a pretty girl with a flower in her hair another."

Laura had nosy neighbors. An older couple sat on a porch a few doors down, and who knew how many other neighbors had noticed them.

Pulling one hand from Brady's, she took a key from her pocket. Still holding his hand, she tugged him up the steps onto the porch and to the door. Then she unlocked the door and pushed it open.

The living room was unremarkable, and Brady would probably consider it plain. The low-pile carpet and flowered upholstered furniture were ordinary.

But Brady didn't seem to care. He put his arms around her and drew her toward him. "Do you believe in free love?"

The heat and hunger in his eyes sparked a like response in her. But she wasn't going to be foolish. "Love isn't free."

Her conclusion made his brows raise. "You've learned that already?"

She nodded. "I have a friend who sleeps with every guy who asks her out. She's not happy. I have another friend who's saving herself for marriage. And she's not happy, either. Neither is her boyfriend."

A slow smile slipped across Brady's lips. "So what's your philosophy?"

"I don't have one. I just know I have to be careful, I have to be cautious and I have to be sure that whatever I do is right for *me*."

"Of all the girls I could have found at the demonstration, I had to choose one with common sense."

Although she smiled, she asked, "Is that why you were there? To find a date?"

His expression sobered. "No. I'm not sure *why* I was there. I guess I had to get a feel for both sides. I wanted to know that going to fight over there was the right thing for me to do."

"Is it?"

"Yes. My dad said he has a friend who could pull strings so I don't get sent to Nam. That's what my mother wants. But I can't let him do that. I have a classmate who came back without his leg. I have to help finish what the guys before us started." His sober expression changed. "But in the meantime—"

He was waiting for some sign from her that they should take whatever was happening between them further, that she wouldn't back away.

She pictured him in uniform, imagined him leaving, thought about him fighting in a war he felt he had a duty to fight. In spite of the warning voice in her head, she let her fingers follow her heart. She lifted her hand and traced a line down the side of Brady's face. She felt his jaw tense and his body go taut.

Her caress was obviously the sign he'd wanted. He kissed her until she was dizzy.

Eventually he murmured, "I'd better go. When can I see you again? I'm going back to school tomorrow night, but I can pick you up after church and you can meet my family."

"Won't they mind if I barge in?"

"They won't mind. You can stay for dinner. Mom cooks enough for an army."

"Oh, Brady, I don't know. You're just going to take me home—?"

"Yeah, I am, unless you'd rather not meet everyone."

All day this man had projected confidence and self-assurance, but now he seemed uncertain. "Unless you'd rather I just go back to college and forget today ever happened."

"No! I *want* to see you again. And I'd like to meet your family. But I don't want to feel like an intruder."

"You won't." He removed the daisy from her hair. "I

think you might need to replace this tomorrow. This one looks as though it's had a long day."

She laughed and it felt so good.

He laughed, too, hugged her and then kissed her again.

With effort, Brady opened his eyes and became aware of his surroundings in CICU. Laura was stroking his hair. She loved to touch. She'd always loved to touch.

Laura.

She'd stood by him through everything. And now she'd probably saved his life. *More* that he owed her.

An oxygen tube was at his nose. He moistened his dry lips. "What happens next?"

"Brady. I'm so sorry. I shouldn't have pushed you—"

Pushed him to tell the kids. To tell Kat, whom he'd never had a problem loving. But most of all to explain to Sean. Laura had loved their son from the moment he'd been settled in her arms by the caseworker. His own lack of response to his adopted son had made her especially protective of the child she'd loved instantly.

"It's okay," he managed to say hoarsely. His mouth was so dry. "Did you do CPR? I thought I heard a medic say you did."

"Sean and I did."

"I guess I might not make that Orioles game," he said, trying to joke. She'd gotten him tickets for the Orioles third home game for their anniversary.

"Maybe not that game. But another one soon."

Laura's forced optimism wasn't going to do either of them much good if he didn't pull through this. "You were right," he murmured.

"About what?"

Right about driving himself too hard, working too much, caring little about his health as long as he'd gotten everything done in a day that he'd planned. "I should have signed up for that gym membership you suggested." He attempted to give her a smile but didn't quite pull it off.

She looked surprised, as if that wasn't what she'd expected.

Keep it on the surface, he warned himself. *Don't make matters worse.* "What happens next?" he asked again.

"You have a catheterization in the morning. Till then, you need to rest. Don't think about anything you shouldn't."

Like reporters in their front yard? Like the condemnation he'd surely see in Sean's eyes after his son read the article?

Don't think about it. Bury it. Like the past.

As Brady floated in a fuzzy haze, he knew he wasn't going to dig everything up again. It didn't matter what anybody thought, including his son. As he'd told Laura, Sean would prefer to believe the worst. If they just let everything die down—

Today's news was tomorrow's garbage. Vietnam was old news. He was not going to unearth memories better off left buried, unearth feelings so claustrophobic they choked him.

His heart was beating harder. Laura wasn't quite in focus....

The sliding glass door opened and a nurse hurried in. "Ten minutes are up," she said kindly. "But you can return in an hour."

"Our son or daughter will be visiting then."

Brady squeezed her hand. "*You* come back."

"It's important the kids see you."

"Kat," he agreed.

"Sean, too. It'll be okay, Brady. I promise."

Okay? He didn't believe that for a minute.

Laura leaned over and kissed him gently on the lips.

He was almost relieved when she left. Closing his eyes, he willed his heart not to hurt any more than it already did.

Chapter 3

When his mom entered the waiting room, Sean stopped pacing. "What's going on?" he asked, anxious to know his dad was still alive. No matter what his mom said, his dad's collapse was his fault.

She mustered up a little smile. "Your father opened his eyes a couple of times and he even talked to me. We have to believe he's strong enough to pull through. He's going to need our support and—"

"Aunt Pat!" Kat jumped up from the sofa where she'd been paging through a magazine and ran to her aunt. "Did you hear? Dad had a heart attack!"

In the doorway Pat put her arms around her niece and gave her a long hug. At the same time, she glanced at Laura. "Has anything changed since you called me? I just got your message."

Aunt Pat, his dad's sister, was a real estate agent. Divorced, she'd never had kids, but she was nice enough, even if she did have silicone boobs and sprayed hair. She was supernice to Kat, had even invited her on a shopping trip to New York last summer. She'd given *him* a hundred dollars his last birthday, and that was way cool.

"He's scheduled for a catheterization at 7:00 a.m.," his mother responded.

"Can anyone visit him?"

"Ten minutes on the hour."

"I won't take that time away from you. He'll know I'm pulling for him. I always have."

Sean wondered what that meant. The realization dawned that he really didn't know a lot about his parents—not really. Apparently they had secrets.

"If you're going to be here through the night, I can drive the kids back to your place and stay with them until morning if you'd like," his aunt offered.

Sean didn't have to be told that a heart cath was serious stuff. "I'm not leaving. I'll stay here."

Aunt Pat studied him as if he were a kid. "There's nothing you can do here."

"I'm staying." When he checked with his mother, he saw she understood.

She understood a lot of things his dad didn't. But even his mom couldn't imagine everything he kept inside. He was a disappointment to his parents. He'd never lived up to their expectations. Until he'd been diagnosed with dyslexia, his dad had thought he was lazy, that he didn't care, that he didn't try. After all, he wasn't their *real* son. Their real son had died, and his father would never forget that. When he looked at him, Sean always felt small, as if he'd never measure up. Maybe he wouldn't.

After all, his biological mother had given him away. He'd had the guts to finally ask questions when he was around ten. He'd learned she couldn't care for him, and she hadn't even known who his father was! He had no desire to find her or meet her. He had a mother. He didn't need another one. And since his father's identity was a mystery... Brady Malone was his dad and they were stuck with each other.

"Mom, should I go with Aunt Pat?" Kat asked.

"That's up to you, honey. You'll only be five to ten minutes away. I can call if anything happens."

"What do you mean if anything happens?" Kat sounded afraid. "Dad's not going to *die.* He'll be all right, won't he? You said he will."

Laura went to Kat now, too, and draped an arm around her shoulders. "We have to believe he will."

Sean felt as if he were standing in the middle of nowhere, all alone, the way he always was.

Kat's eyes were wet now and tears dripped down her face. "I don't want to stay here. I don't want to smell these awful smells and see all these sick people."

Usually he tolerated his sister. But sometimes... "You're such a spoiled brat," Sean muttered before he could help himself.

Kat's "I am *not*" protest and Laura's warning "Sean" hit the air at the same time.

Aunt Pat held her hand up like a referee. "Whoa, everyone. Take a deep breath. Kat, it's okay if you don't like the hospital. I don't, either. If you come home with me, we'll gather some things for your dad, your mom and Sean. Was this about the article?" she asked, staring at his mom as if what had appeared in the paper was no secret to her.

"Yes," his mother said softly. "Don't answer the phone if it rings. I'll sort through the messages eventually."

Aunt Pat gave a knowing nod, clasped Kat by the elbow and led her down the hall.

After a few seconds of silence, his mom suggested, "Try to be a little understanding with your sister right now. She's only fourteen."

"And most of the time she acts like ten."

His mom's face was drawn as she told him, "We all have our own way of coping. Yours and Kat's are different."

His way of coping started with shots from those bottles in the toolshed. "How do *you* cope, Mom? How have you coped all these years knowing what Dad did? How have you lived with that?"

He hadn't meant to bring the matter up again now, but the questions were doing a slow burn in his stomach. Gary had shown him the article in the paper at baseball practice. Maybe his dad's heart attack *was* really about the article being published. But what did *he* have to do with that?

"Was that article in the paper true or was it a lie? *Did* he kill women and kids?"

For once in her life his mother was at an absolute loss for words. Finally she answered him. "I know you need to talk about this. I know you have questions. But there are two sides to every story and you have to hear your father's."

Maybe a part of him was glad this had happened. Maybe a part of him wanted to kick the pedestal out from under his dad's feet. But another part…

Sean suddenly realized Kat wouldn't be here and *he'd* have to visit his dad alone. Panicked, he asked, "What am I going to say when I go in to see Dad?"

"You don't have to say anything. Just *be* with him. Let him know you're there. If you do want to talk, just tell him you're sure he can fight through this."

When his mom's voice cracked, Sean felt something breaking inside him. He glanced away and told himself his dad would be all right. His dad *had* to be all right.

As the monitors beeped, Brady floated, trying not to think or even feel. There had been times over the years when he'd blocked out all feeling. In Nam, for sure. As well as after he returned home. After Laura's miscarriages. After Jason died—

He didn't want to go there.

He wished there was a clock in the cubicle. But doctors probably thought patients shouldn't think about time or count the minutes until their next visitor. Would Laura come back? Or would Sean or Kat visit?

In spite of his struggling to stay in the here and now, his mind wandered. To the day he and Laura had moved into their first house—one with a mortgage instead of a landlord. She'd discovered she was pregnant one week and they'd found the split level the next. They'd been so happy…so ready to prepare a nursery.

But then he'd returned home from work one night and—

"Laura! Laura, are you home?" he'd called as he'd set

his briefcase in the kitchen. There was no answer. Yet her purse sat on the counter.

Returning to the living room, he called up the short flight of stairs. "Laura."

A sixth sense urged him to climb them, even though she didn't call back. At the top of the stairs he heard her crying coming from the bathroom.

Rushing in, he found her on the floor by the bathtub, with blood on her white summer dress. "Sweetheart, what's wrong? What happened?"

She was sobbing now. "I lost our baby. Oh, Brady. I lost our baby."

He had to get her medical attention. But her tear-stained cheeks, the sense of loss in her eyes, had him holding her and rocking her. "It's okay. It's okay. We'll have another baby."

"I wanted this one. I *wanted* this child. What if I can't get pregnant again?"

"You're young and healthy. You'll get pregnant again. We'll have lots of kids. You'll see. I love you, Laura."

Then he scooped her into his arms and carried her to his car to drive her to the hospital.

The doctor had performed a D&C. Visiting Laura and holding her through her grief had been difficult for him. He'd tried to bury his. When she'd returned home, they'd talked about trying again as soon as the doctor said they could. He'd brought her daisies. He'd bought her her favorite perfume. He hadn't bought a charm. Charms were for the happy times. The times they wanted to remember.

Eventually her smiles had become natural again.

Until the next miscarriage. There had been a third. Then she'd become pregnant with Jason.

His son.

"Mom?"

An hour later, Sean's strained voice told Laura she'd been staring into space for at least ten minutes. "How'd it go?" she asked.

Her son dropped down onto the sofa beside her and raked his hands through his hair. "He was sleeping. He didn't know I was there."

"He might have."

Now Sean stretched out his legs and slouched against the cushion. "Tell me something about Dad you've never told me. Not about now, but—" he pointed to her bracelet "—tell me what he was like when he was in college. He wasn't that much older than me."

"He was twenty-one when I met him."

"Did he always want to make robots?"

She smiled. As an engineer, Brady had been ahead of his time. "Yep. When he took me to meet his parents, he showed me his workroom. Uncle Matt and Uncle Ryan had an HO train set up year-round."

"They would have still been in high school."

"Right. Your dad did all the electrical work on the trains, but on his side of the room there were electronics kits."

"What about Aunt Pat? Did she have a space in the workroom?"

Laura laughed at the thought of Pat playing with trains or experimenting like Brady. "No. She wanted no part of it. She liked it when her brothers were busy down there because they weren't annoying her."

"That sounds like Aunt Pat." Sean was quiet for a couple of seconds, then murmured, "When you talked earlier about the way you and Dad met and all, he seemed so different from the way he is now. Was he?"

How much should she tell Sean?

Maybe that was the problem. She and Brady had always filtered everything they'd told the kids, instead of just laying it all out. At eighteen, Sean could vote, he could enlist, he could fight in a war. When should parents stop protecting children from heavy truths that would color the rest of their lives if they understood them?

"When I met your dad..."

Her voice trembled and tears blurred her eyes, but she blinked them away. "He wasn't like anyone else I'd ever met. The first time I looked into those blue eyes, I wanted to stay there. When he took my wrist and dragged me from the demonstration, I felt safe being with him. He knew where we were going even if I didn't. It was so odd, really, because I'd learned not to depend on anyone. I'd learned I had to make my own way."

"You were only twenty."

She nodded. "Losing my parents made me feel so alone. Even though my aunt Marcia took me in, I still felt...abandoned. Your dad changed that. He opened this great big window for me. He let in light and love and warmth. He had this amazing sense of humor and he knew how to relax. We'd sit for hours—"

"Making out?" Sean asked with a smile.

Her cheeks warmed. "Just being together. Before he left, we took walks in the park and fed the squirrels. We flew kites. We went to a party with his friends."

"Before he left?"

"Before he went to basic training at Fort Dix. Before he got sent to Hawaii. Before he went to Vietnam."

If she told Sean about that night with Brady's friends, he'd learn an important truth about his dad.

Six weeks into her dates with Brady—he'd come home every weekend—they'd gone to a party at Jack Crawford's. His apartment was small, on the second floor of a row house on West Princess Street. Jack had gotten a medical deferment because of a heart murmur and sold shoes at Thom McCann.

When Brady had introduced her to Jack, his buddy had said in an aside, "I guess we have to watch our language tonight."

Laura had worn a lime-green A-line dress, not sure what kind of party they were attending. She'd tied up half her hair with narrow lime-and-fuchsia grosgrain ribbons. Pretending to appear worldly, she'd remarked offhandedly to Jack, "I've heard all kinds of language. Don't worry about me."

When Brady had draped his arm around her shoulders, she'd felt trembly and weak-kneed, as she always did when they were close. Although they made out every time they saw each other, they hadn't gone any further than that, not because they weren't eager to, but because Brady had said more than once that he respected her dreams, understanding that they had to learn to trust each other—that they'd know when they were ready.

Would they? Was she putting them both through weekends of frustration because she was afraid she'd get hurt? Because the wrong decision could mean an unhappy turn in her life? Because the war was standing between her and Brady and they both understood that?

That night she wanted to forget about it all, and she suspected Brady did, too.

Two more friends—Tom and Luis—showed up. They seemed surprised that she was there, but Brady made no excuses for her presence, just introduced her to Luis, who went to Penn State, and to Tom, who was earning a degree at Shippensburg.

Tom, who defied longer men's hairstyles by wearing a crew cut, held out a box. "It's a game called Pass-Out. We can talk and play and drink, all at the same time."

While Luis and Tom moved the coffee table into the middle of the room, Brady lifted the cushions from the sofa and positioned them around it. Luis took out three packs of Lucky Strikes and tossed then onto the coffee table next to the game. "My contribution."

Brady produced a bottle of Burgundy from a paper sack he'd carried in and set it on the counter in the narrow kitchen. Laura had never been to a party like this, with a lava lamp glowing blue-green on top of the TV console, smoke filling the room and scents of wine and whiskey wafting up from juice glasses. She tucked her legs under her on the cushion and felt really grown up for the first time. While Luis strummed his guitar, Tom and Brady talked about the courses they'd enrolled in, the ones they'd hated and the ones they'd liked. Jack told funny stories about how picky some of the customers at the shoe store were. The guys reminisced about their high-school days.

At a lull in the conversation, Brady leaned close to her.

"I might have met you in high school if you'd stayed in Catholic school."

"My aunt didn't intend to pay anything extra to send me there."

When they started the game, Brady rolled the dice and moved his marker. The square said All had to take a drink. They did. The talking and playing went on as the sun set and traffic noises outside the open windows became quieter.

After she'd downed two glasses of wine, Laura switched to soda. Jack, Luis and Tom started mixing more ginger ale into their bourbon. But she noticed Brady wasn't diluting his. At some point, pink-elephant cards from the game forgotten, Jack flipped on a transistor radio and they listened to the Saturday-night countdown. The Beatles' "Get Back" pounded through the room.

By midnight, Laura realized Brady and his friends had talked about absolutely everything except the thousand-pound gorilla in the room. None of them had mentioned the war. None of them had mentioned friends who hadn't come home. None of them had mentioned that Brady, Tom and Luis would be drafted into service for their country after they graduated. It was almost one in the morning when Luis and Tom left. As Brady stood, he wasn't quite steady on his feet.

"If you two would like some privacy, you can have my bedroom. I can bunk on the couch," Jack told them.

Since Laura had worked at the Bon Ton until five, she and Brady hadn't had any time alone. Tomorrow his family was going to have dinner with his uncle, then he'd be leaving to return to school. She wouldn't see him again until next weekend.

"Why don't we take him up on his offer for a little while," Brady suggested. "I shouldn't drive yet. We can leave when my head clears."

She wasn't sure what her aunt would say if she came home in the wee hours of the morning, but right now she didn't care. Being with Brady was more important than anything else.

"All right. Let's stay," she agreed.

Ten minutes later, they were lying on top of Jack's cotton spread, breathing in sweaty socks, Aqua Velva and smoke that had drifted in from the living room. The room was black except for the glare of the street lamps battling against the rolled-down shades.

Brady lay on his side, his muscled arm resting across her waist. He kissed her longingly, deeply, passionately.

Afterward, he brushed his thumb along her hairline. "So what did you think of everybody?"

Still reeling from the effects of his kiss, she didn't filter her thoughts. "You have good friends, but I'm not sure you should have brought me along tonight."

"Why not?"

They'd kicked off their shoes, and Brady's stockinged foot rested against her nylon-clad one. "Because none of you talked about what was on your minds."

"Sure we did. We talked for hours."

Their body heat, Brady's face so close to hers, his scent and pure maleness tempted her to kiss him instead of talking to him. But she spoke her mind anyway. "You didn't talk about the draft, or about you and Luis and Tom going to basic training in a few weeks. Or about your friends who are there now and what's happening."

Brady shifted away from her, rolled onto his back and stared up at the ceiling. "Damn it, Laura, not everything's about the war. What did you think we should do? Analyze the last news report? Talk about how we're giving up real life for the next two years? Share notes on why our mother's cry because they don't want us to go? What good would any of that do?"

Brady had never been angry with her, never shut her out, never turned away. She suspected what was at the bottom of it all.

Although his long, hard body was tense and rigid, she turned into his shoulder, laid her head against his arm, hugged him as best she could. "I know sometimes when you get really quiet, you're thinking about it," she said softly. "I imagine when you're lying in bed at night, you can't get to sleep because pictures are going through your head—pictures from TV and stories you've heard. You don't have to hide what you're thinking or feeling from me, Brady."

His body was so still, so stiff, she couldn't even feel him breathing. She wished there was a little more light in the room and fewer shadows. She wished she could see him.

Finally she felt his breath. It was fast and shallow. She raised her hand to his face, and he suddenly turned away from her. But not before she felt the wetness. Not before she realized there had been tears on his cheeks.

She held on tighter. "Tell me," she whispered into his neck.

He just shook his head and mumbled, "I had too much to drink."

She guessed why that was so. "Nothing you say is going to change the way I feel about you."

His shirt was damp from their combined body heat. Still staring at the wall instead of at her, he kept his voice so low she had to strain to hear.

"In the daytime, I think about our reasons for being in Vietnam and I know I have to do my part. I think about how proud my parents will be when they see me in a uniform. I think about learning skills I don't have now. I think about toughening up so I can really face the world when I get back. But at night— At night I think about Bill's leg being blown off. I think about the guys who haven't come home. I think about the swamps and a strange country, living in God-knows-what conditions." Without warning, he faced her. "Most of all at night, I think about dying. Since I met you, I think about that a lot and I get so damn scared."

He wasn't touching her and she realized he expected her to move away, either to turn away in disgust or to leave him with his misery. She wasn't about to do either.

Winding her arms around his neck, she felt her own voice break when she admitted, "I'm scared, too."

As they held each other, she knew that what had just happened between them was more intimate than making love.

"Mom. Mom?" Sean asked. His voice seemed to come from very far away.

She focused once again on her son. "Yes, honey. I was remembering."

"Remembering what? What Dad was like?"

"I often wonder if children ever really know their parents," she admitted with a sad smile. "I mean, we're people, too, and we had lives before you were born. Believe it or not, we had the same struggles you do."

"Not Dad. He never had to struggle with anything." Sean's voice was almost bitter.

If only you knew, she mused, and then realized maybe it was time Sean *did* know. Not everything. Lots of things Brady needed to tell him. But she could reveal bits and pieces that Brady would *never* tell him. Brady was a proud man. Brady wanted his son to always see him as strong, maybe even as invincible. Her, too, for that matter. But she knew better. She knew he was human just as she was, with flaws and needs, wants and desires that sometimes got them into trouble and other times made life worth living.

"I was remembering the night your dad cried and I held him tight and we prayed he'd return safely from the war."

The shock on Sean's face was reiterated in his words. "You've got to be kidding. Dad cried?"

Had she made an awful mistake? Was this something too private to share with her son? Yet if Sean didn't soon learn that his father had flaws, that he hurt and got disappointed and didn't always succeed, she was afraid the two of them would always be at odds.

Her voice vibrated with the intensity she felt. "I'm talking to you as one adult to another. You wanted to know something about your dad. I just confided in you about a night when both of us were so scared that there wasn't any escape from it. Your dad was twenty-one, graduating from college. You'll be graduating from high school soon. What if someone put a weapon in *your* hands and shouted orders at you? What if you were sent to a foreign land where nothing is easy, nothing is familiar and there's no way to go home? Think about it and then tell me what you'd do with that storm building inside you."

It was a few moments before Sean murmured, "I can't imagine it."

"Vietnam wasn't so different from Iraq. Maybe the cause was more idealistic. I don't know. By the time I met your dad, no one could ignore the clips on the news...our boys dying. The war was touching so many families' lives that the nation couldn't look away."

She tapped her finger on Sean's chest over his heart. "When war touches you personally, when a relative or friend dies or loses a leg, the fight is a prison you can't escape from. A young man walking into hell has *every* right to cry."

She was talking to Sean from a woman's perspective, from *her* woman's perspective, as a girlfriend and a mother, or as simply a lover of peace. Maybe he needed to know her, too, in all this. Maybe he'd never realized what was at her core. Perhaps it was time he did.

After a few very long minutes during which neither of them spoke, Sean asked what she thought was an odd question. "How long had you been dating Dad when that happened...when he let you know he was scared?"

"Six weeks. We'd had six weekends together, letters in between."

"He must have trusted you."

"That night, we started to trust each other. I can't explain what happened between me and your dad that spring. As your mom, I'd tell you never trust love at first sight, never trust that initial excitement because it could fade away, never think the moment is going to last forever. Because what your dad and I shared was so rare, Sean, so very rare. But your dad and I were blessed with knowing from the moment I met him."

"Knowing you were going to get married?" her son asked.

"No. Everything was still too uncertain. But we knew for sure we had a connection, a bond that would never be broken. That weekend was a turning point for me in more ways than one. Up until that weekend, I'd lived with my aunt." Aunt Marcia had died of lung cancer before Sean and Kat had come into her and Brady's lives.

"What happened that weekend?" In spite of the late hour, Sean's eyes sparkled with interest, as if he was intrigued by everything she was telling him.

"Your dad and I had gone to a party. I met his high-school friends, who'd gone their separate ways for a while. Your father didn't take me home until 4:00 a.m."

Slipping back in time again, she remembered how they'd fallen asleep in each other's arms on that bed in Jack's apartment. When they'd awakened, Jack was snoring on the sofa. It had been so late and she'd had no idea what her aunt was going to say.

She'd never expected Aunt Marcia to be waiting up for her.

Brady had driven away after she'd unlocked the door and gone inside. How she wished he'd still been by her side. How she wished she'd felt like a niece to this woman with the angry expression and a slip of paper in her hand.

Marcia Watson had thrust that piece of paper at her. "I can only imagine why you're traipsing in here at 4:00 a.m., but I'm telling you this—I've had enough of looking after you. Here's a place you can stay. If you don't like it, you have a week to find somewhere else. You're old enough to be on your own."

Chapter 4

Hours had passed since Brady's surgery.

Laura's palms were sweaty as she approached the Open Heart Intensive Care Unit, thinking about Dr. Gregano's words after Brady's heart catheterization the previous day. "Your husband has ninety-nine percent blockage in the main artery, eighty-five percent in the…"

His diagnosis had hit Laura like a belly blow. For some reason, she hadn't been able to absorb everything. When she'd managed to concentrate on his voice again, she'd heard, "…surgery as soon as we can schedule him in the morning."

Now, as she stood there after so many cups of coffee she'd lost count, trying to prepare herself for this first visit, all she could think about was the fact that she'd triggered this. She'd caused Brady's heart attack. And she had to face the aftermath of it.

Both the surgeon and Dr. Gregano had warned her that some people didn't want to visit their loved ones the first night after surgery.

Stepping inside the cubicle, she felt her breath catch as she saw Brady, and she almost backed away. The doctors had explained what she'd find, yet she hadn't been prepared.

He looked like death. He was so white she wasn't sure blood pumped through him. His hands, arms and face were swollen, his fingers blue. He seemed to be shivering. He was hooked up to tubes, IVs and monitors, and a machine breathed for him, making his chest heave. There were markings and dye on his body.

She felt as if she'd stepped into a science-fiction movie.

Still, even if a machine was breathing for him, this was her Brady and he was alive.

A nurse touched her arm. "He's doing fine."

Fine. What an inadequate word.

Dr. Gregano had told her Brady would be sedated. That was best the first twelve hours. But she wanted to see those blue eyes of her husband's. She needed to see those eyes. She needed to know he was still her Brady.

After approaching Brady slowly, Laura sat on the edge of a chair next to the bed. This was so different from when she'd visited him after his heart attack. She wasn't sure exactly why. Maybe because she knew that during the operation, the surgeon had cut through Brady's chest and cracked open his sternum. Brady had been connected to a heart-lung machine and his heart had stopped. The surgery had been traumatic, and she really didn't fathom the results of that yet. Maybe because she was afraid that the Brady who would wake up wouldn't be the Brady she'd married and loved for more than half her life.

The lump in her throat made it hard for her to swallow. Her stomach roiled with fear and she felt nauseated. Yet she had to be here for him, just as she'd been there for him after other kinds of nightmares, just as *he'd* been there for her after her miscarriages and after the death of their son. That was what she and Brady did. They held on to each other through the difficult times, even when they didn't feel like it, even when it was hard, even when they didn't want to. When had they stopped going out for dinner on the odd evening the kids were both involved in activities and Brady was home? When had kisses become short and perfunctory rather than long and passionate? She couldn't remember when making love had joined their souls. More tears came to her eyes and once more she blinked them away. Making love with Brady had always brought them back together when distance found its way between them.

She laid her hand on Brady's arm and whispered, "I'm here."

He didn't respond and she recognized the fact that he couldn't.

Because the sight of Brady like this was so overwhelming, because she had to stay and touch him, yet felt he wasn't really here, she sank into memories again, desperately wanting to escape the complications of everything happening now, to be anywhere else with Brady.

All over again it was May 1969. Each day that month had brought her and Brady closer. Each day had shown her how much he cared.

After Aunt Marcia had ordered her to rent a place of her own, Laura had gone to the address on the slip of paper her aunt had thrust at her. She'd found a boardinghouse that smelled like sour cabbage. As the landlady had taken her to the second floor, a disheveled man had opened his door and leered at her. When Mrs. Treedy had told her she'd be sleeping on the third floor with another "gentleman" across the hall from her, Laura had made her escape.

On her return to her aunt's, she'd found a note:

I'll be back around five. I put some boxes in your room for you to start packing. See you later.
Aunt M.

Laura had replaced the note on the red Formica table but had brought the Sunday paper with her to the sofa. Sinking onto it, she'd told herself she was *not* going to cry. She was twenty. She was old enough to be on her own. She'd get extra hours of work somehow or add another job. *And* she'd find a place better than Mrs. Treedy's.

About three o'clock, a car pulled up outside. Brady hadn't said anything about getting together again. He'd been silent the night before as he'd driven her home. Today was the dinner at his uncle's with his family, then he'd be headed back to school. Maybe he'd call her before he left. Maybe he wouldn't. She had the feeling he was embarrassed about last night. As far as she was concerned, there was nothing to be embarrassed about.

She sensed rather than heard the footsteps on the porch and realized she was holding her breath when the bell rang. Running to the door, she broke into a full smile. It was Brady.

"Are you busy?" His tone was nonchalant, but his hands dug deep into his jeans pockets.

"I thought you were having dinner at your uncle's."

"I was…I did…but I needed to see you."

She opened the screen door and motioned him inside. "Aunt Marcia's not here. I…need to talk to you, too."

He saw the paper spread out on the sofa, the black circles around ads. "What's going on?"

"You wanted to talk about something."

Now he shifted uncomfortably. "Actually I don't really want to. I'd rather forget all about last night. You must think I'm a coward."

When she clasped his arm, she looked him in the eyes. "I don't think that. I'd never think that. There's nothing wrong with feelings, Brady. Last night, you felt everything that's been piling up inside. You have every right to be scared."

He winced at the word and protested, "I'm not scared. I know what I have to do."

For a moment he studied her, then he took her hand and pulled her to the sofa. When they were seated, facing each other, he ran his hand down her cheek. "I don't let anybody see what you saw last night. Don't you get that?"

She rubbed her cheek against his large strong hand. "You can be who you are with me. You don't have to pretend. I want to know you. Last night, I felt closer to you than I've ever felt to *anyone.*"

Wrapping his arm around her, he drew her against him on the sofa. He tilted his head against hers and they just sat there, their bodies touching, just like their hearts.

A few minutes later, he motioned to the newspaper., "So tell me what this is all about."

It seemed so natural to pour out everything to him. "When I got in so late last night, Aunt Marcia was up. She said I have to move. She gave me this address for a rooming house and I went there this morning. Oh, Brady, it was awful!" Her voice quivered as she told him about the condition of the place, the man in the hall, the attic rooms.

"You're dead-on you're not staying there. I don't want you anywhere around a creep like him."

She pointed to the paper. "I have about ten possibilities circled here. I probably shouldn't call on a Sunday, but I'm going to. I have to find a place as soon as possible. Aunt Marcia put boxes in my room—"

Brady pushed himself from the sofa and rose to his feet.

"What's wrong?"

He headed for the kitchen. "I'm going to make a call."

"Who are you calling?"

"No questions yet. Just give me a couple of minutes, okay?"

She gave him about ten minutes, and privacy, too. If whatever he was trying to do for her didn't work out, she didn't want her disappointment to show.

When he returned to the living room, he was grinning. "Let's take a ride."

"Where are we going?"

"You'll see."

At that moment, she'd follow him anywhere.

Fifteen minutes later, Brady had veered off North George Street, down an alley and into a small parking lot in back of a flower shop.

"Are we window-shopping for flowers?" she asked, not understanding at all what they were doing here. She'd heard of Blossoms, a shop with a wonderful reputation, especially for providing wedding flowers. Last year on her aunt's birthday, she'd had a small arrangement delivered to her.

"It's my mother's shop," Brady explained with a hint of pride.

"Your mother owns Blossoms?" His mom had talked about working with flowers, but Laura hadn't realized she owned her own shop.

"Yep. But it's not the flower shop we're interested in today. Come on."

He was out of the car and around to her door before she could even open it. When he took her hand, she followed him to the back door of the store, thinking they were going inside. But they weren't. Instead they started up the stairs to the second floor. On the small porch, he produced a key and opened the door.

When they stepped inside, Laura saw trellises and plant stands. Then she noticed the sink, small refrigerator and gas range. "It's a kitchen."

"This apartment was here when Mom bought the shop. She rented it for a few years but then decided the renters were more trouble than they were worth. She's been storing odds and ends here. So when I told her about your aunt kicking you out because I brought you home too late—"

"Brady, that's not the reason. She's just using it as an excuse."

"I know that, but I wanted to keep things simple. Anyway, I asked Mom if she'd consider renting it to you. She said she would if—" he stopped and gave her a mischievous grin "—*if* I convince my brothers to help me move everything out of here."

"But where will you put it all?"

"Mom's going to pick out what we should take downstairs to her storage room. The rest she said she might donate to the Salvation Army. The apartment isn't very big—just a kitchen, a bedroom with a sitting area and a bath...."

As Laura peeked into the other room, her chest felt tight. "Brady, it's wonderful. But I'm not certain I can afford this."

"Mom said you could pay whatever you were going to pay for the room in that boardinghouse."

That wasn't nearly enough. "Maybe I could help your mom in the shop when I'm not working at the store."

"I'm sure she'd like that, especially during her busy times. It really gets crazy at Christmas, Valentine's Day, Easter—most of the holidays."

Jubilant over the idea of having an apartment of her own, she threw her arms around his neck. "Thank you. You don't know how much this means to me."

His fingers laced in her long hair. "I think I do."

When Brady's lips captured hers, she melted into him, wishing they could start a life together right now...wishing the war waiting for him would simply go away.

A nurse came through the sliding glass doors into the OHICU cubicle, bringing Laura back to reality again—the reality that Brady wasn't breathing on his own and seemed too ill to ever recover.

"Time's up," the woman informed her gently.

Laura had so many questions. How soon would it be

before Brady could breath on his own? What did she need to know to make his recuperation successful? Would he look better tomorrow? Would he really be ready to go home in a few days?

Yet she understood the nurse couldn't answer those questions. She realized that for now she'd have to take one hour at a time. For certain, she wasn't going to let Kat or Sean visit their dad. Kat would fall apart, and Sean, even though he'd pretend to handle this scene, really couldn't.

There were so many tubes and lines and electrodes attached to Brady she couldn't give him a real hug. She didn't even realize she was crying until she leaned over him to kiss his cheek and a tear landed on his jaw. The terror of seeing him like this built inside her until it was clawing at her chest to break out.

After she squeezed his arm, she said close to his ear, "I love you, Brady." Then reluctantly she let go of him and left the cubicle.

Tears from fatigue, from worry about Brady, blurred her vision. Exiting his room, she ran into a nurse, murmured, "Excuse me," and headed for the shelter of the hall. She had to be alone. She needed to cry out the weakness inside her so it was gone and she could deal with the rest of this.

"Mrs. Malone, are you all right?"

Having spoken with Dr. Gregano a few times now, she recognized his voice. She swiped her tears away with her palms. "I'm just—" she finally raised her gaze to his "—tired."

"Stay here a moment," he ordered, his brow drawn.

Where was she going to go?

To her dismay, the tears kept coming, and she

scrubbed at them like a small child who didn't want to be caught crying.

Suddenly Dr. Gregano was back, carrying a box of tissues. He offered them to her. "Here, blow your nose. Then you have to listen to me."

She felt like an idiot, blowing her nose in front of him, but she did, and wiped her tears and stuffed the tissues in her pocket. "I'm sorry, I—"

He was already shaking his head. "You don't have anything to be sorry about. The first visit is tough. I saw my father like that. I thought *I* was prepared. I knew how he'd look. I knew what the machines would be doing. But to visit a loved one like that is devastating. I'm here to tell you, though, the next visit will be better and the one after that better still. Your husband's color will improve. He'll begin breathing with the respirator. He'll be more alert and realize where he is. In a few hours, we'll get rid of that tube down his throat and he'll really start the road to recovery."

"I'm so scared," she admitted. "This couldn't have happened at a worse time. We have some family issues and—"

"Every family does. But as far as being at the worst time—" he shook his head "—this shake-up can let everyone reevaluate what's happening in their lives."

This doctor might be years younger than she was, but he had experience she didn't have and there was a maturity about him. Maybe it came from dealing with life and death every day.

"How old are you?" she asked boldly.

At first he was taken aback, and then he smiled. "Forty-seven. How about you?"

"Fifty-eight," she admitted with a sigh. "But feeling a lot older right now."

"At times I feel a hundred and four," he confided. "But fortunately, once I get out of this hospital, work out at the gym and eat a breakfast that counteracts everything I've done, I feel middle-aged again, ready to come back in here and start the war all over."

"You fight for your patients," she said, "even when they give up."

"Sure do."

Almost reflexively, she glanced at his left hand. He wasn't wearing a wedding ring.

Observant of where she'd targeted her gaze, he said, "I'm not married. No woman would put up with my schedule."

"Maybe you just haven't met the right one." A man like him, dedicated to his profession, determined to give his patients most of his energy, deserved to have somebody waiting for him at the end of a long day. But she didn't say that. It seemed too...personal somehow.

"Feeling a little better?" he asked.

"Yes, and thank you for your concern. You're busy and I know Brady's your patient, not me. I'll be fine. After the next visit I'll try to get some sleep."

"Away from the hospital?"

"Well, I was just going to stretch out in the waiting room again."

"Go home, Mrs. Malone. Sleep in your own bed. Try to get a good night's rest. You'll do more for your husband that way than if he spots those dark circles under your eyes and realizes you're dragging because you haven't slept."

"I just...I just don't want to leave him. It's crazy, but I feel that as long as I'm here watching over him, as long as I'm talking to him and touching him, he'll get stronger faster."

Dr. Gregano gave her a wry smile. "Mr. Malone is a lucky man. I imagine that whether you're here or whether you're at home, he'll feel you pulling for him."

The cardiologist's pager went off. Excusing himself, he checked the number. "I have to get this," he said with a grim expression. "Remember what I said and take my advice. Go home." Then he was rushing toward the elevator.

Laura looked back at the cubicle she'd exited. Dr. Gregano had said Brady would be better in another hour. She couldn't leave yet...she just couldn't. She'd call Pat to pick up the kids, but she was going to stay. No matter what Dr. Gregano said, she wanted Brady to feel her presence. She wanted him to feel her touch.

After thirty-three years of marriage, she didn't know what else to do.

Chapter 5

"Kat looked so grown-up today." Brady laid down his fork and rested his head against the back of the chair Sunday afternoon, four days after surgery, feeling more tired than he could ever remember feeling. The surgery should have fixed him. Had it?

Making conversation took effort. But he didn't want Laura worrying any more than she already was. He could see the guilt in her eyes that she'd caused his heart attack. He could see the questions. But he wasn't ready to face problems that had been around much too long. He needed a hell of a lot more energy than this to do that.

So he concentrated on pushing his lunch around his plate and forced himself to talk just to get this visit finished. "But I got the feeling she couldn't wait to leave." He could still hear the rasp in his voice from being on the ventilator.

After a moment's hesitation, during which he could tell Laura was debating with herself, she said, "She likes to spend time with you. She just doesn't want to spend it with you in a hospital."

"*You* don't like hospitals, either."

She shrugged. "I'm grateful to this hospital and the doctors who saved your life."

Brady closed his eyes for a few moments. "I'm just so damn tired."

"I hear that's normal. You might feel that way for a while."

When Brady opened his eyes, he studied her, a list of everything she'd had to handle since he'd been rushed in here clicking in his mind. "Sean's been okay through all this? No signs of him drinking?"

Last summer Sean had gotten home in the middle of the night two nights in a row. They'd let the first time pass, but Brady had confronted him the second night. He'd been so drunk he couldn't stand without leaning against the wall. Brady had grounded him for six weeks and taken away his driving privileges except for going to and from work. Their son had been resentful and angry the rest of the summer. After the fact, from talking to another parent, Brady had learned the boys partied much too often, and he'd known he'd had to be strict with Sean. It had seemed to work. When the school year started and his son had kept up his grades—knowing he had to in order to get into college—he and Brady had formed an uneasy truce. But it was a truce that could easily be broken.

"Actually, he's been very supportive," Laura replied. "The thing is, he overheard some of our argument. He thought we were arguing about him and that caused your heart attack."

"The blockage in my heart was a time bomb. *That* caused my heart attack. Be sure to tell him that."

"I did."

He knew what she was thinking. He should talk to their son. She'd always expected so much of him where Sean was concerned and he hadn't been able to deliver.

To avoid an argument he commented, "One of the nurses mentioned you had to elude a reporter when you left yesterday. Are they bothering you?"

Laura hesitated.

He hated that she was being so careful around him. He hated that she thought since his heart attack he had to be coddled or protected. She obviously didn't know what to say and what not to say because of that videotape they'd had to watch and the suggestions in the informational binder he'd glanced at but she'd probably read cover to cover. Both had warned that a recuperating heart surgery patient should keep anxiety and stress to a minimum.

"Laura, what's going on?"

"There was a short segment on the local news about the article," she replied quickly.

There was more. "What else?" he prodded. "Don't hide things from me."

After glancing out the window for a moment, she admitted, "We've had news vans in front of the house and reporters waiting for us downstairs. But the ruckus is dying down now. Pat told the reporters to get lost while I was here with you. Since then, they've kept their distance."

Hospital sounds—a metal cart clicking on tile, lowered

voices, a laugh track on someone's TV—filled the silence between them.

It was time to change the subject. Brady commented, "I can't believe Dr. Gregano is going to discharge me tomorrow."

Laura gave Brady a bright smile. "You walked up and down the hall three times today and you're going to do it again tonight. That's progress."

"At home—"

"At home, we'll take things one day at a time. I was thinking..." she began lightly. "Sean could help me bring down one of the single beds in the spare room and set it up in your den. That way you could sleep there and...rest during the day if you need to."

The thought of being an invalid was unfathomable. "I'm going to hate this. Maybe I can just use the recliner."

"They stopped your heart," she reminded him softly. "Your body went through terrific trauma. You're not going to come home and try to act all macho, are you? Because there *are* restrictions."

"I read the list," he admitted, wishing the next few weeks were over.

Edging forward on her chair as if she wanted to reach out to him but didn't know exactly how, she asked, "How much do you remember about surgery and afterward?"

After he lifted his glass from the nightstand, he took a few swallows of water, then shook his head. "Not much. I was hoping I'd see that bright light and maybe find answers in it, but no such luck. I went to sleep, and when I woke up, that damn machine was breathing for me. I couldn't even feel my arms and legs. It was the weirdest thing. Then little by little sensation came back and I felt I was in my body again."

When she moved her hand, her bracelet brushed against the arm of the chair. She studied it, then met his gaze again. "I told Sean about how we met, about the demonstration, about Aunt Marcia kicking me out."

That surprised him. "Why?"

"We spent a lot of hours together waiting to hear about your condition. He asked me about the charms on my bracelet and what you were like back then."

After a few beats, Brady inquired, "And what did you tell him?"

"That we fell in love and it happened fast and we were connected from the moment we met. When I told him..."

He caught the glimmer of sudden emotion in her eyes.

She gave him another smile. "The memories are still so alive and real. They were comforting when you were in surgery. I could recall what I'd been wearing and what you'd been wearing. I could even smell the scent of British Sterling. Remember? You wore it the night we went dancing...the weekend before you left."

Were the memories comforting to her because back then everything had been so easy between them and now nothing seemed easy?

She pointed to the tiny envelope charm. "Do you remember calling me from Fort Dix to make sure I'd received this?"

"I remember." He'd known how much those charms had meant to her. That was why he'd bought another one. "I sent you that charm to remind you that what we had was real."

"You were jealous of Jack."

"I was afraid he was going to take my place. When he asked you to go to the movies, I thought he was moving in."

"He was just being a good friend."

"He still is."

"Have you talked with him?"

"No." He hadn't talked with anyone but Laura, Pat and the kids since the night of his heart attack. After he recuperated, he'd face the rest of the world.

"Angie called yesterday to find out how you were. She and Jack are going to become grandparents again around Thanksgiving."

Brady remained quiet for a while. Eventually he confided, "The other day before surgery, I was thinking of all the things I might never experience. Being a grandfather was one of them."

"Now you don't have to worry about that. You'll be stronger than ever and hopefully we'll have at least five grandkids."

With arched brows, Brady grimaced. "We're older than other parents who have kids Sean's and Kat's ages." He and Laura had been married fifteen years when they'd adopted Sean.

"Not really. We were just before the trend. Lots of couples now don't have kids until they're thirty-five or forty. Besides, isn't age just a number?"

"Yeah, a number I'm feeling right now. Laura, we don't know what's going to happen when I go home."

"Yes, we do. You're going to start rehab and be stronger and even better than you were before."

She leaned over to kiss him on the lips.

Her closeness, her perfume, her silky hair sliding across his jaw, stirred up desire he didn't want to feel... shouldn't feel. They might never have a normal sex life again. The meds the doctor prescribed could cause problems.

At the last second he turned his head so her kiss fell on his cheek instead of his lips.

So much new territory ahead of him. So much old territory he wanted to dismiss. But he knew that Laura wouldn't let him. And sometimes, he resented her for that.

He couldn't resent Laura. After all, she'd saved him. She'd saved his sanity years ago. She'd saved his life after his heart attack.

He owed her too much to ever forget.

After Laura left Brady's room, she needed a few minutes to herself before she joined Kat and Sean in the lobby. She felt close to tears and knew it was because Brady had turned away from her kiss.

His color was better each time she saw him. He was also more alert. She was scared to death of the drive to their house tomorrow, afraid she'd jostle him. She was just as unsure what kind of routine they were going to establish...how much care he'd need. But she wanted him home. She wanted them to become close again. She was going to take care of him. Right now he had no choice but to let her.

For the few minutes that they were remembering his call from Fort Dix, she'd felt close to him. There had been a time when Brady had been open and communicative and she'd practically known every thought in his head, just as he'd known hers. As soon as he'd given her his address at Fort Dix, she'd written to him every day and he'd written to her. Through those letters, they'd talked of their childhoods, their hopes, their fears and…their dreams. Back then she'd considered herself the luckiest woman on earth.

Feeling shaken by Brady's withdrawal, she slipped into one of the hospital's lounges. She just needed a few moments to herself…a few moments to recall where they'd come from so she could figure out where they were going.

Before he'd left for Fort Dix…

Sinking onto one of the couches, she laid her head against the back cushion. After Brady's college graduation, she'd tried to prepare herself for his leaving. They hadn't discussed his service duty or the future or where they were headed. That territory was so foggy, the road so undetermined, just to live in the moment was easier.

Since everyone realized that they had a standing date on the weekend, his mother had made a suggestion while Laura was helping arrange flowers for a wedding. "We'd like to do something special Saturday night before Brady…goes away on Monday. We'd like to take you along, too, to a private club we belong to. A band plays on weekends and it could be a lot of fun."

Laura wanted to spend absolutely every minute she could with Brady before he left, preferably alone. Anna seemed to sense that. She'd patted Laura's hand. "We don't have to make it a late night, and you and Brady will still have some time together. Believe it or not, his father and I understand young love."

Although Laura had blushed, she'd known she couldn't refuse this woman who had been so kind to her, who had given her a place to stay, who had accepted her into her family.

On Saturday night when Brady picked her up, he'd looked so handsome Laura's mouth had gone dry. He'd worn a navy suit, a blue-striped tie and a white shirt. To believe that this terrific man was dating *her* had been hard.

He'd driven her to the club. While they were dancing, as the band played "Stardust," he'd ducked his head and whispered into her ear, "I want to go back to your place. Two more songs ought to do it. If I can't kiss you soon, I'm going to explode."

"I wouldn't want that to happen," she teased, but when she looked into his eyes, she saw the hunger there and felt the same hunger inside herself. She felt it keenly in every atom of who she was.

His voice was rough when he bent to her again. "I bought condoms."

Condoms. She'd heard of them but had never seen one. She had a friend who'd told her that her boyfriend wouldn't wear one.

She understood exactly what Brady was suggesting. He was giving them a way to avoid an unwanted pregnancy, a way to make love without repercussions, a way to be closer to him than she'd ever been before.

Yet was making love with him the right thing to do? Her virginity was important to her. She had viewed it as a gift she'd save for the man she married. But she realized now, that was the ideal. Real life was here and now with Brady. She also suspected she wouldn't be Brady's first.

What if she was just one more girl to take to bed? Even if he got home for a few days after basic training, then he'd be gone again for two long years.

Her doubts must have shone in her eyes.

He brought her closer still, forgetting about propriety. "I wanted you to know I was prepared."

The way she'd been raised warred against what she'd wanted. She'd wanted Brady. But what if she disappointed him? What if her inexperience embarrassed them both? What if she wasn't woman enough for him to come home to?

What if he met someone else while he was gone?

The memories of that night pulled Laura in. The hospital and all its trappings—the smell, the noise, the fluorescent lights—faded. With hardly any effort at all she could see herself standing outside her apartment door with Brady, inserting her key into the lock, not knowing exactly what was going to happen next. Yet she understood that whatever happened next was her decision to make.

As she'd opened the door, Brady had taken her into his arms and kissed her as if it were the last kiss they'd ever experience. She'd found herself drowning in it, her questions lost in the desire that he'd banked until tonight. Before when they'd kissed, he'd been demanding but had always given them both the opportunity to cool down, to remain levelheaded, to understand the situation they were in. The future was so uncertain. Since that night in Jack's bedroom, they'd both buried their fears.

Should she foolishly give herself to Brady for tonight, hoping for forever? On the other hand, if she didn't show him how much she loved him, maybe he would look for someone else while he was away. He'd never said he loved her. He'd never put his feelings into words.

Breaking away, breathing hard, he gazed into her eyes. He'd removed his suit coat, thrown it into the back seat of his car and tugged off his tie on the drive here. Black chest hair curled at his open collar. His hands cupped her breasts and stroked her, while his mouth devoured hers again with almost a fevered desperation.

But now she couldn't let his kiss sweep her away. During the past few months, maybe their dates had been a much-needed distraction. Maybe the phone calls and letters had kept him from thinking about where he was going and what he might be doing. Tonight, was he anticipating the future they could have? Or did he merely need an escape? Did he want to plunge into pleasure and use it as a numbing drug against the turmoil inside him?

Her hands slid over his white cotton shirt as she rested her palms on his chest. She didn't push away, but it was a signal to stop. He'd always accepted her smallest hesitation seriously, but tonight his kiss tried to change her mind. His tongue coaxed her to reconsider.

She pressed her hands against him a little harder.

Suddenly he broke off the kiss and dropped his hands, breathing hard. "What's wrong? Don't you want this? Isn't it what we've been building up to?"

"I've never slept with a man." Her words trembled. "To sleep with you tonight…I have to know we're doing it because we're committed to *us,* not because you'll have someone to write to while you're away, not because I'll be a distraction and an escape, a memory you can take with you."

"What have we been doing, Laura?" he asked angrily. "You think I'm dating you as a distraction?"

She forced the words from her. "I don't know."

Now Brady seemed angry and frustrated. Stepping away from her, he shook his head. "I thought we had something special. Yes, you've been a distraction, but a distraction I haven't needed. I've had coursework to finish. I've had essays to write and blue books to prepare for. I should have been at Lehigh studying all these weekends, but I wasn't. I came home to see *you*. I stayed up till three in the morning to finish reading or squeeze in papers when I could have been spending time with friends at the University Center. I even had my mother give you a place to stay."

She couldn't put into words what she was feeling, the reassurance and love she wanted to hear. Living with her aunt, she'd felt isolated and alone. She'd always been quiet and never attracted the cute boys. She'd always concentrated on schoolwork and hadn't been part of the popular crowd. She wasn't the cheerleader type who found flirting easy. Brady had just dropped into her life like a shooting star. Maybe she didn't feel worthy enough to hold on to him. Maybe she didn't feel that anything good could last.

Not missing a beat, Brady went on. "If you don't want to get closer or have memories we can both live on while I'm gone, that's fine. I understand that. I guess I'm a fool for believing you wanted to be more than a pen pal and a Saturday-night date."

Before she could form a coherent thought, let alone

put words together, he was out her door, charging down the wooden steps, heading for his car.

What had she done? Her fears and her hesitancy had sent him the wrong message. Falling crazily in love with Brady had stirred up all her insecurities as well as brought her joy and excitement. She couldn't let him leave without him realizing how much she loved him.

After she raced out the door, she almost tripped running down the stairs. She hung on to the banister.

He was opening the car door when she caught his arm. "Brady, don't go."

Her voice broke and she realized they were both pushing so much worry aside, both tamping down so much sadness at being torn apart, that their emotions were at the spilling-over point. That was exactly what they had done—spilled over.

He took one look at her face and wrapped his arms around her.

While she cried, they held each other in the parking lot as the breeze whispered by them, as a car horn honked, as moonlight trickled over them.

Finally she pulled away and swiped at her tears. "I can't bear the thought of you going. You've become so important to me. But I feel as if I'm living in a dream. I've never wanted to be with a man the way I want to be with you. I don't expect you to make declarations you don't feel, but I have to know you want *me,* not merely any girl. I need to know you want to come home to me and the life we can have. But I also worry it's too soon for either of us to make that kind of commitment."

He held her face in his hands and lifted her chin.

"Sometimes I forget how your aunt treated you. You're so mature most of the time. I don't see that scared little girl who's still inside you. I shouldn't have said what I did."

"You should have told me you weren't getting enough sleep and were having trouble finishing your work."

He gave her a crooked smile. "Who needs sleep?" He curled his arm around her waist. "Let's go back up to your place. I have something to give you. Now that we've both let off some steam, maybe we can have the kind of talk we have to have tonight."

Once inside her apartment again, they opened a window. Then he clasped her hand and guided her to the sofa.

She'd taken pride in her apartment. When she'd moved in, the only furniture she'd had was her bedroom suite from her aunt's house. She'd bought a small sofa and a floor lamp in a used-furniture store. Brady's mom, who had stored a table for two and chairs in her basement, had told Laura she was welcome to those. Laura had found a couple of throw rugs on sale and curtains for the windows. The night breeze tousled one panel.

Brady settled on the sofa beside her. "I wanted to spend some time with you before we went out to dinner tonight," he admitted, "but the day got away from me. Mom and Dad had people they expected me to say goodbye to and there were a few friends I had to visit. The goodbyes kept getting harder. They were all building up to this huge goodbye I was going to have to say to you."

She could only imagine what today had been for him, leaving everyone he knew and everything he loved.

"Friendships don't last." He added, "I mean, guys swear

they'll be friends forever, but Tom, Luis and Jack are the only ones I've kept in touch with since high school. If I'm gone for two years, I won't have any friends when I get back. People change, their lives move on, and friendships don't mean what they once did."

What Brady was saying rang true for her. She had two friends from high school she'd stayed in touch with who hadn't gone to college, either, and were working in town. The friends who had gone on to college didn't stay in contact and didn't phone. Their lives were about classes and frat parties and whatever was happening on campus.

Yes, people changed, but *she* wasn't going to change. Her feelings for Brady weren't going to change.

Brady clasped her hand and interlaced their fingers. "I thought about asking you to marry me before I left, but I decided that wouldn't be fair to you."

"Shouldn't *I* make that decision?" She would say yes if he asked.

"We've only known each other less than three months. After Fort Dix, I'm not sure where I'm going until I get my orders. And then— Anything can happen over there, Laura."

All the things he wasn't saying played through her head. He could lose an arm, a leg…or even his life.

Scooting closer to him, she assured him, "I'm not going to change, Brady. I'm going to be right here waiting for you when you get back, no matter what." There was so much conviction in her voice he had to believe it was true.

The nerve in his jaw worked. He slid a blue velvet box from his pocket and handed it to her. "Open it."

The box was larger than a ring box and Laura had no idea what was inside. When she raised the lid, she found a gold-link bracelet with two charms. Tears came to her eyes as her fingers slid under the tiny daisy charm and then the small engraved heart.

"Check the back," he directed her.

She turned the heart over. It read *Love, Brady.*

"The daisy is to remind you of the day we met and how great it was and how much we enjoyed being together. The heart— I guess it's kind of symbolic. You've got my heart, Laura. You've had it since the day I met you. When I get back, I want to marry you and begin a real life."

All the questions she'd had earlier fled in the face of this gift. Now she knew what she meant to him. Now she knew they'd formed lasting bonds, not temporary ones. "I love you, too, Brady. I'll wear this every day and keep your heart safe. You'll be taking mine along with you."

After he helped her put on the bracelet, he wrapped his arms around her. He kissed her, but she could tell he was restraining himself. She didn't want restraint tonight. She wanted to love Brady. She wanted to show him exactly how she felt, no restrictions, no boundaries, no fear. She wanted to give him a night that was so wonderful he'd have no doubts that she'd be waiting when he returned home.

Leaning away from him, she stroked the beardline on his jaw. "Will you stay with me tonight?"

"Stay?"

She would have to put it into words. Because of what had happened earlier, he wouldn't push her.

"I want you to make love to me. I want you to be with me all night and wake up with me in the morning. I want to make you breakfast. Can we do that?"

He studied her face. "Are you *sure?*"

"I love you so much, Brady. I want us both to have memories we'll never forget."

Their next kiss changed everything. It was a man's kiss that held nothing back. Where once the possessiveness of it might have frightened her, now it didn't. It filled her with excitement and anticipation and joy. Returning his kiss, meeting each brush of his tongue with one of her own, she began unbuttoning his shirt. She slid her fingers into his chest hair.

Brady's groan was primal. As they undressed each other, Laura felt no embarrassment. She'd never seen a man naked before. Her eyes grew wide as he dropped his trousers and stepped out of his boxers.

"I don't want you to be scared, Laura. It's just part of me that's going to become part of you. The first time might hurt a little—"

"The first time?"

He smiled. "I hope you like it enough to do it again."

She wished she didn't feel so innocent, so naive, so unsophisticated. She'd read books about having sex, but she had a feeling the real thing was going to be very different.

With them both undressed, Brady wrapped his arm around her waist and tugged her with him a few feet to the bed. They lay face-to-face and she noticed he was hard with arousal.

He dragged his thumb over her cheek. "I want to touch you everywhere, but if anything I do makes you feel uncomfortable, or if you don't like it, tell me."

She suspected nothing Brady did would make her feel uncomfortable. She was right.

That night became the epitome of her dreams. That night she became a woman. That night she fell so deeply in love she knew it would never end. Brady touched her in so many ways. He caressed her. He inflamed her desperately. He awakened desire, chased away her loneliness and truly became the center of her world. She never imagined hands could express so much feeling. She never guessed kisses could become so soul deep that she'd burn with a passion that could consume her. Brady cherished her body as she curiously explored his. His mouth on her breast quickened the sensations in her womb. Expressing her pleasure, she murmured his name, surrounded his hot arousal with her hand and felt his pulse beat for her.

After he slipped on a condom, she welcomed him, not sure what to expect. He said she'd feel pain and she did, but just a slice of it and then sensations so wonderful she wanted them to last forever. Brady thrust slowly at first, then faster. Joy rippled down her spine as she urged him deeper. Pleasure suddenly overtook her whole body and she shook from the aftermath of it. When Brady's orgasm hit, she held him through his shudders and knew she could never let him go.

That night, she knew if he didn't come back from the war, she'd be destroyed.

A nurse rushing into the lounge where Laura sat broke the movie of memories. The R.N. was obviously looking for someone. She nodded at Laura, then hustled away.

With the remnants of her reminiscence still vaguely nudging her, Laura realized that in a way she *had* lost Brady to the Vietnam conflict. Because at his return, he was a changed man.

Chapter 6

The sun cast long shadows the following day as Laura drove into the garage and pressed the remote button to close the garage door behind her and Brady. There was still a news van parked at the curb. She didn't know how they ferreted out their information. She just wished privacy could be what it used to be.

"I wish we could make them leave, but we can't. Not when they aren't on our property."

"They'll leave eventually," Brady predicted. "Don't pay any attention to them."

Glancing over at her husband, she thought he looked pale, as if each bump in the road while they'd driven home had cost him.

"Are you okay?" It really was a stupid question. He'd had his chest pried in two, his heart stopped and now he had to figure out what his life meant again. What their life together meant. There were too many silences between them. Too many times they glanced away from each other instead of looking into each other's hearts. Were they afraid of what they'd see?

When he turned to her, his face was lined with fatigue. He still had dark circles under his eyes. She so wanted to do everything she could to help him get well. Not out of guilt, but because she loved him.

"I'm fine," Brady's voice was strong with determination, as if willpower could make him well. He opened the car door.

"I'll come around and help you—"

"Don't," he said tersely. "I'll do this on my own steam."

She shouldn't feel hurt by his attitude, but she did. He was acting as if he *did* blame her for his heart attack, no matter what he said.

The door from the house into the garage flew open and Kat practically danced in. She embraced Brady carefully, but her voice was full of enthusiasm. "Welcome home, Dad."

Laura watched Brady hug their daughter, heard him say something that made the girl laugh. Laura wondered where Sean was and what kind of welcome he'd have.

Snatching the bag of instructions and meds she'd received from the hospital, she followed behind Brady as he went up the two steps, halted, then walked down the hall past the mudroom. Even up until yesterday, he would grab for the oxygen after exertion. He was short of breath and had to use his spirometer to get the fluid out of his lungs. This walk through the kitchen and into the living room would tire him.

To her surprise, when they reached the living room, a wide banner capped the doorway. It read Welcome Home, while helium balloons bobbed where they were taped around the door frame.

Laura felt the past squeeze her heart. The banner, the balloons and Kat's happy expectant face sent her back to the day Brady had returned home from his stint in the army. The day she'd thought their lives together were going to begin.

Instead they'd almost ended.

She'd been so excited. She'd helped Brady's mother prepare the banner, tape up the streamers, attach the balloons. His parents had rented canopies for the backyard and invited family and friends for a welcome-home party. They expected Brady early in the afternoon and Laura had hoped that after the initial greeting with his family, they'd have a bit of time alone.

There was so much to catch up on, so many kisses to give, so many hugs to take. She'd been afraid to admit she didn't know Brady anymore. Two years could have made a huge difference in their lives. After basic training, they'd spent two idyllic nights together with his three-day pass. It had been like a honeymoon. She'd felt torn when he'd left again for the base, as well as when he'd called her before he'd left for Hawaii.

Then he'd been sent to Vietnam.

At first, his letters had been messages of how much he missed her, what conditions were like at their base camp, stories about how some of the soldiers had gotten to know a few South Vietnamese children. Then she'd received the letter about his first firefight, another letter relating how a buddy had been killed. The emotions behind his words had been heart-wrenching. She'd so wanted to put her arms around him and hold him tight, and did it in her dreams, praying he'd feel her love until he'd received her next letter.

In the weeks that followed, his letters came frequently, telling her how much he missed her, how much their time together before he left seemed unreal and that he was holding on to it through the tough stretches. Then she hadn't heard from him for six whole weeks and neither had his parents. They'd all been afraid he'd been injured or worse, but had received no information to verify that.

Finally both she and his mother had gotten letters. Hers was different from previous ones—almost remote, short and to the point. He'd merely stated he'd been out on an operation and was sorry if she'd worried, but he couldn't get a letter to her or his parents. Seven more months in Nam to make up his year, then he'd be stationed elsewhere.

He'd been sent to Fort Lewis in Washington State, but now, after two long years, he was coming home. He'd received a Bronze Star for valor and she was so proud of him. Yet deep in her soul, she knew they weren't as close as they'd once been. Although she kept filling her letters with news of everything from work to the flower shop to how much she loved him, his had remained short and sporadic and different. She'd gotten a few phone calls from Fort Lewis, but those had been awkward and brief. He'd dissuaded both her and his parents from flying to Washington.

Unable to help herself the day of Brady's return, Laura had stood at the front picture window for much of the afternoon, watching for him. The party had been in full swing, in anticipation of the guest of honor's homecoming, when a truck had parked in front of Brady's childhood home and she'd caught sight of his profile in the passenger seat. She'd been scared that everything had changed between them and nothing would ever be the same.

She'd been right.

When Brady stepped out of the pickup, rounded it and stood looking at the house where he'd grown up, all the feelings Laura had ever had for him rushed through her. She ran out the front door, barely registering the fact that he wasn't in his uniform but a casual chambray shirt, jeans and boots. He'd sent her a few pictures, so that his weight loss and the gauntness of his features didn't throw her. But when she flung her arms around his neck, the expression on his face did.

He dropped his duffel, and his arms went around her loosely, not in the tight embrace she desired. When she gazed into his eyes, they were the same blue but so very different. His lips were unsmiling, and she had the feeling he might push her away.

"Brady?"

He closed his eyes and the nerve in his jaw worked. He held her a little tighter. Looking at her again, he said, "You're more beautiful than I remembered."

"I've missed you so much," she responded, wanting to get them further than this, needing to connect with him as she once had.

They didn't have a chance to connect because at that moment his family and friends poured out the door and they were surrounded. He was being clapped on the back and his hand shaken. Although she was beside him, she felt so separate from him.

That evening, Brady's gaze didn't leave her, whether they were across a crowded room, on opposite sides of the yard or nearby each other talking to his parents. Yet there was a wall between them so tangible that she could almost reach out and touch it. A remoteness surrounded him that didn't invite a kiss or an embrace. Still, she saw longing in his eyes, the same longing that had made a home in her the two years he'd been gone.

Maybe they just needed time together again. Maybe after the party everything would go back to the way it had been. She waited.

Once the party was over, Laura found Brady outside, looking up at the sky. Coming up beside him, she asked tentatively, "Do you want to go back to my place?"

His shoulders straightened. "That's probably not a good idea tonight."

"Because you're tired? We can just hold each other and sleep." Didn't he understand how much she loved him? Didn't he understand how she'd waited for this moment for two long years? They had to get to know each other again.

His expression was so sad it terrified her. "Give me a couple of days, okay? Coming back from Nam, getting out of the service, hasn't been easy."

"You didn't want to come home?"

He rubbed his hand across his forehead and then looked up at the sky again. "Those stars are the same stars that shone on us over there. But, Laura, you were in a different world than I was."

An awful thought occurred to her—the reason he might be acting so removed. "Did you find somebody else?"

His hands were on her shoulders then and holding her

hard. "This isn't about finding someone else. I'm not the same person I was two years ago. You don't understand, but believe me, you don't want to be with me right now."

Bitterness, anger and regret were evident in his voice. She didn't comprehend those feelings or know what to do with them. She only knew how she felt.

"Do you still love me?" she asked softly.

He still didn't answer her. Instead he asked her a question. "Remember the weekend before I left for basic? Remember when I kissed you and you pushed away?"

"I remember."

"If I start kissing you, I won't be able to stop for so many reasons you don't want to count all of them. I need you, Laura, but that need isn't based on love right now. It's based on being without a woman way too long. It's based on needing to know I'm alive. It's based on wanting to bury the past, use sex to forget, use you to find a way out of what I'm feeling now. I can't do that to you."

The intensity in Brady practically hummed. His vehemence almost shoved her away. But this was Brady, and she wasn't going anywhere. She'd heard what the war had done to Luis, and she had to convince Brady she wasn't the innocent she'd been when he left.

"Jack said Luis came back pretty messed up," she told him. "He won't leave his apartment. He smokes pot. He drinks…and that's his life." Luis had been injured in action and received a medical discharge, but from the moment he'd arrived home, he'd isolated himself.

"Tom is still MIA?"

She nodded. "I don't know what you went through, but I want to understand it, and I want to be with you."

Releasing her shoulders, he shook his head. "Go home, Laura. Just go home."

When she lifted her arm, her bracelet glittered in the moonlight. "Do you want me to forget we ever meant anything to each other?" That thought practically devastated her.

The haunted look in his eyes tore at her. "Like I said, you don't want to be with me."

"I do."

The symbolic words weren't lost on either of them.

At last Brady blew out a long breath. "Give me a few days. Maybe finally being home, things will be different."

She wanted desperately to know what those things were, but he obviously wasn't going to tell her. If she gave him the space, she could lose him. If she didn't, she could lose him.

"What happens after a few days?" she couldn't help asking.

"After a few days, we'll figure out what we do next."

There was an unassailable aura of control around Brady. She could imagine what decisions he'd had to make on a daily basis—life-and-death decisions. She could only imagine how much had been *out* of his control.

Pictures she'd seen on TV flashed through her mind. Would Brady ever tell her what had happened to him?

If he didn't, she wasn't sure they could find each other again.

One of the balloons in the doorway bobbed against Laura's arm, tugging her back to a homecoming she hoped would be very different from the last.

Suddenly beside her, Sean asked worriedly, "How's he doing?"

"Coming home tired him out. After I fix lunch, we'll have to give him peace for a while. Why don't you tell him you're glad he's home."

They both noticed Kat fetch a pillow to help Brady settle in the recliner.

"Kat already did that," Sean remarked in a monotone.

"I'm sure he'd like to hear it from you."

"Right." Moving away from her, Sean warily approached his dad.

She wanted to shout, *Don't be afraid to talk to him, Sean.* Yet she couldn't do that. She had to let them find their own way and that was so painful for her to watch.

One hand in his pocket, Sean stood to the side of the recliner. "Mom said you're thinking about turning one of the rooms in the basement into a gym."

Brady glanced at Laura. "I don't start rehab for about five weeks. After that, I could use at least a treadmill here."

"I've been checking out machines on the Internet. There are good ones available for home use now."

To Laura's relief, Brady responded with some enthusiasm. "Thanks for doing that. If you print out a list, in a few weeks we'll check into it."

Sean shifted on his feet. "My graduation will be May twenty-fifth. About four and a half weeks. Think you'll be able to come?"

"I'll make sure I'm there. I know how important that day is to you." Brady's answer sounded heartfelt.

Sean ducked his head for a moment, then said in a low voice, "I'm glad you're home."

Laura hadn't realized she was holding her breath, but she had been. Maybe Sean's almost losing Brady, Brady's almost losing his life, would make a difference to them both. The next step would be for Brady and Sean to have a heart-to-heart about that article. But Brady had to get his strength back before he could do it.

The doorbell rang. Two dings rather than a chime meant someone was at the back door. A neighbor? She doubted it. She thought about not answering the summons.

But the doorbell dinged again.

Sean crossed to her. "Do you want me to get it?"

If it was a reporter, she was afraid Sean would be no match for him. "I'll take care of it."

After hurrying to the kitchen, Laura opened the back door, hoping beyond hope she'd glimpse a friendly face.

Two men were standing there, neither of them happy at the other's presence. The man on the left looked to be in his early thirties. Dressed in a blue oxford shirt, tie and khaki pants, he wore a press badge. "I'm Kev Norris from the *York Spectator.* I'm here to find out exactly how Brady Malone is doing. Is he your husband?"

Her gaze fell on the second man, who wasn't wearing a press badge. He was wearing a suit that was rumpled. He appeared to be in his late fifties, with receding hair and hazel eyes that seemed more interested than predatory, though that could be her imagination.

He produced an ID from his pocket and opened it so she could see it. "Bob Westcott. I freelance."

Laura gripped the door. "I don't have anything to say to either of you."

The younger reporter, obviously tired of waiting,

replied curtly, "Well, you should have something to say. Stories are buzzing about your husband and his service record. We hear he had a heart attack. Was it really a heart attack, or did he try to commit suicide?"

She was so shocked that she couldn't find a word to say. Then suddenly she could. "Get off our property."

"Mrs. Malone, I'm just trying to let the public know the truth. I have every right—"

"*We* have a right to privacy," she reminded him.

Neither man moved away, and she was about to shut the door, when Bob Westcott said quietly, "We're not cut of the same cloth, Mr. Norris and I."

"Don't believe a word he says," Norris protested. "He's a reporter just as I am."

"I told you to leave, Mr. Norris, unless you want me to call the police."

"Can I just have three minutes?" Westcott asked her.

Why she was even considering talking to him she didn't know. But she didn't feel threatened by him or invaded.

Making an impulsive decision, she opened the door a little wider and let the man slip inside. To Norris, she repeated, "Get off our property."

After she closed the door, she wondered if she'd made a huge mistake.

"I'm here, Mom." Sean's voice came from the doorway to the dining room.

"It's okay. I'm going to talk to this gentleman for a few minutes. If I yell, call 911."

Westcott gave her a wry grin and shook his head. "We really do get a bum rap these days."

"Whose fault is that?"

"The fault doesn't belong to all of us, Mrs. Malone."

This time instead of his ID, he took a business card from his pocket. "I suspect that when your husband recovers from his bypass surgery, he'll want to tell his side of what happened."

Astonished, Laura asked, "How did you know he had coronary bypass surgery?" They'd all been careful not to give out any information. And with privacy policies these days, the hospital didn't tell anyone anything.

"I have my sources." He handed her his business card. "I was in Vietnam. I know what it was all about. If Mr. Malone feels he needs to be heard, tell him to call me. I sell to all the local papers and I'm sure that on this, they'd certainly buy the story."

In spite of herself, she was interested in his work. "What kinds of stories do you write?"

"Do you recall the piece about a year ago about a casino possibly coming to Gettysburg? I wrote that one."

She had read the story, although she hadn't paid any attention to the byline. It had actually been well balanced, giving both points of view. Would Brady consider talking to this man when he was well?

"I can't promise anything, but I'll give my husband your card."

"I figured this whole thing is probably causing a lot of turmoil for all of you. I'm not here to harass you, but with what your husband might have to face from the public when he's out and about again, he might want to do something about it. I'd like first shot, that's all. Okay?"

Now, instead of interest, she saw understanding in his eyes, and she didn't believe it was feigned.

"All right."

Westcott nodded, then went to the door and opened it. "I'll think good thoughts for your husband." And he was gone.

When she returned to the living room, Brady studied her curiously. "Who was that?"

The kids seemed to sense she wanted to talk to Brady alone. Sean said, "I'll be upstairs."

Kat followed him up the steps.

Laura went to the recliner where Brady sat. "It was a reporter. He's a freelancer. He said he was in Vietnam, and if you ever want to tell him your side, he'll listen and write up a fair article."

"Everyone has an angle," Brady muttered.

"He didn't seem to. I think he really wants to help."

"He wants the byline."

"Brady—" She stopped. That night of Brady's heart attack she'd started the argument. She'd pushed. She wasn't going to push now. Brady's health came before anything else.

Yet she was afraid that if he didn't lay the ghosts from the past to rest, he'd never be really healthy again.

Sean and Kat stood in the gallery window at the front of the house, watching another news van roll up to the curb. A woman in a suit climbed out and hurried up to the front door.

The doorbell rang.

Shielding his eyes against the glare of the April sun, Sean spotted his mother on the front walk. One sign of trouble and he'd be down there. The thing was—he just didn't think his dad would appreciate his interference right now. And Sean didn't want to do anything to upset him. He didn't want him having another heart attack. He sure didn't want to be the cause.

It still bothered him that his parents had been arguing about him when his dad collapsed. On one of his visits to his father in the hospital after surgery, his dad had thanked him for doing CPR. But it had been a duty thanks. He'd also told him his heart attack had had nothing to do with Sean.

Those were words…only words. He and his dad just didn't get along that well. They never had. They never would. That was why he still felt responsible for his dad's collapse. If his mom and dad hadn't been arguing about *him*—

He could still hear his dad say, *He needs to learn how to handle life on his own.*

"What do they want to know?" Kat asked anxiously beside Sean as she peeked out the window.

They hadn't talked about anything that had happened. Maybe because neither of them knew what to say or do or believe. "Didn't you read the article in the paper?" Sometimes his sister lived on another planet.

"Yeah. I read it. But I don't believe it."

The article was folded in his wallet. He didn't know why it had seemed important to keep it. It just had. He'd read it at least fifty times, wanting to understand. But he didn't understand and his sister surely didn't, either.

"It's probably the truth, Kat. How could they print it if it wasn't? And if the reporter's not lying, it means Dad was a son of a bitch who never owned up to what he did."

"Don't say that." Tears shone in Kat's eyes. "Don't say that about Daddy."

With that parting protest, she ran to her room and slammed the door.

Blowing out a sigh, Sean knew Kat might have some unpleasant truths to face, and some fast growing up to do.

He'd wait a few minutes, then he'd go out to the toolshed where he'd hidden the bottles Boyd's brother had given him. Having a few swigs of a minibar's liquid samples was the best way to deal with what was going on. If he was numb, he wouldn't care about any of it. If he was numb, maybe he could eventually tell his parents he didn't want to go to the college he'd been accepted to…maybe he wouldn't feel he was always on the outside looking in.

Chapter 7

The pitch-blackness of his den surrounded Brady as he lay on his back in a single bed from one of the spare rooms, staring up at the ceiling. Every once in a while, he could hear Laura shift on the sofa. She'd insisted on sleeping down here with him in case he needed anything. It wasn't going to be long until he climbed those damn stairs, got to the second floor on his own steam and stopped feeling like an invalid.

You are *an invalid...at least for a little while.*

He swore, keeping the epithet silent so Laura wouldn't hear.

If he had to put into words what he was feeling tonight, he couldn't do it any more than he could have done it the night he'd come home from the service. Just as then, he felt he'd been out of touch with the world as everyone knew it, but now had been thrown back in and he was supposed to live in it again as if nothing had happened. Kat had been the only one tonight he could relate to normally, but then, Kat never pretended something she wasn't feeling.

Sean, on the other hand…

Their relationship had so many knots he didn't know where to begin untying them. Maybe he and his son could relate over the gym, putting it together, exercising. But as soon as he was feeling better, he'd be getting back to work. Work, where he had complete control, where the adrenaline rush of winning contracts and creating innovative designs kept other emotions buried.

Like the past. He wasn't going to dig it up. He wasn't going to talk to Sean about it, and he wasn't going to talk to a reporter about it. No talking about the past. That had been his vow from the moment he'd gotten home from Vietnam.

That night, he'd climbed out of the truck and Laura had run to him. He'd seen in her eyes what she'd wanted, and he'd realized he couldn't give it to her. Over the months he'd been stationed at Fort Lewis, he'd thought about ending their relationship, setting her free. But he'd so hoped that once he was discharged, he could believe in a life with Laura again. The memory of her smile had gotten him through long dark nights in Nam. The echo of her sweet voice had kept him sane.

Those first few days at home after his discharge he'd holed up in his room as much as he could. He'd had trouble having normal conversations because nothing was normal for him anymore. He couldn't begin to explain how protecting his fellow infantrymen and how being willing to die for a buddy paired up with killing the enemy. The dichotomy tore a man's soul apart.

How could he have slipped *that* into normal conversation?

His parents had wanted to discuss jobs, interviews, résumés and where he was headed next. His brothers had wanted to talk about sports and girls and next year's classes. It was as if they'd all been speaking a foreign language. Thank God Pat had gone back to Atlantic City, where she'd been working for the summer. She wouldn't have respected his privacy, wouldn't have left him alone when he closed his bedroom door. After a few days, he'd phoned a friend who had been through some of it with him. Carl had gone home to Illinois. But in the here and now rather than in the trenches, everything had been different. They hadn't been able to talk about anything that had mattered. Their words had been surface, the silences long, their goodbyes terse.

By the fifth day, all Brady had thought about was how loyally Laura had written to him. She'd poured her heart out. She'd said she wanted to be with him now. She wouldn't want to be with him once she realized what was going on with him. He didn't sleep at night. If he did doze off, he had nightmares. She wouldn't want to be with him because the way he needed her was too damn fierce, too damn raw, too damn scary. At twenty-two, she'd thought she was mature and could handle anything. But he'd known in his gut that she'd turn and walk away as soon as she glimpsed the garbage inside of him.

Still, she'd seemed to be the one person he'd wanted to reach out to…wanted to try to connect with again.

When he hadn't been closeted in his bedroom, he'd gone for long walks, needing the physical activity. Sometimes he'd driven to the track at the nearby high school and just run. He'd stopped running that Friday night after a game of basketball—one-on-one with Ryan. They hadn't talked, simply played as hard as they could. Afterward he'd showered, picked up his car keys and told his parents he didn't know when he'd be home.

They'd cast worried looks at each other, then his mother had asked, "Are you going to see Laura?"

"Yes," he'd replied. In Laura's letters, she'd told him she worked full-time at his mother's shop and part-time at Montgomery Ward's at the mall.

"She'll be working till nine," his mother had reminded him.

"I'll go over to her place and wait for her."

That was what he'd done.

Settling on the wooden stairs at her apartment, he'd let the night breeze blow his hair as he'd blanked his mind to wait. The end-of-the-day heat dissipating from the asphalt, the petunias and marigolds planted in Laura's window box, were conflicting scents.

On alert when Laura's car drove into the parking lot, he finally heard her car door slam and her footsteps on the sidewalk.

When Laura saw him, she jumped, startled, and put her hand over her heart. "Brady, you scared me."

"Sorry."

"Why didn't you go inside?"

"It's been a long time, Laura. I didn't know if you would want me to."

As he stood, he felt like a stranger to her. How could that be? They'd dated for almost three months, made love in a consuming way that had shaken him to his core, yet had wrapped them in a bond he'd decided would never be severed. They'd written to each other for the past two years. Still, he was painfully aware that feelings just were and there wasn't a hell of a lot he could do about them.

"I probably shouldn't be here," he said.

From the light of the porch lamp he could see color stain her cheeks. "If you don't want to be here, you should go."

Damn it! He was doing a terrific job of pushing her away. One part of him screamed at him to take her into his arms. The other part knew he should warn her to run, run as far as she could away from him.

The quiet of the night was almost eerie with the main street only about forty feet away. But there wasn't a sound.

He didn't move and neither did she. The fact that he was still there must have convinced her to say, "Come on in."

When she brushed past him on the landing, the touch of her arm against his was electric. He was aroused and didn't want to be. Her perfume wafted behind her. He sucked in a breath because he remembered it so well.

Once inside her apartment, he concentrated on noticing differences—furniture she'd added, curtains that were new, a watercolor on the wall. It was a home for her now, not just a place she might stay for a little while.

He didn't feel as if *he* had a home. He was living in his parents' house, but he'd outgrown it. Before he could rent a place of his own, though, he needed a job. Next week he'd work up his résumé. Next week he'd start looking. Next week he'd take back control of his life. If he could only slip into a routine that fit, maybe the agitation and restlessness would ease up.

"Something to drink?" Laura asked brightly—too brightly—as if she was on the verge of tears.

"Sure."

"Root beer? You used to like root beer so I bought some."

"Root beer's fine."

They took their sodas to the sofa, sat and had nothing to say. The awkwardness became so unbearable he set his drink on the coffee table. "This was a mistake. I shouldn't have come."

She laid her hand over his. "But you did. Because you didn't have anywhere else to go? Or because you wanted to be with *me?*"

He'd forgotten the clarity in her brown eyes, her honesty, so he answered honestly, too. "Both."

"Your letters changed."

It wasn't an accusation. It was a statement, and a "why?" was behind it or coming next. "I wrote what I could when I could."

Her eyes were shiny now. "You don't want to talk, do you?"

"No."

"We don't have to talk, Brady. There are other ways of communicating."

Blond strands in her light brown hair shone like gold under the floor lamp. Her skin was tanned, as if she'd been in the sun recently…and it looked so soft. Her lips… They were the lips he'd dreamed about kissing again for two long years.

"I'm not afraid of you kissing me, Brady. I would never be afraid of that."

She'd obviously remembered what he'd said the night of the party, the night he'd warned her that everything was different. Her invitation was almost a dare and it was a dare he couldn't resist. He needed something to ease the ache inside him. Alcohol didn't do it. Pot didn't do it. Running didn't do it. Maybe Laura could pour some sweetness on the acid that felt as though it was burning a hole through him.

Their kiss wasn't like any other they'd ever experienced. He could tell from her intake of breath. He could tell by the degree of his hunger for her. Furiously desperate, searching for the old and the new, their tongues tangled, their lips clung, their hands explored. She was unbuttoning his shirt as he unzipped her dress. The heat they generated seemed to melt their clothes away.

He wanted Laura for so many reasons. She was innocence and purity and life before hell. She was sweetness and woman and softness and home. The sofa became too confining. They kissed and touched and caressed on the braided rug on the floor, their bodies slick with desire that became almost too explosive. He was still afraid having sex with her was all wrong. But he didn't know which way to turn, and Laura was pulling him toward her.

When he entered her, he wasn't thinking about consequences or the future or commitment or vows. He was responding to pure need—the need to feel alive and be alive, the need to forget about guilt and regret and pain so fierce it would never go away. As he thrust into her, she lifted her hips higher, as if sensing he needed deep and consuming and fast. She reached for her orgasm first, wrapped her legs around him and cried out his name.

He came in a hot heavy surge that left him spent.

After Laura kissed his neck, he rolled to his side, taking her with him, and held her tight. Then, right there on her living-room floor, he fell into a deeper sleep than he'd experienced in two long years.

A few hours later, when he felt the touch on his shoulder, he was back in mud and grit and foliage so thick it could swallow him up. He responded reflexively as months of experience had taught him. He grabbed for the knife on his belt but didn't have it. Before he was even consciously awake, he'd pinned down his attacker.

"Brady! Brady! It's me! It's Laura."

Her name penetrated, and he froze. When he opened his eyes, she was beneath him, looking scared. Thank God he hadn't wedged his arm across her throat. Thank God he hadn't hurt her. Had he?

Hastening to his feet, he saw that he was still naked and so was she. Making love with her rushed back.

He sank to his knees beside her. "Are you okay? Damn it, Laura, I'm sorry."

She was gazing at him with wide eyes, and her voice trembled. "I'm fine, but are you?"

"I told you this wasn't going to work. I told you I was different. I can't stop these reactions."

"You were defending yourself," she said as if she understood, yet not completely.

"I don't know what I was doing. I just know I'm not who I was. If we can't even sleep together—"

"We can sleep together. I just shouldn't wake you

suddenly. Or—" she hesitated for a moment "—I just have to do it from a distance."

"Laura—"

She sat up, sat before him naked, pleading for what the two of them could have. "Give us a chance. Let me figure out how to help you."

For a year and a half, Laura attempted to make them into what they'd been before. Brady had worked hard at trying to be normal, trying to forget, trying to go on. But normalcy was something he'd feared he'd never really feel inside again. Before he'd left for the service, he'd loved Laura. He'd fallen hard and fast. But after he came back, he couldn't get there again. She still turned him on. Sometimes he felt a sort of peace in her presence. He didn't want to be with anyone else. But his soul was confused. Ethics he'd learned in his childhood had gotten smashed. Wasn't a life a life? Was one person's life more valuable than another's? After World War II, Americans cheered their soldiers when they returned home. Now they didn't.

How could he take Laura to the latest Robert Redford movie and feign interest in it as if he'd never gone to Vietnam? How could he go dancing with her and just slough off a burden he couldn't seem to put down? How could he pretend they could find happily-ever-after when he had trouble merely getting through today?

If they had sex—always with protection after that first homecoming union—he didn't stay the night. He'd hold her until she fell asleep and then he'd leave. He couldn't take the chance that she'd witness one of his nightmares. He couldn't take the chance that he'd hurt her if she awakened him.

A month after he'd gotten home, he'd found a job in the design department of an air-conditioning firm. It wasn't what he wanted to do. He had ideas for vending machines already on paper. There were more running around in his head for robots that could do assembly workers' jobs. But he needed a paycheck. He needed a place of his own. He needed to feel he had control over something.

There were too many times he didn't. Flashbacks occurred when he was startled. He'd scared Laura out of her wits a couple of times.

One Sunday afternoon they'd gone to the park to feed the squirrels. A helicopter had flown overhead. As soon as he'd heard the *thwat-thwat* of the rotor blades, he'd had a flashback, started shaking and taken cover behind a line of bushes. For a few awful minutes, he'd been back in Nam. He'd been oblivious to everything after the helicopter passed over. By the time he'd stopped shaking and realized he was in a park with squirrels and swings, not in a fight for his life, Laura was by his side, as white as a bleached shirt.

She'd wanted him to get help...had begged him to. By help she'd meant a therapist. He'd stubbornly refused. How could he ever explain panic crawling up his spine, hypervigilance that turned a snapping twig into a gunshot, restlessness that made it impossible for him to relax? But most of all guilt he knew could never be washed away?

When he'd rented a small house, he'd transformed the basement into a workshop. In his spare time, and when he couldn't sleep, he'd work down there, driven to make prototypes, apply for patents, sock away enough money to open his own company someday. Neither he nor Laura had mentioned marriage.

Unexpectedly, his turning point had come on a Sunday in late January 1973. His mother had invited Laura and him for dinner. Snow had begun falling that morning, but they hadn't paid much attention to it. They could always stay the night at his parents'.

As usual, he'd been going through the motions that day, attempting to deny the sadness in Laura's eyes…as well as disappointment and something even deeper that made him feel he'd betrayed her in some way.

She'd gestured at the picture window and the falling snow beyond. "Let's go outside."

"Are you serious?"

"You're as restless as a caged tiger. Outside you can breathe easier."

To his dismay, most of the time Laura saw too much. But he didn't argue with her. He went to get his coat.

They didn't know what to do at first, but then Laura smiled. "I'll race you to the oak."

The three-story oak was the tallest tree on the property. "I'll give you a head start," he offered.

"Don't you dare. If I win, I win fair and square."

Then she took off, lumbering through the snow in her boots. He raced after her, and for all of three minutes, he felt free with the wind and snow brushing his face, the cold air stretching his lungs. When he passed Laura, he didn't feel triumphant, just grateful she'd suggested this. As he reached the tree, he put out his hands to stop himself and grabbed on to the trunk to keep from sliding in the snow.

Soon Laura stopped beside him, bent over, her hands on her knees, breathing hard. She looked up at him and her blue tam pressed her bangs to her forehead. Her cheeks were red and her breath came in white puffs. "Okay, so you beat me. No surprise there. Now let's do something *I* can be good at."

"Such as?"

She grinned at him. "Making snow angels." She fell down onto her back and swished her arms and legs, impressing an angel into the white powder.

Brady didn't follow suit.

"Come on," she coaxed. "Didn't you do this when you were a kid?"

Watching Laura lying in the snow with the abandon of a child, making wings for herself and an angel's robe, struck him as...ludicrous. He couldn't do something so inane. It was silly, so childlike. They *weren't* kids. He couldn't pretend to have fun with her. He couldn't play when everything inside him told him he had no right to play...or to be happy.

His expression must have shown what he was feeling because Laura sat up. "Brady?"

The snow fell heavier, almost like a curtain between them. He felt such a separation from her. His insides twisted, his stomach hurt, his chest became tight. "I can't do this, Laura."

"Do what? Make angels? Are you cold?"

He was cold, all right, cold to his very bone marrow. So cold he felt as though nothing would warm him up again, except maybe the fires of hell the nuns had talked about when he was in grade school. Did hell really have fire? Or was it just a place with complete aloneness. He couldn't be any more alone than he was now.

"I can't do this, Laura," he repeated. "I can't pretend we're a couple and everything's fine."

Since he'd returned home, she hadn't criticized him, she hadn't turned away from him, she hadn't gotten angry with him. But now he saw anger and the spirit that was Laura's.

She got to her feet. "I've tried to give you time to heal in your own way. I've tried to give you space. But I want *us,* Brady. I want to marry you and have lots of kids and plant daisies along our picket fence. I love you, but I can't be with you anymore, not unless you get help. You can't do this on your own. Your mother made some calls—"

"You talked about me with my mother?" The wind swirled snow around them and rustled through the trees.

"Why not?" Laura asked defensively. "We're both worried about you. Don't you think it hurts us to see you in pain?"

It hurt him to see the disillusionment in Laura's eyes. "It's never going to go away, Laura. It's never going to get better. I've got pictures in my head that are burned there."

"You won't get better if you don't do something to *make* it better. I don't know if a therapist can help, but you've got to try something. You can't keep living like this, closed off from everyone. We can't be together if you close yourself off from me. If you want me in your life, you've got to put *yours* back together again. I love you too much to watch you slowly destroy yourself like this."

"I can't talk about—"

"Yes, you can."

She almost tripped in the snow struggling to get closer to him. Grabbing on to the tree where he stood, she pleaded with him. "You've got to do something. If you don't, we can't be together anymore."

The truth and resolve in her words hit him like a deadly blow.

At his complete silence, she waited a moment and then walked away from him.

He wanted to call her back, but he couldn't. He just stood there in the snow, letting it collect on his lashes and his shoulders, feeling a burden of guilt so great it almost brought him to his knees.

Brady spent the next three weeks without Laura, in no-man's-land until his sister, Pat, called him. "What's this I hear about you and Laura breaking up?"

"Did you talk to Laura or did you talk to Mom?"

"Both, but neither of them are saying very much. What did you *do?*"

"I didn't do anything."

She let the silence lie for a while. "I guess that's the problem, huh? You haven't done anything about Laura since you came home. You've been pushing her away. I guess you pushed too far."

"I don't need a lecture, Pat."

"Well, you sure as heck need something. Do you want her to find another man, marry him and have his kids?"

The truth of it was, he hadn't thought about that, and now at Pat's words, his heart hurt. "No!" The word was gruff and immediate and full of vehemence.

"Then what are you going to do about it? If you don't do something, you *will* lose her."

What had Laura said? *If you want me in your life, you've*

got to put yours back together again. He didn't know if he could. But maybe it was time he put a more serious effort into trying.

"Brady, I'm sure you risked your life over there for something you might not have believed in. Maybe you think you've already taken too many risks. I don't know. But it seems to me Laura is worth fighting for no matter what you have to do."

No matter what you have to do.

The idea of baring his soul and letting memories flood back terrified him. What was the worst that could happen?

He'd freak out and they'd lock him in a psychiatric ward.

"I'll think about it."

There was impatience in his sister's voice as she warned him, "Don't think about it too long. Laura could meet the man of her dreams tomorrow."

Pat was goading him. Yet she was right. But could he ever again be the man of Laura's dreams?

Chapter 8

The March wind whipped against Brady's car as he parked beside Laura's blue Challenger in Montgomery Ward's parking lot, his conversation with Pat still echoing in his mind. The spaces were all but empty now, except for those taken by the clerks in the stores. Laura would be walking through those doors in about five minutes.

They were a very long five minutes.

When he spotted her, he felt a hint of joy again, the old excitement and longing for what they'd once had. It had been seven weeks since he'd seen her. Maybe the most important seven weeks of his life.

She was wearing a coat with a faux-fur trim around the hood, down the front and around the calf-length hem. A mint-green scarf wrapped around her neck, and the fringes blew behind her in the wind. When she saw his car, she recognized it immediately. She just stood there staring at him.

If she was as angry with him as she should be, or as hurt as she must be, she might just hop in her car and drive to her apartment.

So she wouldn't even consider that option, he climbed out of his car and went to meet her. "Will you talk to me for a few minutes?" he asked, gesturing to his Camaro.

"All right," she agreed.

He couldn't tell from her expression whether she was glad to see him.

When he opened the passenger door for her, she politely murmured thank-you and slid inside. This wasn't the Laura he knew. This Laura was keeping her feelings hidden, her countenance neutral. His heart pounded because he wasn't certain how she was going to react to what he had to say.

After he closed his door, he shifted to look at her. She wasn't taking off her gloves or in any way making herself comfortable. He had the feeling she was ready to bolt. He knew he was on the verge of losing her, but hopefully just on the verge. If he had the courage to do it, he could still turn this around.

He plunged in. "A month ago, I started going to a counselor who was recommended to my dad. He has an office in his house, so I can maintain my privacy. I've had seven sessions with him."

"Is he helping you?" Laura was concerned.

Although he couldn't see her clearly in the car's shadows, he started to hope again. He had to be honest with her. "I'm not sure. The sessions aren't what I expected. I mean, I don't know what I thought therapy would be. He doesn't have answers. He just leads me so that I examine what's there."

Silence built in the car. Then Laura moved slightly, facing him a little more squarely. "Why did you come tonight?"

His voice was husky when he admitted, "Because I pushed you away."

"You didn't just push me away. You shut the door." It wasn't an accusation as much as a statement of fact.

"When I came home, I wasn't ready to be with anyone. I haven't been able to let you in."

"You don't trust me to understand what you've been through."

He shook his head. "I don't think it's a matter of trust. I'm afraid that if you see what's inside me…you'll hate me." His therapist had led him to understand that this was his deepest fear.

"Brady! How could you ever think that?"

"I've done things—" After he closed his eyes for a moment against the guilt, regret and self-recriminations, he looked at Laura, felt the root of love that had sprouted at the antiwar demonstration and plunged ahead. "I'm here tonight to ask you to come with me tomorrow to my therapy session. John—that's the counselor's name—believes that's what's needed here. He wants me to tell him what happened in Nam and he believes you need to hear it, too."

"*He* believes?"

"I know you and I can't go on the way we've been. We either have to really be together or break apart."

Perceptively, she asked, "You think if I hear what happened over there, I'll walk away?"

"It's possible. You need to know who I've become."

She considered everything he'd said. "If I come tomorrow, what then?"

"We just have to do this and decide where we are afterward."

"You can't just tell me about your experiences?"

"John feels it would be safer for me if we do it there. My nightmares are like a horror movie, Laura. He doesn't want me to get stuck in one."

"I don't understand."

"When I have flashbacks, it's as if I'm there again. He explained it to me."

Suddenly Laura clasped his arm. The old warmth was back in her voice. "I'll do anything to help you, Brady. Just tell me where to go and what time to be there."

Her hand on his arm, her touch, her presence in his life were so necessary to him. Relieved she'd agreed to accompany him, he was worried about what would happen after the session. He'd tried to bury his time in Nam. He'd thought that was the best way to go on. But John believed burying it instead of examining it was why he still had nightmares and flashbacks and wouldn't let Laura get close.

Brady knew one thing for certain. If he looked at it all again, it would be for the last time. After tomorrow, he and Laura would either move on together or be torn apart. Now he just wanted to get tomorrow over with, no matter what it brought.

He opened his car door. "Give me your keys. I'll warm up your car and then I'll follow you home to make sure you get inside okay."

"Are you going to come in?"

"Not tonight, Laura." Maybe not ever again. It all depended on what happened tomorrow.

"Brady! Brady, look at me." John Markowitz's usually calm voice was firmer and louder than Brady had ever heard it.

"Brady, focus on my eyes and listen to me," John ordered. "You are home. You are safe. You're in the present and all that you remembered is in the past."

Brady could feel the sweat dripping from his brow. His shirt stuck to his back. His body was taut with memories he didn't want to recall ever again—the booby-trapped Chicom grenade, the smell of cordite, Ricky going down, the shouts, the squad of VC, the arms' fire, the anxiety and fear…the dead bodies.

Dropping his head into his hands, he took a deep gulp of air, as if that could drive all the images away.

Beside him on the couch, he felt movement, then a light hand on his arm. "It was war, Brady. It's over. You're here with me."

If he looked at Laura, he was certain he'd see the condemnation he deserved. She might pretend she could handle what he'd just told her in front of John, but when they left this office, they'd be over.

John was sitting in a chair in front of the sofa, and Brady didn't know when he'd moved there. The counselor said soothingly, "Sit back and breathe deeply. Relax for a minute."

Relax? When he'd just stepped out of a living nightmare? No one could understand what the retelling, the reliving and the rethinking did to him. Only another

Vietnam vet could. John was the same age as his father and had served in the army, but, stationed in Europe, he'd never been in combat. Brady could tell Laura liked the therapist. In just a few minutes at the opening of the session, John had put her at ease. He'd asked her how she'd felt waiting for Brady and what she'd experienced since Brady had come home and tried to find his way. She'd been forthright, letting her tears spill out, and Brady had felt all the more guilty for them. He'd never meant to hurt her. Since he'd returned home, he had. He'd hurt her by withdrawing, by distancing himself, by walling himself off and not letting her in. But now…

"Laura, can you tell Brady what you're feeling at this moment?" John encouraged her.

"I hurt for him." Her voice broke.

"Can you look into his eyes and tell him that?"

She brought her leg up onto the sofa and faced Brady. "I hurt for you. I understand that you believe you did something terrible. But you had to make a two-second decision. You had to think about Carl and the rest of your squad."

"I killed them." His voice was raw and he wasn't going to let her pour any sugar on this.

Intervening, John asked, "Do you understand what war is, Brady? It's both sides fighting to survive. You survived. Are you sorry about that?"

He took a few moments and examined it. "No."

Before he could comprehend what Laura was going to do, she slipped off the sofa, knelt in front of him and held his hands. She gazed into his eyes and he saw nothing hidden, nothing guarded on her face.

"I love you, Brady." She stopped for a moment and he

imagined she was still thinking about the horrible scene he'd described. With determined certainty, she went on. "I can accept what happened to you."

"You mean, what I did." She had to realize he'd had an active role in what had happened.

"All right, what you did. I can't begin to understand all of it. But I don't think less of you. I still want to be with you. I want a life with you."

Brady glanced over her head at John, hardly able to accept what she was saying.

The therapist gave him a smile and a shrug. "She's making herself perfectly clear. You've got two options. You can believe her and have a long, happy life together. Or you can not believe her and be alone. No matter what happens, you've made a breakthrough just in the telling."

Standing, Brady pulled Laura to her feet. "I need fresh air. Let's go."

If John was surprised, he didn't show it. He stood, too, and went behind his desk. "We should make another appointment, and I want you to join a therapy group I'm leading."

"No. No more appointments. No more of this."

"Brady—" John's voice held a warning tone.

"I came to you because Laura pushed me to get help. You've helped me put everything into perspective. I've got a life to live now."

"Do you think the flashbacks are going to stop? Do you think the nightmares won't trouble you anymore?" the therapist asked, obviously concerned.

"Of course not," Brady replied. "But I'll work through them. I promise if I ever really need you again, I'll call you."

A worried expression crossed Laura's face, and he squeezed her hand. "Let's go," he repeated.

Once they were outside in Brady's car, he switched on the ignition, backed out of John's driveway, went about two blocks and then pulled over to the curb.

"What are we doing?" Laura asked.

"I have to know what's going through your head. I have to know if you meant what you said in there."

Her face took on such a tender expression, his chest grew tight.

"Yes, I meant it."

Her eyes were shimmering with love, and although he was still stirred up by the memories, still carried guilt and regret and remorse, a door had been opened in his heart that Laura could walk through. He couldn't believe everything he'd told her hadn't affected her. There was only one way to truly find out if they were going to make it. One way for him to tell if she could love him freely, accepting who he was…and what he'd done.

"Do you want to go to your place, or do you want to come to mine?" he asked, all churned up by the pictures he needed to blot out, yet led by the hope he might have a future with her.

"Let's go to your house," she answered quietly.

They hadn't spent much time at the house he'd rented, maybe because inviting her there was symbolic of letting her into his life. "My place it is."

He hardly remembered driving there. He was too busy pushing away pictures and sounds that haunted him, focusing his awareness on Laura and the next hour or so that would determine the course of his life.

Since he was making good money, he'd bought new furniture when he'd rented the house. The sofa and armchair were green plaid, the recliner a solid green. The two end tables were bare except for the lamps, and the coffee table held a few professional magazines. There was no dining room, so a maple table and chairs stood in the kitchen. Although dishes were piled high in the sink and Brady didn't clean much, the rest of the place was straightened up.

Why shouldn't it be? He was never there. Or else he was downstairs in his workroom.

When he led Laura into the bedroom, the mahogany furniture gleamed in the sunlight pouring through the side window.

"Do you want me to close the blinds?"

Laura shook her head. "No, making love in the sun is just what we need."

Part of him couldn't believe this was happening. Part of him expected her to recoil and run away. He was ready to accept that.

But she didn't run. She let him undress her.

When she started on his buttons, he took her hands. "I can do it faster."

Stripped and lying in bed beside her, he realized he wanted making love with her today to be different from all the others. He knew they couldn't get the first time back. That had been all romance and closeness and pure innocence because she'd been a virgin. Their weekend together after basic had been a honeymoon-like dream. Over the past twenty months, when they'd had sex, it had been a release and an escape for him. It had been a way for him to get rid of stress, a way to stay close to Laura, even though they weren't close.

Today, he knew he was expecting too much, but he wanted more.

"What's the matter?" she asked, running her fingers through his chest hair.

"I need to be here with you, really *be* here with you. Do you know what I mean?"

"I think so. Since you got home…I almost felt as if I could have been any girl and it wouldn't have mattered to you."

He wrapped his arms around her. "Oh, Laura, I'm so sorry."

"Don't be sorry, Brady. Just…make love to me."

As Brady kissed Laura, he was gentle at first, maybe expecting hesitancy, maybe expecting her actions not to match her words. But she didn't hesitate at all and her hands were on him as if she wanted to touch him everywhere. He took his time, prolonged their pleasure, studied her face again and again, searching for regret or revulsion. All he saw was love.

How could that be?

The need to possess her tore his control in two. When he entered her, he found not only desire on her face but joy. In that moment he finally understood that it wasn't what he'd done that had kept them apart, but his refusal to trust Laura's love. He could still hardly believe she was giving him such a gift.

His pleasure became hers and hers his. When he cried out, so did she. In that timeless, endless interlude, they were absolutely one.

As he rolled onto his side, taking her with him to keep

them joined, he realized he'd gotten the answer he'd never expected. She loved him! She really loved him.

The tips of their noses touching, he kissed her softly, then leaned back a bit so he could see her face. "Will you marry me?"

Her eyes widened and she smiled at him with a radiance that tightened his throat. "Yes, I'll marry you."

"Mom and Dad will probably want us to have a big wedding so they can invite everyone they know."

"We can have any kind of wedding they want."

"I'd prefer sooner rather than later."

"Big weddings take time."

He groaned. "We've wasted enough time already."

She shook her head. "It wasn't wasted. We learned an important lesson. Whatever we have to face, we have to face it together."

Wrapping his arms around her, he was sure he didn't deserve this gift she was offering him. He would give her the moon and stars and the whole world if he could. He would give her absolutely everything she'd ever wanted. Wasn't that what a husband was supposed to do?

As he hugged her, desire bit him hard again. There was no doubt in his mind that he could push his demons into the cellar and keep them buried. He and Laura *would* live happily ever after.

Now as Brady tried to change position in the single bed in the den, he realized resting on his side was out of the question. He hated lying on his back. He couldn't sleep that way.

Maybe he wasn't as uncomfortable with the position

as he was with his thoughts. He couldn't believe how naive he'd been, thinking happily-ever-after was even a possibility. Throughout the months after he'd proposed, he'd still had nightmares that brought him awake sweating, shaking, sometimes calling out. But he'd let Laura stay with him. If she awakened him, she did it from a distance. They'd bought an old school bell. She'd ring it until she got through to him, until he realized where he was and who she was, and that he was no longer in danger. She was there, by his side, choosing to stay rather than go.

They'd married in March 1974 because both the church and the Yorktowne Hotel could accommodate them that particular Saturday. Laura's bridesmaids had stayed with her in her apartment the night before the wedding. Brady's dad had taken him and his brothers and Jack to a pub, where they'd talked about sports and cars. He hadn't gotten drunk. He'd had no desire to get drunk. He wanted his full faculties about him when he said, "I do." Each day he had trouble believing Laura hadn't walked away. In fact, the morning of the wedding…

He'd left his house before the first light of day and gone to her apartment.

When he knocked, *she'd* answered the door.

"I'm not supposed to see you until later!" she said seriously.

"Tradition isn't as important as our future. Is anybody else awake?"

Slipping outside, she closed the door behind her, her hair all tousled around her face. She was wearing a pink chenille robe with a wide belt and was barefoot. He simply stared at her, amazed that this woman was going to be his wife in just a few hours and he could look at her every morning like this for the rest of their lives. She wrapped her arms around herself because the March air was cold.

"Did I wake you?"

"I've been awake since five," she admitted. "I'm too excited to sleep. We all talked until about one, but I'm so full of energy I don't think anything's going to slow me down today. How about you?"

"Yeah, we got home about one. But I woke up around five, too, and I knew I had to talk to you."

Her smile faded, her eyes became worried and her arms dropped to her sides. "What's wrong?"

"I just need to make sure you want to get married. The nightmares might never go away. The flashbacks can still happen anytime. I want to give you so much, Laura—"

The worried look faded and she wrapped her arms around his neck. "When you asked me to marry you, I said yes and I meant yes."

"I'm not that boy you met on the courthouse steps."

"No, you're not. I'm not that girl you dragged away from trouble that day. We've both changed. I think that's what being married is all about—growing and changing together." She leaned back, worried again. "Now, if *you're* having doubts..."

"No doubts. From today on we're only going to talk about the future—not the past. Agreed?"

She searched his face, then nodded. "Agreed."

He pulled a tiny box wrapped in gold paper out of his pocket. "Here. I wanted to give you this. I know we'll be exchanging rings later, but I thought you'd like these for your bracelet."

After tearing off the bow and paper, she stuffed them in her pocket, then lifted the lid. Inside she found two tiny entwined gold rings to attach to her bracelet. "Oh, thank you, Brady! They're perfect. Wait right here. I have something for you, too."

She was back in an instant, holding a box wrapped in blue paper with a darker blue bow. He tore the wrappings from it and opened the lid. He found gold cuff links and a gold tie bar engraved with the letter M.

"They were my father's," she said softly.

Embracing her, he settled his cheek against hers and murmured, "I'm honored you gave them to me."

After a soul-deep kiss that made him want to forget all the hoopla and take her to a small chapel somewhere, marry her and forget about the crowd that was going to witness their ceremony, he left her standing at her apartment door.

When they returned from their honeymoon to the Poconos, she'd be moving into his house with him. Then they'd start their real lives and he'd make some serious money. She'd have babies and time would take care of the nightmares and regrets.

At least, that was what he'd thought. That was what he'd hoped. That's what he'd prayed. But what he'd envisioned hadn't happened, and worse yet—

Suddenly he heard Laura stirring on the sofa across the room. "Brady, are you awake?" she whispered.

"I'm awake."

"Do you need pain medication? Something to drink?"

"You don't have to wait on me."

She was silent and he knew he shouldn't have said it in just that way.

After a few moments, she asked, "Do you want to go back to sleep? Or do you want to talk?"

Talk. That was Laura's solution for any problem, but not his. Talking didn't change the course of events. Talking didn't change the past. Talking was simply that, hearing yourself go over what was in your head. If he said he wanted to go back to sleep and kept tossing and turning and moving around, she'd hear that. Then she'd know he'd simply tried to shut her out again. Lately, shutting Laura out had become more comfortable than letting her in. Was their marriage unraveling after thirty-three years? He'd tried and tried to be the husband she'd needed. But sometimes he'd felt he was pretending…doing all the right things but not feeling what he should when he did them. Maybe trying wasn't enough. Maybe love wasn't enough.

"Go ahead and turn the light on," he said. "I'm wired. I can't seem to shut down. I don't have enough energy to walk for more than five minutes, but I can't sleep."

The light beside the sofa came on and he blinked at the sudden brightness. Pushing himself up to a sitting position, he tried to ignore the residuals of surgery, the pain from the incision, the tingling in his chest and arm which he'd been told was quite normal.

She was about to throw off her afghan, when he suggested, "Stay there." He made his way to the sofa and eased himself down. The afghan she'd covered herself with was between them.

"Why aren't *you* sleeping?" he asked, deciding that if she wanted to talk, they could discuss what was bothering *her.* Though that might not be any safer than what was bothering him.

"Because my mind's probably going as fast as yours."

She gave him a smile that was so innately Laura he reached out for her hand. "This hasn't been easy for you."

"Life isn't easy. We'll deal with it."

He withdrew his hand. "You know, Laura, it's okay to collapse after you've been through an ordeal. That's normal." Sometimes her strength wasn't a virtue but a barrier, and her love a bittersweet gift.

"If I collapse, then what? I collapsed once and it wasn't pretty. I don't ever want it to happen again."

Laura's collapse, as she called it, had been a long time coming. Three miscarriages and the death of a child would do it to anybody. But she hadn't seen it like that. She'd seen herself as weak. After Jason's funeral, she'd broken down and cried day and night. He'd called John Markowitz and the psychologist had recommended that both join a group he ran for parents who'd lost children. Laura had attended the sessions. He hadn't.

"Do you believe everything happens for a reason?" she asked, gazing at him with expressive brown eyes.

They'd had this discussion before in their marriage, but not lately, maybe not for the past five years. "Are we talking about the master-plan theory again?" He couldn't keep the cynicism from his question.

"If you don't want to talk about this, we don't have to," she said softly, looking tentative now instead of open.

He raked his hand through his hair. "I don't think I'm up to a philosophical discussion about why I had a heart attack. I had it because of genetics. My grandfather died of a heart attack and so did my mother. My dad had a stroke."

Her silence was louder than any words could be.

"Say it," he said gruffly, his heart pounding a little harder.

"Say what?"

"Say what you're thinking."

"You don't want to hear what I'm thinking." She stared straight ahead rather than at him, and he felt those degrees of separation again that had crept between them one by one.

"I can practically read your mind," he told her. "You're thinking I brought this on myself by what I eat, by not getting enough exercise, by working too hard. I don't believe hard work ever killed anyone. And the rest…" He sighed. "I was predisposed to this. Even if I become a vegetarian, it won't change my genes."

"I wasn't thinking about your diet, Brady. I was thinking maybe this happened so we could all become closer as a family."

That logic absolutely escaped him. "Sean will be out on his own soon. Three years and Kat will be off to college, too. They'll both forget they even have parents."

"Maybe." She didn't sound happy about it.

To make her feel better, he suggested, "Daughters seem to stick closer than sons. Even Pat did. She stayed in York and helped Mom after Dad's stroke. Matt and Ryan went off living their lives."

"I want to keep Sean close, too," she murmured.

"And you want me to do the same. It might be too late. I wasn't around enough when he was little and there's nothing I can do about that."

"If you'd tell him what happened in Vietnam—"

"No." Brady's heart was definitely racing faster now. And he could feel the ache in his chest, the sweat beading on his brow. He felt himself flushing.

"Brady?"

"Leave it, Laura. Just leave it."

Then he went to the bathroom for a pill that he hoped would take care of more than one kind of pain.

Chapter 9

"No!" Brady called out in bed beside Laura.

She came awake with a jolt, as she had many other nights since his surgery a month ago.

He was tossing…kicking the covers…mumbling about mortars and Carl and the VC. He would hurt himself if he kept this up. He still had to heal.

Pushing away the fear of waking him, she grabbed his shoulder. His pajama shirt was damp with sweat.

In an instinctive response, he grabbed for her arm and gripped it.

"Brady. Brady, it's Laura. Laura."

His grip loosened. Quickly he heaved himself to the edge of the bed and switched on the lamp. "Did I bruise you?"

The information they'd received from the hospital had explained that bad dreams might be one of the aftereffects of open-heart surgery. But Brady was having more than bad dreams. Tonight he'd been back in Vietnam. She'd been through this with him before.

She didn't even check her arm. "No. I'm fine. Are you?"

"Just great," he muttered, not looking at her. "I'm just great."

Her mouth went dry. This was her fault.

She'd caused his heart attack. These dreams were a reminder he couldn't deny. *She* was responsible. And he wouldn't let her help him. He wouldn't let her in. The past few weeks had almost been packed with as much tension between them as the time after he'd come home from the service. Although he denied it, she knew he blamed her for having to go through this recuperation, the nightmares and the life changes he didn't want to make.

Tomorrow he'd have another electrocardiogram. But it wouldn't really tell the doctors what was going on in his heart.

"Brady, what can I do?" She had to fix this. Somehow she had to fix *them*.

"There's nothing you can do. You know that. They'll fade. Eventually."

But *would* the nightmares fade? Pandora's box had been opened, and this time Laura didn't believe the lid could be put back on again.

Pushing himself up off the bed, Brady didn't even glance at her as he headed for the bathroom.

She wrapped her arms around herself, holding back tears. If only they could go back—even just to this year's anniversary. What she wouldn't give to go back in time merely two months.

On their thirty-third anniversary, Brady had come home around eight.

She was in the kitchen, cleaning up pots and pans from cooking his favorite dinner. She'd tried to paste on a smile. "Hi. I just put dinner in the refrigerator."

"I didn't forget what today is."

No, he hadn't forgotten. She could see that. Her smile almost faded away as she said, "I made your favorite—coq au vin. Do you want me to warm it up?"

"Sure." He looked away from her, down the hall. "Are the kids upstairs?"

"They went to the movies. I…" Her voice faltered and she took a deep breath. "I was hoping we'd have the evening to ourselves."

When he crossed to her, he stood very near. "I *didn't* forget," he said again.

"If you didn't forget today was our anniversary, then I guess you just didn't want to be here!"

"I didn't know you'd cleared the deck for us. I'm not a mind reader. Maybe you should have told me."

Those tears were so close. "Maybe I should have."

He sighed. "I thought about buying you something. But you have everything. What you could use is a smaller car to run errands. Your van's getting older. Maybe we can buy one of those yellow Mustangs."

She didn't know what to say to that. She took an envelope from a kitchen drawer and handed it to him. The card she'd bought seemed meaningless now. Too much sentiment that could embarrass them both. "I thought you'd like those."

He opened the envelope and pulled out the tickets. "An Orioles game. That's great."

"I couldn't get the home opener. It's the third game at Camden Yards."

"Will you go with me?" he joked.

"I can. Or maybe Jack would like to go." She didn't suggest he take Sean. But that suggestion was there between them, too. She understood why Brady often didn't come home for dinner. He and Sean didn't talk. Whenever Brady asked their son questions, he got monosyllabic answers that frustrated him.

"Thank you," he said a bit too enthusiastically as he put his arms around her and kissed her. The kiss had some of the old passion in it. At least, she thought it did. She kissed him back with the fervor she felt…with the fervor she'd always felt. They could still salvage the evening.

When Brady broke off the kiss, she smiled. "I have strawberries and whipped cream for dessert."

"The kids will probably be home till I eat."

"We could start with dessert first."

His brows arched as he caught her meaning. "Yes," he drawled. "We could. I'll go get a shower. You bring the strawberries."

Then he kissed her briefly again, smiled and left the kitchen.

They'd fed each other the strawberries and made love. It had felt forced, as though they were both trying too hard. More a ritual than a joining of hearts.

Somehow, feelings that had once been so strong didn't awaken desire as they once did.

That was what she'd thought in March. But now she wondered if Brady's feelings for her had faded altogether.

Because now their marriage was falling apart.

* * *

"The test go okay?" Laura asked Brady on Friday afternoon as he climbed into her van.

Last night, after his nightmare, neither of them had fallen asleep easily. He'd listened for Laura's breathing to deepen, but it hadn't for over an hour.

This morning Pat had dropped him off at Apple Hill Medical Center and Laura was picking him up during her lunch break. He was damn tired of all the tests, probing and questions. He was also tired of being chauffeured.

"It was just an electrocardiogram," he answered briefly.

After his checkup next week, he'd be able to drive himself. Then Laura might stop hovering. There was so much tension between them. He could feel her expectations, her willing him to be well and at peace once more, her desire to assuage her own guilt. Although he'd been told bad dreams might be one of the aftereffects of his surgery, he hadn't been prepared for the recurring pictures that he'd believed he'd erased from his memory years ago.

Laura was so patient with him that sometimes he just wanted to shake her. Why couldn't she see that he needed to be left alone until he recovered…until he felt like a man again? He saw the longing in her eyes for the intimacy they used to share. But he couldn't wrap her in his arms right now because he knew where it would lead….

In another week or so they could consider attempting sex.

Sex.

He had no idea how his heart would respond even if he could get it up and keep it up. His medication might prevent a normal response. On top of that, the idea of his pulse racing out of control brought back visions of his heart attack.

Maybe after he started rehab and felt comfortable with the treadmill and his heart going faster…

Since his heart attack, he'd been reexamining his life, wishing he could do some of it over. When he looked at the whole of his marriage, he could see how much he owed Laura…how much he'd always owed Laura. She'd saved him from hell. That was why he worked so damn hard. She deserved the best of everything. She deserved a lot more. But sometimes he couldn't give her what she desired most—the connection they'd found on the courthouse steps.

"That could be your last test for a while. You've got to be happy about that." She was obviously trying to engage him in conversation.

"I am." There didn't seem to be more to say.

"Brady, talk to me."

"About?" he asked with restrained patience.

"About what you're thinking, how you're feeling. You wanted me to go back to work at Blossoms and I have. But we hardly ever talk."

After uncomfortable beats of silence, she added, "I'm wondering if you're blaming me for all you're going through—your recuperation and…and the bad dreams you're having again."

"I've told you before. The heart attack wasn't your fault."

"I feel it was. Ever since you got home, you've been shutting me out."

He kept silent.

"Did you know that after my miscarriages, I thought you might blame me for them?" she asked quietly, as if she'd been reexamining their lives, too.

"Why would you possibly think that? I never gave you any indication that I did, did I?"

"No. But I kept losing the babies. I kept worrying about what I was doing wrong. If I shouldn't have been working. If I should have found another doctor."

"Laura, your miscarriages were probably *my* fault. Because of the defoliant used in Nam. We didn't know it then, but we know it now. When rumors about Agent Orange began trickling out, we discussed it."

Shooting him a quick look, Laura sighed. "Guilt isn't always rational. I know you wanted lots of kids like I did. And when I was pregnant with Jason—"

She paused and he knew why. They didn't talk about Jason because it was just too painful.

But this time she didn't stop. "When I was pregnant with Jason, you were there for me every moment…during our worry until I was at eight months and then nine months along. When he was born, you were happier than I've ever seen you."

Reluctantly Brady recalled that time, too. "My flashbacks had quit. The nightmares were almost nonexistent." Their son had been the hope who could finally eradicate everything bad that had gone before.

After silence wedged between them, she sent him a weak smile. "So many good memories. Like Jason's first Christmas, all the lights you put on the tree, the train set you assembled. You kissed me under the mistletoe and gave me the Christmas-stocking charm that year."

He heard the catch in her voice as she faced the windshield once more.

Then her small smile faded and the good memory became one both wished they could forget.

"After Jason died—" She slowed for a red light and glanced at him. "Afterward…since there was no specific cause to blame with SIDS, I ran what-ifs through my mind over and over again. What if my milk had been more plentiful and I could have breast-fed him? What if I'd put him to bed later? What if I'd put him to bed earlier? What if I'd checked on him more often? If only we'd had a baby monitor. If only I'd gotten up early." After a few moments, she added, "We haven't had a smooth road. Your almost dying in front of me has brought a lot of the old times back."

Old times. Old memories. Brady vividly recalled rushing into the nursery, finding Laura holding Jason… His son had been three months old when he'd stopped breathing. His throat tight, Brady skipped ahead.

The day of the funeral—

He'd stood gazing at the little maple casket. He remembered thinking he'd wanted to be alone with it. He'd wanted to tell his son everything he'd never have a chance to tell him. He'd wanted to imagine Jason going to kindergarten, picking out his first pup, racing a bicycle. Yet he'd known that if he'd actually dwelled on any of that, he might fall apart.

Laura had held herself together until the last of their friends and relatives had left their house. Then she'd begun crying inconsolably. He'd held her day after day until finally weeks later, she'd begun attending John's group. He just hadn't been able to do that. There had been no way he could talk about how he'd felt.

Laura's voice now penetrated the reflections and brought him back from a place of sorrow he rarely visited. "Brady?"

"Sorry. I was thinking. What did you ask me?"

"Do you remember the night I got home from Blossoms after talking to that customer who'd adopted?"

"I remember." That night Laura's face had been glowing, her eyes bright, and she'd looked like the twenty-year-old he'd fallen in love with.

"I gave you the business card from the lawyer in Harrisburg."

"And told me how your customer had adopted three children and how they were so adorable and that you'd held the two-year-old for a long time. You asked me if we could adopt."

He'd known no other child would ever take Jason's place. But Laura had believed adopting could make them happy again.

Ever since Brady had come home from the service, he'd been afraid he'd lose Laura. It was as simple as that…and as complex. When she'd gotten pregnant with Jason and the pregnancy had gone to term, he'd felt a little more secure in their happiness. But after they'd lost Jason, he realized that if they didn't have kids together…and that meant adopting, she might leave. So he'd agreed to fill out the paperwork for the lawyer.

When Sean had been placed in Laura's arms a year and a half later, Brady had felt…*nothing*—no connection to this child he was going to raise as his son. He'd tried his damnedest, but it was easier to work than to be around the baby. It was easier to devise a business plan for the company he intended to build than to watch Sean take his first step, hear him speak his first word, witness the bond between this child and Laura. Because he worked so much and spent so little time with Sean, they'd never established those basic ties to carry them through the years. It was *his* fault, not Sean's.

When they'd adopted Kat, he'd had no trouble taking her quickly into his heart, possibly because she was a girl. His love for his daughter had become another wedge between him and Sean. If anyone asked Brady if he loved his son, he would say he did. And he did. But it was a love of distance, a love of responsibility, a love that had never tied the two of them together.

Beside him now, Laura softly said, "If we hadn't adopted Sean and Kat, think of what we'd have missed."

Part of him agreed.

The other part…

He was glad Laura was turning into their driveway, glad they wouldn't have more time to reminisce.

There was a black BMW parked in front of the garage.

"It's Jack!" Laura said brightly.

Brady hadn't been answering calls. Since he worked in his home office a few hours a day now, he let the machine pick up.

As they stopped in the driveway, Brady watched Jack get out of his car. His old friend smiled and waved.

Brady climbed out of the van, leaned in and said to his wife, "Don't work too hard."

She forced a smile and nodded. "I'll probably be home around seven."

He should have kissed her. Just a fast kiss. Nothing would happen with that. But with Jack waiting…

Laura waved as she backed out of the driveway.

He went to meet his old friend.

"You've lost weight," Jack said to him.

Jack, like many men their age, had added about five pounds a year the past five years. His face was fuller than it used to be, hiding some of the wrinkles. His brown hair was laced with gray, but his hazel eyes were as sharp as ever, and in his yellow polo shirt with brown slacks, he appeared every inch the successful businessman he was. He now owned three shoe stores in the surrounding area.

Brady's T-shirt and jeans made his loss of fifteen pounds since the surgery obvious. He'd needed to get lean again and he wanted to stay that way.

"Want a cup of coffee?" he asked. "It will have to be decaffeinated, though."

"Make it strong, and I don't care."

Brady chuckled. Jack had always been practical.

Inside the house, Brady led Jack to the state-of-the-art kitchen, with its stainless-steel appliances, mahogany cupboards and bay-windowed breakfast nook that overlooked the backyard.

Once the coffee was brewing, Jack said, "I called and left lots of messages."

Brady captured two stoneware mugs from one of the cupboards. "I know."

"You don't have to avoid me, Brady. We've been friends too long for that."

"I've been putting most of my energy into my recovery."

"No, you've been hiding out. Has the flak from that article in the paper blown over?"

Jack went for the bottom line. "For the most part. I

wasn't in any condition to deal with it when I got home from the hospital. I didn't turn on the TV, so I didn't hear local reporters doing a two-minute bite about it, either. No doubt everybody's forgotten about the story now. It's old news."

After they stared at each other for a long moment, Brady inquired, "Aren't you going to ask me if it was true?"

"No, I'm not. You never wanted to talk about Nam and I guess there are good reasons for that. When I saw what Luis did to himself after he came back, I was just so damn grateful I didn't have to go."

A few years after Luis had been discharged, he'd died of a drug overdose. Brady, Laura and Jack had attended the funeral together.

After filling the mugs, Brady handed one to his lifelong friend. "Reporters wouldn't stop calling for a while. Laura dealt with most of that and just told them we had nothing to say. There's a pile of letters, not all of them condemning me. Two of them counted. Those were from servicemen who'd been there."

"I think it was rotten the Chamber of Commerce rescinded the Man of the Year Award and gave it to someone else. Why didn't you fight that?"

"Fight it? Jeez, Jack. I couldn't lift over five pounds after I got home. I was having palpitations and didn't know if my heart would ever function properly again. I couldn't waste my energy on that."

"I guess not," he conceded. "When are you going back to work?"

"My secretary's been faxing me anything I have to okay. I can access files on the computer from here." After he could resume driving, he'd go into the office part-time until rehab was finished. When he did go back, there would be whispers and stares and lots of speculation. He'd have to let it all roll off his back unless…

"I got an offer I might not be able to refuse."

"What kind of offer?"

"A firm in Maryland wants to buy my company. If I sell it, Laura and I will be set for life."

Jack whistled low. "Are you going to do it?"

"I haven't told Laura about it yet. I'm mulling the offer over and weighing our options. It's something positive that could come from all this."

"That depends on how you look at it. Truthfully, Brady, I can't see you planning sea cruises for the rest of your life. Even if you go deep-sea fishing, it's still fishing. Your mind's too fast to ever relax."

"Maybe I could learn."

"Or maybe you should stop staying in the background. That's what you're trying to do, you know."

"I like the background."

After a moment of reflection, Jack asked, "Who talked? Who gave all that crap to the reporter?"

"Only one man might have. He was there."

"Why did he do it?"

"I have no idea." Since his surgery, Brady had been thinking about Carl Miller and the experience they'd shared. He'd been telling himself it would do no good to get in touch with Carl. As before, he just had to move on.

Jack sipped his coffee. "I'd want to know."

Maybe it *was* time Brady called Carl and got some answers.

Chapter 10

"I'm home," Laura called lightly as she pushed open the door to Brady's den late Friday night, hoping to glimpse some sign in his eyes that he was glad to see her.

She'd expected to find him at his computer when she walked in. Instead he was on the other side of the room, sitting at his drafting table, blueprints curling at the edges unfolded on its surface. She knew he was itching to get back to a regular routine and shove off his invalid status.

Then they could have sex again. Then maybe she'd feel close to him again. This afternoon in the van, he'd seemed so far away.

He was wearing a T-shirt and jeans and looked lean and fit. Although lines cut deeper around his eyes and mouth now, he was handsome…and virile. She felt old desire stir with new as she approached him.

He glanced up, but she could tell he was distracted. "Busy night?" He checked his watch.

"We're always busy this time of year." Did he even remember Mother's Day was on Sunday? She'd hired extra staff who were reliable and creative so she didn't have to be tied to the shop, though she loved Blossoms. It had been Anna Malone's legacy to her.

"Are you working tomorrow?" he asked.

"In the morning. I have errands to run in the after-noon—pick up dry cleaning, get my hair trimmed, stop at the pharmacy. Sean's baseball game is at six."

Nonchalantly he pushed aside the schematics and stood. "I thought I'd go along."

"Really?"

"I have nothing but time on my hands. Jack seems to think I'm ashamed to show my face since the article appeared. I have to prove him wrong."

"You don't have to prove anything to anyone, least of all Jack."

"Maybe I have to prove something to myself. When I go back to work, I'll have to deal with stares and comments."

"And maybe questions."

"I don't intend to answer any questions." He focused on the drafting table and she followed his gaze.

"What are those?"

"Ideas that never materialized." He picked up the sheaf of papers, rolled them and inserted them into a protec-tive tube. "I've had an offer from a Maryland firm wanting to buy the business. We wouldn't have to worry about our retirement."

"We don't have to worry about it now." She yearned

to go to Brady, wrap her arms around him and lay her head against his chest. But he was still healing and he'd given her no indication that he wanted any kind of intimacy.

A doctor actually had to clear him to have intercourse. She remembered the nurse saying one way for Brady to test himself and see if he was ready for sex was to climb two flights of stairs. If he didn't become short of breath or overly tired, then he could probably resume intimate relations.

For the past few weeks, she'd wanted to be intimate *without* having sex. She'd just needed Brady to hold her. She'd just wanted to hold him. But every night they lay on separate sides of their king-size bed, waiting for the next nightmare. It was as if he was afraid to get close. Maybe it was simply male ego. If he couldn't perform, he didn't even want to get started. She'd always loved touching Brady and kissing him. She missed both.

Corralling her thoughts and returning to their conversation, she asked, "What would you do if you sold your company?"

He arched a brow and smiled. "Spend all my time at the gym."

"You'd get bored with bodybuilding in about three days."

"I'm going to have to exercise for the rest of my life…and eat vegetarian burgers, too." He grimaced.

"I bought a few new cookbooks for nonfat casseroles and entrées."

"I can't wait," he said wryly. After a long pause, he suggested, "You could sell Blossoms, too. We could travel."

Over the years, Brady had never taken enough time off for them to travel. "I've always wanted to visit Florence."

She walked up to him then and stood toe to toe. Was that the old hunger in his eyes? She couldn't be sure. "Do you know what I'd really like?"

"What?" His voice was gruff.

"I'd like us to go on a second honeymoon."

"That's different from traveling?" He sounded amused.

"I think so." After a few heartbeats, she had to say more. "I miss you. I miss you holding me and making love to me."

"You know I can't—" His cheeks flushed.

"We can't have intercourse yet. I know you're worried about what will happen when we do. But that doesn't mean we can't hold each other and kiss."

"It's not that simple."

"Why?"

He kept silent.

"We're slipping further away from each other," she murmured.

Stepping away from her, he shook his head. "I don't feel like a man right now. Don't you get that? The one thing we've always had going for us, no matter what was happening, was great sex. Since we can't—"

"The one thing we always had going for us was a connection," she cut in, realizing not having intercourse was only one aspect of what was and wasn't happening between them.

"The connection was based on chemistry," he insisted.

"No. It was based on feelings we had from that moment on the courthouse steps. We couldn't have stayed together this long if all we had was chemistry. Your caring and your compassion and your support kept me whole through my miscarriages. After Jason died, you were my lifeline. I don't know what would have happened if you hadn't been there."

"You're a strong woman, Laura. You would have survived."

She felt he was purposely driving a wedge between them. "Don't downplay your commitment and love."

"Then don't give me more credit than I deserve."

The silence in the den was stifling and she brought up a subject that had drifted under the radar with everything else that had happened. "You deserve the Man of the Year Award."

Brady's back grew stiff. "The executive board of the Millennium Club didn't think so."

"You didn't return their calls."

"I had nothing to say to them."

Biting her lip, she murmured, "Sometimes you're so stubborn."

He picked up the tube of blueprints and carried it to the closet. "And sometimes you can't see the obvious."

"Exactly what's so obvious?" She didn't want to rile him or entangle them in an argument. But she was tired of trying not to do or say something that would upset him. She was tired of not being honest. She wanted to know his real feelings and she wanted to know them *now.*

He finally let them free. After only a moment's hesitation, words burst from him. "Years ago, you forgave me for something that shouldn't have been forgiven, no matter what rules of engagement allowed for. I thought you were giving me a miraculous gift at the time, but your forgiveness has been a weight I can't escape. I can never do enough, say enough or *be* enough for you."

She was absolutely stunned by his words. As Brady stood there, holding drawings he'd made years ago, she felt as if he'd slapped her. All she'd *ever* done was give him her love. From the sound of it, he hadn't wanted it. In fact, he'd *resented* it in some way.

Although inside she was trembling, she forced out, "What should I have done that day in John Markowitz's office? Condemned you?"

"Morally I deserved to be condemned." His voice was so flat and stoic it scared her.

"You defended yourself…and Carl."

"I killed women and children." The truth was stark and he said it without emotion.

"Who were trying to kill *you*."

He kept silent.

Your forgiveness has been a weight. Had her love been a weight, too? What had happened to the strong bonds they'd felt from the beginning? Apparently they'd been a casualty of war, also. "You never should have gone to Vietnam. You should have burned your draft card and left for Canada."

She didn't even realize she'd spoken until he swore. "You make it sound so simple. I wanted you and my family to be proud of me. I wanted to do my duty. I wanted to stop Communism. I didn't want to take what most people thought was the coward's way out."

"*I* never would have thought that."

"We'd known each other for three months! What we felt hadn't been tested."

When she considered all they'd been through, she blurted out, "It's certainly been tested since then. Are you saying you stayed in this marriage all these years because you felt indebted to me? You owed me for forgiving you?"

When he was silent, when no words of protest came to his lips, she felt sick. So she struck out at him the way he'd struck out at her. "If you want to sell your company and travel, that's fine. But maybe you should travel alone." As she rushed out of the den, she choked back a sob.

Halfway down the hall, she heard him call her name. But her ears were ringing, her pulse was racing and she didn't want to face what else he might have to say. Was he intentionally sabotaging their marriage? Or had his heart attack finally brought truth into the light?

"Mom! Mom! Are you home?" Kat called from upstairs.

Taking in a gulp of air, steadying the beat of her heart, Laura stopped to compose herself. She felt as if her world was falling apart…as if everything she'd created with Brady was a sham. If he'd resented her all these years, where could they go from here?

She didn't have time to answer that question as she managed to call back to their daughter, "I'm home. I'll be up in a minute."

But Kat didn't give her even the minute. She galloped down the stairs. "Suz Cochrane is having a party tomorrow night. Can I go?"

When faced with granting permission, Laura always considered if there was a good reason she should say no. If there wasn't, she said yes.

Focusing on Kat, she asked, "Will her parents be there?"

"Yep."

Amanda Cochrane kept a tight rein on her daughter. She probably decided to have this party at their house so she knew exactly what was happening.

"All right, you can go. I was hoping you might want to catch Sean's game with us. Dad's going."

Kat bit her lower lip. "Mrs. Cochrane is going to phone for pizza around six. I'll skip Sean's game this time. Can you drop me off on the way to the game and pick me up around ten?"

Laura could hardly keep her mind on their conversation. She was still back in that den, listening once more to Brady's words.

"Mom?"

"What did you say, honey? I'm sorry."

"Can you drop me off on the way to the game and pick me up later?"

"Sure."

Feeling raw and vulnerable, Laura knew she had to pull herself together. As she mounted the steps toward Kat, she asked, "Is Sean in his room?"

"No. Didn't Dad tell you? He's over at Boyd's house. Dad told him he could go as long as he was home by midnight. I can't wait until I can drive and get my own car."

Kat's words didn't sink in. Laura was thinking about what she should do. Had everything she'd ever done and felt in her marriage been a mistake? Had the commitment to Brady she'd never questioned been too intense, too naive, too…foolish?

She reminded herself again that Brady had been through a traumatic surgery. He *was* still recovering.

Climbing the stairs, she decided to get a shower and

wait for him, hoping that somehow they could find their way back to each other…hoping Brady's turmoil wasn't a cancer that would eat away at their marriage until nothing was left.

Wincing, Sean tried to make sure the floorboards under the carpet didn't creak as he unsteadily made his way to his room. The last thing he needed was for his dad to see him and ground him again. After the summer, he'd be away from here and could do whatever he wanted.

He'd almost maneuvered down the hall, when Kat's door opened.

"I have to talk to you."

"Can't it wait?"

"Something's wrong with Mom. She looked as though she was going to cry and Dad hasn't come up to bed yet," his sister whispered desperately.

Sean leaned against the wall for a moment.

"Are you drunk?" Kat's eyes were wide and worried.

It was midnight. He'd just made his curfew, hoping no one would be up. He shouldn't even *have* a curfew.

As he focused on what Kat had said, he realized his dad hadn't slept downstairs since those first nights he'd been home from the hospital. Maybe his parents had argued again.

"Come on," Sean finally commanded, silently opening the door to his room, crossing to his bed and collapsing onto it.

Obviously not chancing their voices carrying, Kat closed the door.

"So are you drunk?" Kat asked again.

"I only had a few beers. But I felt sick afterward. Boyd had to stop on the way so I could puke out the door."

She knelt beside his bed. "Why do you do it? Why do you drink?"

He had cooled his drinking for a while. He'd had to. He wanted to get away from home even if it was to a school he hadn't chosen. But he was going to work up the courage to change that. The thing was, lately, when he was out with Gary and Boyd, he did whatever they did. That usually meant drinking or smoking pot.

"Go to bed, Kat." He wasn't going to talk to his sister about it.

"Mom and Dad will find out."

"Are you going to tell them?" he shot back.

She sighed. "No, I'm not. But if you keep this up, I won't have to say anything. They'll catch you again."

Kat wouldn't rat on him. They might fight, but they were brother and sister. He mumbled, "They won't notice. Dad's been too sick to care. Mom's been too worried about him to think about much else."

"Do you drink because Gary and Boyd do?"

A few long seconds later, he ran his hand over his face. "No. I drink because when I do, I'm numb. I float. Everything's easy."

"Until the next morning."

He scowled.

"Something's wrong with Mom," she said again, returning to her reason for waiting up for him. "When I asked her if I could go to a party at Suz's, she said all the right stuff, but it was like she wasn't really there. Do you think she's still afraid Dad could die?"

Sean used his elbows to hike himself up. "Maybe she is."

"She left Dad's den looking really weird. She pretended she was fine, but she wasn't."

"Did they fight?"

"I doubt it. She's too afraid she'll upset him to fight with him."

"I'm staying out of his way so *I* don't upset him."

Considering the past few weeks, Sean came to a conclusion that made sense about their mom's behavior. "Mom's been taking care of Dad and working and chauffeuring you. She's probably just tired."

Kat wrinkled her nose, as if that couldn't possibly be the answer. "Sunday is Mother's Day. Did you get her anything?"

"Not yet. Did you?"

"No. You know what I was thinking?"

"It's hard to tell."

She swatted his arm. "Dad's always been the one to get her charms for her bracelet. He hasn't given her any for a while. What if we bought her a Mother's Day charm?"

Sean lowered himself to his pillow again. "That bracelet means a lot to her. Yeah, maybe she would like that." He cracked a grin. "You *do* think about more than makeup and boys."

Standing, Kat planted her hands on her hips. "Just when I figure I might be able to put up with you, you say something stupid." She went to the door. "If you get sick again, don't call me."

Turning onto his side, Sean asked, "When are we going to get the charm? We could go to the mall tomorrow."

"Better make it in the afternoon, so you're sober."

"I never drive when I've been drinking."

"A lot of good that does when you drive *with* someone who's been drinking."

"Boyd only had one beer. He was fine."

"Mom said Dad's going to your game tomorrow night."

"He is? I guess I'd better hit a home run," Sean murmured.

Kat frowned. "Dad just might want to see you play. He might not care if you get any hits."

"Sure," Sean grumped sarcastically. He did have an attitude where his dad was concerned. And that was why he often said and did the wrong thing…the thing that *would* get him into trouble.

Kat was about to leave, when she seemed to decide Sean was sober enough to discuss something else. "Did kids at school give you a hard time about that newspaper article?"

After a long silence, he finally answered. "Not a lot. I just told Gary and Boyd I didn't want to talk about it and they were okay with that. One day when I was alone in the parking lot, Dave Valenti asked me how I liked having a dad who was a murderer. When I threatened to deck him, he backed down."

"I just wish none of it had happened—the article… Dad's heart attack," Kat said. "I wish we could just go back to the way we were before."

"You can never go back."

After a long moment, Kat opened his door. "See you tomorrow."

As Kat exited Sean's room, he closed his eyes, trying to forget about anything that might keep him awake.

★ ★ ★

Laura ran into the bagel shop Saturday afternoon attempting not to think or feel. Brady hadn't slept in their bed last night. When she'd checked the den this morning, it had been empty. A note on the refrigerator told her he'd gone for a walk. If she'd waited longer for him…

The truth was, she'd fallen deeper into hurt that had accumulated hour by hour as she'd waited for Brady to come to bed. This morning, tired and becoming angry as well as hurt, she'd left for Blossoms knowing he wouldn't talk to her until he was ready.

Maybe she didn't want to hear more of the resentment he'd kept inside. Maybe he was planning a divorce. Maybe loving him for all these years had been a mistake.

Was her life a mistake? *Had* she attempted to "fix" Brady when he'd returned from the army? Or had she mistakenly believed their love would be strong enough to cement them for life? She hadn't thought about much else as she worked at Blossoms this morning, mixing up orders, finally retreating to the workroom to arrange flowers.

She heard his words again and each one stabbed her as it had last night: *Your forgiveness has been a weight I can't escape.*

There were two lines in the bagel shop, five customers in each. Most of the tables were full. The Saturday lunch crowd streamed in. As she quickly determined which line to join, she took a good look at the customers in each and spotted Dr. Gregano. She almost hadn't recognized him in the red polo shirt and navy slacks.

Should she say hello?

He probably didn't want to be bothered during his free time by patients or their families.

He finished paying his bill and turned to head toward the only empty table, a bagel sandwich and cup in hand. When he spotted her, he instantly recognized her.

Smiling, he nodded. "Mrs. Malone! Are you getting lunch?"

"Just a bagel, and a dozen to take out."

After a moment's hesitation, he motioned to the table for two that had just been vacated. "If you need a seat, you're welcome to join me."

Her heart beat a little faster as she looked into his eyes. She remembered how kind he'd been the night of Brady's surgery. She could use a little kindness right now. "Thanks. You'll probably be finished before I get my order."

"I drink at least two cups of coffee. This afternoon, I'm not rushing anywhere for a change unless I get beeped."

The line moved fairly fast, and when she carried her cheese bagel, bag and bottle of water to Dr. Gregano's table, he'd just finished his sandwich.

"That's lunch?" His tone was teasing.

"I'm not really hungry, but I can't go all day without eating."

"I'll say you can't. In fact, you've lost some weight."

Surprised he'd noticed, she said, "About five pounds. Life has been hectic."

"And stressful?"

In his eyes, she found that kindness again as well as compassion. Her throat tightened and tears were much too close to the surface.

"Mrs. Malone..."

"It's Laura," she managed to say.

"Laura. You know, don't you, that recovery from bypass surgery can be as stressful for the caretaker as for the patient?"

Breathing deeply, she admitted, "Especially if the patient doesn't want to be taken care of."

"You went to the cardiac workshop for family members and watched the video?"

She nodded.

"Then you heard how traumatic the experience is for the patient. The list of problems to deal with is long. The surgery was a shock to your husband's body—a violation, if you will. And not only for his heart. Muscles were disturbed. His sternum was cracked."

"When he first got home, he was rubbing his neck and shoulders a lot, but, Dr. Gregano—"

"It's Dominic."

She could almost settle into the comfort of his smile. He understood what both she and Brady were dealing with, and to her surprise, his first name came easily to her lips. "Dominic, the physical repercussions are just the tip of the iceberg. He seems to be reviewing his whole life."

"That's not unusual, either. Neither is depression. Remember, he faced death."

"He's done that before," she confided softly.

"The service?" Dominic guessed.

"Yes."

Dawning flared in the physician's eyes. "*He's* the Brady Malone in the newspaper article!" He gave a low whistle. "So that's the family complication you mentioned."

"Yes. Reporters were at our door, on the phone and even at the hospital." She was admitting a confidence she should probably keep to herself, but she felt so raw today that his empathy was a balm.

"Sometimes my newspapers collect for a week and I don't have a chance to read them until I have a day off."

Not giving in to the inclination to confide more, she followed the change of subject. "Do you get many days off?"

"I'm on rotation with two other cardiologists. Once in a while I have a weekend to call my own. What about you? Do you work outside the home?"

She smiled at his politically correct phrasing. "I have a flower shop—Blossoms."

"I've seen the ads." He pointed to her untouched bagel. "I've asked you too many questions and you're not eating. I'm going to get that second cup of coffee. You have your lunch—such as it is."

"Yes, sir," she replied jokingly as if there weren't an age difference between them, as if they were two friends meeting for coffee, as if—

She observed Dominic Gregano as he went to the sidebar of coffee carafes and filled his cup. He was an attractive man. She hadn't looked at a man—at least, not in a man-woman way—since she'd met Brady. No effort had been required to keep her heart and mind on her husband. No effort at all.

So why was it that today she was noticing the clean cut of the doctor's hair, the straightness of his nose, the darker silver rim around his gray eyes? Because she was hurt? Because she felt alone? Because Brady was pulling away and she didn't know what to do about it?

She finished half her bagel.

Dominic returned to their table and seated himself across from her again.

The noise in the shop was reaching a crescendo. Two teenagers shouted to a friend across the room and chatter rose a notch.

Dominic gestured outside. "If you'd like to talk more, why don't we take a walk. We can't hear ourselves think in here."

Tempted. She was *so* tempted. But did she really need a shoulder to lean on? That was what she'd be doing. Did she need a distraction that could make her feel better for the moment but in the long run cause havoc?

Maybe she was crazy. That wasn't interest in her that she saw in Dominic Gregano's eyes, was it?

"It's only a walk, Laura. I enjoy your company and you deserve a break from caretaking."

If she deserved a break, she'd better take it with her kids or Pat or Jack's wife, Angie. It would be dangerous to take it with this man. Every moral fiber in her body told her that.

"Thanks, but I really can't. My son has a baseball game. I have errands to run first and I don't want to be late. I appreciate you…talking to me."

"Anytime," Dominic said as if he meant it.

With a smile, she picked up her bag of bagels, said goodbye to the doctor and left the shop without looking back. She could feel his gaze on her, but she realized she had no response to it. He was a nice, kind, attractive man. But her husband was waiting for her at home and he was the one she wanted to be with.

Even if he doesn't want to be with you?

That was a question she had to find the answer to… because the answer could change her life.

Chapter 11

The sun was dropping onto the horizon as Brady watched Laura turn the steering wheel and veer into the parking lot at the baseball field. She'd been silent during the drive and he knew why. He'd seen the hurt in her eyes last night and he'd hated the fact that he'd caused it. He never should have been honest with her. He never should have acknowledged his resentment. Even *he* hadn't realized it was there to that extent.

"There might be a crowd," she said and he understood she was attempting to keep some kind of line of communication open between them.

He obliged. "We're early enough. We'll get seats."

Just that interchange made the strain between them even worse. It was almost painful being here with her tonight. They couldn't seem to talk anymore without a difference of opinion. Because they were both stressed by his heart attack, surgery and nightmares? Because if he reached out for her, if he even attempted having sex, he was afraid he'd have another heart attack?

Only time and strengthening and healing would help. Even if he could do the stairs, that wasn't sex. How would he know for *sure* that he'd waited long enough?

After climbing out of the van, they walked through the gravel parking lot to the baseball field. He noticed other families exiting their cars and SUVs, heading that way, too. The top seats of the bleachers always filled up first.

"Second row okay?" Laura asked him.

"The second row is fine," he answered her. She'd chosen it so he wouldn't have to climb higher. He was ready to try to climb to any height to feel like himself again.

His gaze on Laura, he realized she looked almost young tonight with her hair tied back in a ponytail, a baseball cap sporting the name of Sean's team shadowing her face. The jeans she wore fit her way too well. Her running shoes were almost new, and they weren't the ones she used in the garden. No one would ever guess she was fifty-eight.

They stepped over the first bleacher, then plopped down close to each other, their hips rubbing, their elbows brushing. Brady caught the scent of Laura's perfume. It had teased his nose in the car. Or maybe it was the lotion she wore. She didn't make any move to slide away from him, and suddenly he felt he could use some space. He shifted, putting a couple of inches between them.

He should apologize for what he'd said last night. On the other hand, should he apologize for the truth? How in the hell had his marriage gotten so complicated after thirty-three years?

"That's him," he heard someone murmur a few rows behind him. "That's the man who did those awful things when he was in the army."

He could feel Laura stiffen beside him.

Maybe she was afraid he'd get into a fight and defend his honor. Have another heart attack. He should have put more thought into attending the game. But he'd been distracted. His conversation with Carl from this afternoon was still running through his head. Still, he'd needed to get out…needed to support Sean. Yet he should have realized people didn't keep their opinions to themselves.

There was a hum of voices and he caught his name being mentioned. He caught words like "Bronze Star," "deplorable," "Vietnam should have never happened."

Then one of his neighbors, Jim Stavros, who had a son a grade behind Sean, sank onto the bench beside Brady. He was a huge man, barrel-chested, with a beer belly that hung over his belt. But he was always genial, and now he clapped Brady on the back. "Good for you, coming out here like this. You guys who were over there were heroes. Don't you listen to what anyone else says."

In spite of the hurt between them, in spite of what he'd said to Laura, he felt her arm lodge against his, felt the support that had always emanated from her.

He gave Jim a short nod. It was supposed to be a thank-you. Then he waited for the game to start, his gaze on his son, who was standing on the sidelines near the fence with his friends. At least Sean couldn't hear. At least his mind was on the game.

Brady stared straight ahead, hoping Sean's team would run away with the score, hopeful the game would be a short one. Then he could congratulate his son for winning instead of dwelling on the spectators' comments.

"Your dad has guts," Boyd said to Sean before the game started.

Sean thumped his bat on the ground and cut a glance toward the bleachers where his mom and dad were sitting. For his dad's sake, he wished he hadn't come.

"Don't pay any attention to Corey Mason and his father," Gary directed him. "They're a bunch of assholes."

When Sean's mom and dad had walked to the bleachers, Corey's father had pointed to Sean's dad and muttered something like, "I can't believe he's showing his face."

Sean didn't know how his dad was doing it, pretending people weren't pointing him out, pretending not to hear the whispers. Dave Valenti hadn't been the only one to razz him at school. Corey had gotten in Sean's face about the article, too. Since Mason was a lot bigger than Sean, Sean had threatened to reveal how Corey had bought an essay off the Internet to send in with his college application. That had shut him up.

"Just pretend that ball is Corey's head when it comes toward you," Boyd decided.

Boyd and Gary were Sean's best friends. They'd all been assigned to the same homeroom as freshmen, taken the same English class together. They were good friends and understood things about him he didn't like to explain.

When Sean had entered high school, he'd known he'd have to work harder than most of the other kids. His mind didn't focus the same way. Sometimes words and lines got jumbled when he was reading, and it took him a lot longer to do his homework than it took Gary or Boyd. They accepted that…and him. As well as the reality that he was good at sports, not to mention the drawing he kept under wraps. No way was he going to let his other classmates find out he liked to sketch in his spare time. They'd think he was artsy-fartsy or something. Boyd and Gary didn't make anything of it…didn't even kid him about it.

"I got some weed this afternoon," Gary told Sean now. "We can get wasted at my place after the game."

Gary's parents weren't around much. His dad was always going on business trips and his mom did her own thing. There was a housekeeper, and Gary often said he saw her more than he saw his parents. He was flippant about the arrangement and acted as if it didn't matter. Sean knew that routine. He himself acted as if lots of things didn't matter.

But tonight…

"I'd better go home after the game. I don't want my dad to feel as if I've deserted him or something." Sean still felt guilty his parents had been arguing about him when his dad had his heart attack. If he got a few hits tonight, he could make his dad proud. How he wished he could make his dad proud.

What would happen if he told his parents he didn't want to go to a private college in western Pennsylvania? That he'd rather go to Scranton to a school where he could do a two-year program in graphic design. They'd be disappointed if he did that. But it wouldn't be the first time. He'd disappointed them, especially his dad, since he'd been adopted.

His dad hadn't been around much when he was really little. For some reason Sean had felt that was his fault. School had been a nightmare. He'd felt stupid, as the other kids seemed to learn so much faster than he had. He simply couldn't grasp spelling. He *still* mixed up letters and saw them differently from everyone else. His mom had started helping him after his report card in first grade…after a conference with his teacher. When he was in second grade, things got even worse. There had been talk about holding him back and an educational psychologist had tested him. That was when they'd found out he was dyslexic. Tutoring had begun in the summer. In third grade he'd started catching up.

Near Halloween that year he remembered one night in particular. His mom, following strategies his tutor had set out, had been helping him with spelling. After supper, they'd sat at the kitchen table with cutout pictures for each of his spelling words with a tape recorder so he could sound out the words, then play them back. They'd gone over his list while Kat strung beads and buttons.

When his dad had come in, he'd told Kat how pretty the necklace was she was making. Then he'd asked Sean, "Ready for your spelling test?"

"Yes, sir." Sean had wished he could look at the list and remember how to spell every word on it.

His dad had picked up the cutout of a truck. "Can you spell *truck* for me?" He'd caught Sean off guard. His dad had looked so expectant, so sure Sean could do what he'd asked.

Sean had known he could spell the word. He'd done it for his mother earlier. But suddenly the letters and sounds had gotten all mixed up in his head. He'd spelled it *t-r-u-k*. He'd forgotten the *c*.

His dad seemed embarrassed for him. He'd patted Sean's shoulder and said, "We'll try it again later. I know you'll do well on your test this week."

But Sean had felt his dad's words had just been words, that he really didn't mean them. Kat often told him he misread their dad. But he didn't misread the disappointment his dad was feeling. His mom loved him no matter what, but his father… Sean never felt good enough when he was around his father, even when he tried his hardest to please him.

At an early age, Sean had seen pictures in the family album of a baby boy, of a proud expression on his dad's face when he looked down at the infant, of the family his mom and dad and that baby had been when someone had taken their picture in front of the Christmas tree. He'd known then that he could never measure up, just as he knew it now.

The coach's whistle broke into Sean's reverie and the three of them headed for the bench. Boyd bumped Sean's elbow. "How about a party *tomorrow* night?"

Sean thought about more whispers, more rumors, more jibes.

"It's at Valerie Johanssen's house. She goes to Red Lion High School. You probably wouldn't even know anybody there except Gary and me."

"I can just crash it?"

"You won't be crashing. Girls always want more guys around. You're going to be graduating. You've got to celebrate."

Gary added, "We're going to do a lot of celebrating. I invited Kent and James to the cabin the Friday of

Memorial Day weekend. We can stay overnight and play music as loud as we want."

Maybe the parties were just what Sean needed. Maybe he should just go all out. He didn't have to worry about his grades now, not with graduation coming up fast.

"Okay. Maybe it *is* time to start celebrating."

After brushing her teeth, Laura ran water in the navy porcelain sink as she stared into the mirror, not knowing the woman she'd become. There were tiny lines around her lips now, at the corners of her eyes, and one in the middle of her forehead.

Attending Sean's game and being with Brady had been hard. Even harder when she'd heard the whispers and seen the stares. Brady had acted as if they'd just rolled off his back. She knew better. He'd been silent as they'd driven home.

After she turned off the brass spigot, she picked up her brush and ran it through her hair in long, swift strokes. What if Brady didn't sleep with her again tonight? She was still so hurt by what he'd said. *I can never do enough, say enough or* be *enough for you.*

Maybe her hurt had tempted her to flirt with Dr. Gregano. Why had she considered going on that walk with him? Considered getting to know him better?

Tears came to her eyes as she thought about longings she'd only ever had for Brady. For a few moments this afternoon after her lunch with Dominic, she'd wondered what his arms would feel like around her, what his lips would feel like on hers. She'd pictured the kiss.

Perhaps that was because she saw her life as an attractive woman nearing an end. Perhaps it was because Brady didn't reach for her anymore at night. Because she felt alone even when she was with her husband. She was reminded of a country song about it being easier to be alone with no one around than to be alone with someone only a short distance away. How true!

There had been stretches in her life with Brady when she'd been ecstatically happy—those three months before he went to basic training after his therapy session into the early years of their marriage. Through her pregnancy and the three months they'd had with Jason, her life couldn't have been more perfect. Sometimes she hadn't known where she'd left off and Brady had begun. Even through her miscarriages, when disappointment could have torn them apart but didn't, she'd known he loved her. She'd known he wanted her. She'd known they were soul mates. But ever since Jason's death, Brady had put a wall up between them, a wall he sometimes lowered but a wall nonetheless. It had been high and thick and wide for a while now. Oh, they pretended it wasn't there. They acted happily married at his business functions, during social interaction with other couples. But even when they made love—only fleetingly could she recapture what they'd once been.

Where had all the feelings gone? Their marriage felt as if it was built on sand instead of rock, as if the wrong word, the wrong gesture, could cause irreparable harm. Could she ever forget what Brady had said to her? Even if it had been said out of frustration…because of his surgery…because he was reexamining his life and didn't like what he saw.

Today she'd realized why men and women had affairs. When doubt crept in, when love was just a word, when affection wasn't part of what a couple was, when vows didn't mean very much at all, commitment became a chain wrapped around the heart. Sometimes she just wanted a release from everything that had happened and everything they'd been and everything they were now.

What *was* happening to her? *Was* she getting tired of fighting battles she couldn't win? Was she just plain weary of struggling to make a connection with Brady that hadn't been there for a long time? Was she angry at him for the distance he always placed between him and Sean? Did she resent the way he cared about their daughter but couldn't seem to love their son?

She hadn't closed the door to the bathroom, and suddenly Brady pushed it open. He was wearing pajamas—black-and-red plaid. He'd worn them ever since he'd come home from the hospital.

Before his surgery, he'd slept naked.

In spite of all the questions she'd just asked herself, in spite of the turmoil from today and the past few weeks, in spite of what he'd said, when she looked at Brady her heart fluttered. With his weight loss, he was as lean now as he'd been in his thirties. He'd always had terrifically broad shoulders. Some men as they aged appeared to shrink—their shoulders stooped, their backsides vanished and they grew old in spirit as well as in their bodies. But Brady…

Brady had always possessed a bigger-than-life stature. He'd always walked with confidence and held his head high. As she stood there in the bathroom with him, remembering how he'd walked away from the bleachers tonight, how he'd shaken Sean's hand after his team won and ignored comments and whispers, she felt such a longing to be wrapped in his arms. She wanted to hear him say that their marriage was strong enough to handle anything.

His blue gaze took in every aspect of her fuchsia chemise gown. The silkiness of it showed off curves she still had. The thin fabric couldn't hide her nipples beading hard under it. The snap and sizzle that reverberated between them wasn't just in her imagination, was it? Yet maybe she'd deluded herself about their whole marriage. She had to find out.

"Why don't you sleep in the nude anymore?" she asked softly, her voice trembling.

His voice was low, husky, as if he, too, could feel the sexual awareness between them. "My chest scars are ugly."

In a few steps, she was right there in front of him, needing so much from him she couldn't put any of it into words. That wasn't like her, not to have the words. Her hair swung against her cheek as her hands went to the buttons on his pajama shirt. One by one she began unfastening them. If they could only touch each other again…

His large hands caught hers and stilled them. "Don't."

"I want to see," she whispered. "I want to see how it's healed."

He remained silent as she undid the last button and then separated the plackets. The scar was nasty and it reminded her of the trauma his body had been through. Putting her lips to it, she gently kissed it.

She heard Brady suck in a breath. His hands went to her shoulders and he set her away. When she looked down, she saw his erection pressing against the fly of his pajama bottoms.

"Not yet," he muttered.

"I don't care about having sex, Brady. Just hold me."

She hated asking. She felt less somehow because he didn't love her enough to take her into his arms simply because he had missed her, too. Was she still desirable to him? She felt as vulnerable as she had when she was twenty and hadn't been sure about his feelings.

Brady wrapped his arms around her then and hugged her. Yet it wasn't a full-body hug. It wasn't a hold-on-tight hug. It was a stay-removed-as-best-he-could hug.

"I'm sorry about what happened at the game," he said. "I suppose I shouldn't have gone."

When she leaned back, his eyes were full of regret. As always, she wanted to wipe it away. "I felt bad for you, but I was proud of the way you handled the situation, too."

"I didn't handle anything. I pretended it didn't matter. Do you think Sean and Kat have been affected at school by the article appearing in the paper?"

"Neither of them has said anything."

"That doesn't mean they haven't gotten flak."

"They both have good friends who will stand by them."

Brady dropped his arms, though she hadn't had nearly enough of being close to him. She was so needy tonight. That was what had almost gotten her into trouble with Dominic—the neediness.

Suddenly Brady said, "I called Carl Miller this afternoon."

She hadn't heard that name in years. About thirty-four years. He was the soldier who'd been with Brady when—

"Why did you call him?"

Brady leaned against the counter, his hands on the edge, his knuckles almost white. "I figured he was the source for the reporter. He was."

"Why did he talk to the paper?"

"The reporter phoned and pretended to know what had happened and Carl let the story spill out."

"Pretended to know?"

"Yeah. Carl didn't realize until he started talking that the reporter didn't know as much as he seemed to. I got the feeling Carl was unburdening himself. He'd never told anybody about it."

"Not even his wife?" Carl had been older than Brady, married before he went into the service.

"No. They divorced years ago, about a year after he got out of the army. He had nightmares and flashbacks, too, and she couldn't deal with them."

Silence bounced around in the bathroom. Laura *had* dealt with it, she'd thought. Back then aftereffects of the war had been called post Vietnam syndrome. Now the term was post-traumatic stress disorder. It was the same diagnosis psychiatrists often gave to rape victims, abused children, anyone who'd experienced something traumatic that affected the rest of their lives. Labeling it only named the devil...didn't exorcize it.

"Did Carl ever remarry?"

"No. And he never had kids."

Laura wondered that if, after his return home, Carl Miller, like Brady, had never again felt worthy enough to experience happiness. Success wasn't the same as happiness. Although Brady was a successful man in so many ways, she didn't believe he was happy. Her heart still ached because of what he'd said last night. She still didn't understand how her forgiveness had been a burden to him. Was it a burden because his experience in Vietnam had made him feel unworthy to love anyone…to let anyone love him?

Brady motioned to the sink and the lotion Laura smoothed on every night. "I'll let you finish."

"We can use the bathroom together," she suggested, wanting that intimacy at least.

"I'm going to get a shower and loosen up my neck muscles. I don't want to steam everything up while you're in here."

She could offer to give him a massage, but he'd refuse. He must have seen how deep-down sad she was feeling, because he said, "Soon I'll be doing those two flights of steps as if I were a teenager again. Then we'll try having sex."

If he thought sex would fix everything, he was wrong. But then, he was more adept at separating his emotions from his actions. She just couldn't do that.

Ignoring the lotion on the counter, she managed to say, "Go ahead and get your shower. I'm finished."

Then she went into their magnificently furnished bedroom, with its canopy bed, cream damask drapes and plush champagne carpeting. She turned down the silky navy-and-tan spread and crawled between the sheets, not missing sex…but missing her husband.

Chapter 12

As Brady emerged from the trail through the woods behind his house Sunday morning, he realized he wasn't absolutely worn out. He was getting better…getting stronger. Some days he still felt he was staring death in the face in an entirely different way than he had in Nam. There his death would likely have been sudden, with no time to think about. At fifty-nine with a heart condition, death would come in degrees.

Would this operation he'd had give him twenty more years? Could he push it to thirty? Could he really change his eating habits, exercise habits, his whole damn lifestyle? He'd been wrestling with that question for weeks. The bottom line was he was facing the end of his life. How did he want to live the rest of his days? The way he'd lived them up till now?

Last night in the bathroom with Laura…

He hated the tension, the awkwardness, the I-don't-know-what-to-do-next feeling that always seemed to be there now. He hated seeing the worry in her eyes. Most of all he hated seeing the disappointment. Why couldn't she realize he had to be one hundred per cent before he made love to her again? She'd say his ego was getting in their way, but he knew, in the deepest layer of his soul, more than his ego was getting in the way.

As he crossed the yard and approached the patio outside the dining room, he spotted his son, sitting on the corner of the glider, some kind of tablet in his hand. As Brady got closer, Sean flipped the tablet shut.

"Are Kat and your mom back from church yet?" Brady asked.

"Nope. I waited until they left to check the refrigerator. We have eggs, bacon and pancakes for brunch for Mother's Day."

"Mother's Day!" Brady swore.

His son looked up at him, surprised. "What's wrong?"

"I forgot about Mother's Day." He swore again, his mind clicking into gear, running possibilities but missing some, grasping others. "I need you to drive me someplace."

"Now? Nothing's open. It's Sunday morning."

"Wal-Mart's open."

"You've *got* to be kidding."

"I'm not. Grab your car keys. Did you get Mom a present?"

"Kat and I went together. We bought it yesterday."

Mother's Day brunch was a tradition. Brady made the pancakes and kept an eye on the bacon, while Sean scrambled eggs and Kat set the table. Then they gave Laura their presents. How could he have forgotten a day that was so important to her, always had been, always would be?

Obviously seeing Brady's discomfiture, Sean said, "Give yourself a break, Dad. You've had a lot going on. No wonder you forgot." In place of the resentment or rebelliousness he usually heard in Sean's tone, this time there was understanding.

"Must have been the anesthesia," Brady muttered. "Do you mind taking me to Wal-Mart?" He asked this time, instead of ordering.

"No, I don't mind. But what are you going to get *there?*"

"Your mother keeps saying she'd like a digital camera similar to the one we got you for Christmas. Do you have pictures on yours—of you and Kat?"

"Maybe. Aunt Pat snapped a whole bunch at Easter."

"Can you bring your CD to the den? I'll go through the photos and print one out. We can find a frame for that at Wal-Mart, too. I'll write Kat a note and slip it under her door, telling her she should keep your mother occupied until we get back."

A half hour later, Brady and Sean were in the camera section at Wal-Mart, in the thick of early-morning shoppers. Almost as familiar with electronics as Brady, Sean picked up a camera with features he liked. "You have to get her six pixels."

"I know. Maybe I should buy a combination video-still camera."

"If you buy one too complicated, she won't use it."

His son was right about that.

In that moment of complete agreement between them,

Brady recalled his last shopping trip with Sean. His son had been twelve and Laura had suggested they go Christmas shopping. But they'd both come home frustrated and in a bad mood. Sean hadn't wanted to go. He'd preferred spending Saturday with his friends. He'd argued with Brady over anything he suggested for Kat, Laura, Pat or for his uncles and their wives. He'd simply not cared. He hadn't wanted to be with his father. Brady knew his inattention during Sean's early years had caused that.

From the time Sean had been tested for his learning disability, teachers and tutors had emphasized how important praise was to him. His parents should build his self-confidence. They needed to point out his intelligence and his gifts and work with his learning capabilities the way they were, not as Laura and Brady wanted them to be. Brady hadn't really understood how Sean could conceptualize data until his son had taken geometry. He had grasped the subject surprisingly easily. Spacial concepts were different from words and Sean had felt more at home with triangles and trapezoids, lines and circles, than with letters of the alphabet. But by then, Sean hadn't wanted Brady to help with homework or his input. If Sean needed help, he turned to friends, or a tutor who worked with him when he got stuck. When Sean was small, Brady had taken only the most perfunctory responsibility for him. By the time Sean was ten, he was pushing his father away.

After that Christmas-shopping trip, Brady had commented to Laura that maybe when Sean matured, they'd find common ground. But Laura had suggested his problem with Sean was deeper than that because Brady held back who he was with his son.

When she'd awakened this morning, Brady's side of the bed had been empty. He'd already left for his walk. It was just another avoidance tactic. He was avoiding *her* and she hurt every time he did it.

She climbed onto the stool and reached for the small antique chest that had been her mother's. This morning, she had an urge to reread Brady's letters to her. It had been years since she'd done so.

Did she want to read them simply for the comfort they gave? Or did she hope to find a clue that would help her get close to her husband again?

Her charm bracelet jingled as she pulled the chest to the edge of the shelf. Intricate designs decorated all four sides of the cherry-wood lid. She carried the chest into the bedroom and settled on the love seat in the sitting area.

When she opened the lid, the musty smell of old paper wafted out. Over a hundred letters filled the chest and she fingered them reverently, as if they'd fall apart at her touch. They were arranged sequentially. She was tempted to start at the beginning and read through them all. Instead she plucked one out of the first group, tied with a yellow satin ribbon. These were the basic-training letters.

As she opened the first letter, a two-by-three-inch photo of Brady fell onto her lap. When she picked it up, she smiled. Brady and a crew cut. All that thick black hair lopped off. The weekend before he'd left for Fort Dix, she'd run her fingers through it over and over. She still loved to run her fingers through it.

She unfolded the lined tablet paper and read,

Dear Laura,
I didn't know whether to send you this picture. I think I miss the sideburns most of all. Please tell me you don't love me for my hair!

Basic training is what I expected. If I had any past lives, I must have been a general, because I like giving orders a lot better than taking them! Learned responses are necessary. Obedience is expected. Once in a while I tend to want to rebel, to shout back and take the chance of doing something my way instead of the "right" way, but all in all, I'm fitting in. I actually like the physical challenge.

Even though I don't have a spare minute, you're always on my mind, no matter what I'm doing or where I'm going or who I'm with. I think about our night together and how I want to spend every night like that with you. I love you, Laura. I never knew what real missing was until I had to leave you behind. Letters aren't the same as hearing your voice, but letters will have to do for now. I'll write to you whenever I can. I don't want you to ever forget or doubt how much I love you.
Take care, sweetheart.
Love, Brady

Sweetheart. How long had it been since Brady had called her sweetheart?

She pulled a letter from the second stack. The envelopes were mostly cream-colored, with a brown-and-orange band down the side. Brady had been in Hawaii when he'd sent those.

She slid out the pages, yellowed now from time. Unfolding them, she spotted the first line and felt an old, yet new, stream of joy pour through her at Brady's words:

> Laura,
> The moon's full tonight. The waves are breaking on the beach and I wish you were here with me to see them. But there's no point in making us both long for what we can't have right now. So I'll answer your question.
>
> You wanted to know whether I'd mind if you went to the anti-war protest in D.C. I know how you feel, sweetheart. I know how much you want to see this war end and you want me back home. I would never tell you what you could and could not do. You're the type of woman who makes up her own mind and I respect that. I'm proud of you for standing up for what you believe in. So my answer really doesn't matter. If you want to go to D.C., then you go. Patriotism isn't about standing up for our leaders and cheering them on whether they're right or wrong. Patriotism is about searching for truth and believing in what's good for our country. If I'm sent to Vietnam, I'll be there to fight Communism. I've got to believe it's a war we can win, but I also understand your desire for your voice to be counted. I just want to caution you to be careful. I can only imagine the crowd that will be there. The demonstration is supposed to be peaceful, but you know what can happen. I want you safe, Laura, just as you want me safe.

So you're going to help paint the bus with flowers and peace signs? Sounds groovy. Write to me as soon as you get home. I want to know everything about it.

In some ways, the days here are going quickly. Yet when I think about our last weekend together and how long it will be until I see you again, each day feels more like a year.

I love you, Laura.

Brady

As she slipped that letter back into its envelope, she remembered that antiwar demonstration. The idea for the Peace Moratorium scheduled for October 15, 1969, had swept across the country. Students, working men and women, even schoolchildren, had attended round tables, religious services and rallies. She and a friend from work had traveled to D.C. with a group from York the day before the protest rally and had participated in the candlelight vigil on the steps of the Capitol. She'd sung her heart out, she'd cried, she'd prayed the war would end soon. The massive protests that month and the next in D.C. had made an impact. But not soon enough for Brady.

Next she chose a letter from the stack with the blue ribbon—the Vietnam letters. As she smoothed it open, a smaller piece of paper fell to her lap. She fingered it, then began reading the longer letter first:

Laura,

Do you realize we've never spent a Christmas together? I bet you're saying what a way to start a letter, but it's all I've been thinking about lately—being here at Christmas without you and without my family. Mom loves Christmas. Maybe she'll let you help decorate. She does a lot of it, even garlands around the doorways, lights down the stairs. Can you do me a favor? Can you buy some presents for me? I've already written to Pat. I took five hundred dollars out of my savings before I left and gave it to her for this kind of thing. She'll reimburse whatever you spend. A bottle of Mom's favorite perfume would be great. It's Chanel something or other. You probably know better than I do. Dad's tough. Maybe you can buy him a box of his favorite cigars. Pat or Matt will know the brand. I thought that for Pat, maybe you could find a necklace with her astrological sign. Chocolate for Matt and a carton of cigarettes for Ryan. If you don't have time to shop for everyone, I'll understand. Whatever you can do will be great. I just want them to know I haven't forgotten them.

It's good to hear you and your aunt are talking again and you're going to spend New Year's Day with her. I'll bet she was surprised when you called.

Thanks for sending the Kool-Aid. It helps kill the taste of the iodine in the water. I never go anywhere without that new picture of you in my pocket. Keep smiling for me. I can't wait to leave this rat-infested hooch, come home and feel you in my arms again.

Pat wrote to me about her friend facing the draft lottery. It's hard to imagine a guy's fate determined by his birthday and then the order it's pulled from a jar. That's almost worse than just simply being drafted. Pat said one of her friends was lucky enough to get a high number. He's pretty sure he won't go to Nam. But another guy she dated has number twenty-seven. At least we don't have to worry about that. Ten more months here, then I'll be back in the States.

I volunteered to help the LT write up the after-action report from our last operation so I'd have the chance to write. But I have to close now. Know that I'm dreaming of you, longing for you, waiting for the day when I can hold you in my arms again.

Merry Christmas, my love.

Brady

That Christmas had been both wonderful and lonely. The Malones had embraced her as one of the family and she'd taken part in all their Christmas activities, from trimming the tree to helping prepare Christmas dinner. That had been the wonderful part. Yet she'd been so lonely for Brady, so eager to get each letter, so worried about his safety and the conditions he was living in. He'd described his hooch after he'd arrived. When he was in camp, he was living in a sort of hut made of plywood, with a tin roof and screen for windows. She couldn't imagine living like that. But he never complained. He was where he had to be...doing what he had to do. But at what cost?

Absently she touched the charms on her bracelet, until she came to the angel holding a tiny diamond. Then she picked up the note in her lap. Brady had sent it to his sister for her to tuck into his present for Laura. He'd bought the angel charm before he'd left for basic training. When Laura had opened the charm, the note in the box read:

> If I were there with you, I'd be offering you a diamond ring. I'd be proposing and we'd be getting married. This angel will watch over you until I can give you that diamond in person. I love you, Laura. Merry, merry Christmas.

How she'd longed for him that Christmas. How she'd yearned to start her life with him.

When she extracted another letter from the pile, she saw the date and breathed a sigh of relief—February 2, 1970—before the six-long-week gap in letters.

> Laura,
> Whenever I write to you, I try to focus on us, on what you're doing and on the future because it takes me away from here for just a little while. You and the family are like a light I try to keep my eyes on. I don't usually tell you what I do each day, what I see each day because I don't want that tainting us. But—
>
> Yesterday I watched a buddy—Michael Wolf—get blown up beside me by a booby-trapped mortar round and I couldn't do anything about it. I felt powerless, Laura. I asked myself what in God's name I was doing here. What was Mike doing here? What kind of war are we fighting? The VC will use anything as a weapon…anything. We have to bury our C-ration cans so they can't use those for makeshift bombs.

I know I should thank God the rest of us made it back safely, but the truth is, when we go on an ambush, God seems so far away there's no point in praying.

Laura stopped reading, thinking about everything Brady hadn't told her in that letter—how he had saved another soldier's life that day and helped the wounded. How she wished he could focus on the Bronze Star he'd received for that instead of what happened a couple of weeks later.

Her eyes fell again to his strong handwriting on the pages in front of her.

If I could see your face, if I could touch your cheek, if I could look into your eyes, maybe I'd have some balance about all this. You know, I've heard soldiers say they're forgetting what their girl looks like, how her voice sounds. That's not true for me. Every day, I look at the pictures of you and the family that you sent me. The photos are wrinkled and not in great shape. A couple have peeled from the heat. They've gotten wet, too, but it doesn't matter. Even without them, when I close my eyes, I can see you on the courthouse steps with that daisy in your hair. I can hear you singing along to "Let the Sunshine In," and if I concentrate really hard, I can feel your skin against mine. My body needs yours, Laura. It could be another sixteen months until I can see you and touch you. Today, that seems like forever. I know you're praying for me and the guys over here. Thank goodness, because I can't seem to. Seeing Mike die like that— When you get this, maybe you can light a few extra candles.

I love you, Laura.

Brady

Her throat was tight, her heart beating fast as she finished reading. With each letter, with each new part of himself Brady had revealed, she'd fallen deeper in love with him. Every day she'd pushed aside her fear for him and imagined the life they'd share when he got home. She'd imagined his guardian angel protecting him wherever he was. She sent him her love by picturing her arms around him. She'd pictured them getting married.

Then abruptly her mailbox had been empty for six weeks, the six longest weeks of her life. His father had kept assuring her that if Brady had been injured, killed or even been missing in action, they'd hear something. They heard nothing for forty-one days. On the forty-second day, both she and his family had received letters.

Laura separated the first letter from the rest of the next stack, which she'd tied with a lavender ribbon. There were only twenty-one of them. His letters had dwindled to one about every three weeks, whereas before that she might get one or two a week. When she drew the single piece of paper from the air mail envelope, she could read it in practically a glance:

Laura,

I just wanted to let you know I'm fine. I was out on an operation, but I'm back now. I really don't have much to say. We're all beat and ready to turn in. I hope all's well with you. It might be longer between letters.

Take care.

Love, Brady

She'd received letters like that every few weeks until he'd come home. There was no feeling in them, no sadness, no passion, no joy, no despair. They were words on a page that represented his responsibility to write to her. He'd always signed them "love" and she'd hung on to that. In her letters to him, she'd asked him if something was wrong. But he didn't answer most of her questions, at least not the ones that mattered. When he was sent to Washington State, his messages became more descriptive, about the people he met and the places he saw, but he didn't mention getting married. On their second Christmas apart, he'd sent her perfume.

When he got leave, he discouraged her as well as his parents from flying out. He always had plans. In one of their few phone calls, he'd told Laura he'd be home soon and they could talk then. Seeing each other while he was stationed at Fort Lewis simply wasn't a good idea. She'd stopped asking why because she'd realized he wouldn't answer her. She'd told herself that seeing him, then being torn apart from him again, would be worse than not seeing him at all. But she'd known something had changed. *He* had changed. Did he still love her?

She was about to pull another of Brady's first letters out of the chest, when the bedroom door flew open. Kat bounded in, with Sean and Brady close behind her. They were all smiling.

"Happy Mother's Day, Mom. We've got your brunch all ready. Let's eat before it gets cold."

Laura's gaze met Brady's. Now that the bedroom door was open, she could smell pancakes and bacon.

"Before you say it," her husband joked, "I made Egg Beaters for me. I'll just pretend they're real eggs."

"They *are* real eggs, Dad. They just don't have the yolks in them," Kat informed him.

"And we're having turkey bacon," Sean added, as if that should impress her, too.

It did. They were not only celebrating the holiday, but thinking of Brady's health.

Kat motioned to the chest. "What are you doing?"

"Reading old letters." This time when her gaze met Brady's, his smile faded away.

"I'm surprised they're not falling apart." His voice was bland.

"I'm glad they're not. They mean a lot to me." She wondered if he remembered what he had written. She wondered if he remembered how he'd felt.

Sean looked from her to his dad, then reminded her, "Brunch will get cold. Come on."

Closing the lid to the chest, she left her memories on the love seat and went to the kitchen to make a new one. Maybe slipping back into the past wasn't a good idea. Instead of comforting her, the letters simply made her feel more empty now.

Brady sat in his kitchen, getting an erection, and he was angrier than hell about it. Angry because he couldn't control desire he wasn't ready for.

Laura's brown eyes were big and surprised as she opened Sean and Kat's present. She was holding the little charm as if it were the biggest diamond on earth. She was beautiful this morning, with her hair loose around her face, her lips pink from the lipstick she'd applied, her figure trim but curvy under her pink blouse and striped capri pants.

Right now he wanted to strip her clothes off her and take her to bed.

However, more than a lack of sex was causing the rift between them. He really didn't blame her for his heart attack. If it hadn't happened during their argument, it would have happened eventually. She and Sean had saved his life. The rift had to do with his blunt words Friday night and her drive to resolve something that couldn't be resolved. She wanted to remake him, transforming him back into that man she'd met.

He didn't want to be remade or fixed…or forgiven. As he'd told Laura, there was something about forgiveness that wasn't a gift but a burden. Forgiveness didn't wipe away a sin; it just muted it.

Laura took the charm in the form of a number one with the letters "MOM" beside it and held it up to her bracelet. "It's perfect. This is the first charm you've given me."

"We know Dad gave you all the other charms," Sean said. "But we thought it was time we got you one."

Laura turned to her daughter. "You two actually went shopping together?"

"How else was I going to get around?" Kat joked. "Really, it was pretty easy."

He could tell by the warm affection in Laura's eyes that

she knew "easy" wasn't the only reason Kat had bought the charm. She knew her daughter respected her, even when she wanted her own way. Kat might come to him when she suspected her mother would tell her no. But she believed Laura was a great mom just as he was a great dad. Sean appreciated Laura, too. What Sean felt about Brady was something else entirely. Especially now. Though this morning Brady had felt they were actually relating as father and son.

"We went to a jewelry store at the Galleria. They'll attach it free," Sean explained to his mom.

A faraway look played over Laura's face as she mused, "I used to always go to the jeweler across the street from the Bon Ton building to have your dad's charms attached. But they went out of business a few months ago." She paused for a moment, then added, "I wish the two of you could have seen what a real department store used to be. Someone even ran the elevator back then because they weren't self-service. There was a mezzanine with a restaurant…that's the same floor I bought my records on."

"Those old vinyl things you have in your closet?" Kat asked.

"Those are the ones," Laura replied.

Laura had never been able to make herself part with her original Beatles forty-fives and albums. She also had recordings of Gary Puckett and The Union Gap, The Mindbenders and Frankie Avalon, Kenny Loggins and Air Supply. Laura loved music. She always had. In the flower shop when she was arranging flowers, she played everything from Elton John's "Aida," to Bon Jovi, to Il Divo. She liked passion in her music.

They'd had passion between them...until it had been stunted by the hours he put into his company...by the needs of Sean and Kat...by an undercurrent they'd both denied. Especially the past couple of years. He hadn't acted on desire when he'd felt it. He'd put everything else first.

When had Laura stopped waiting up for him?

When had he decided not to wake her for early-morning loving?

When had living started interfering with loving instead of adding to it?

After Jason died? After they adopted Sean? When Sean reached his teenage years and had started visibly rebelling against Brady?

Why was he being so damn philosophical this morning?

Because he felt Laura slipping away.

She wanted some kind of spiritual connection they'd had early in their marriage. The memory of it was what kept them together. Their history kept them together. Ironically, their children kept them together as well as pushed them apart.

But what would happen when Kat went to college, too, and he and Laura rambled through the house? Then what? They would have to either begin all over again or—

"So Dad, give her your present now," Sean urged him, with an enthusiasm Brady thought was a bit forced.

Brady suddenly realized he and Sean might be more alike than he ever imagined. They were both pretenders. For all these years, Brady had pretended he was fine, that he could live a normal life, that he could have a family and find satisfaction in that. Since his heart attack, however, he now saw clearly that he'd just been going through the motions. That was what Sean was doing now with him—saying what he had to say to encourage harmony, going along instead of fighting against, biding his time until he left and was on his own.

Brady pushed his chair back, went to the counter and lifted the package he'd set there. He'd bought one of those gift bags at Wal-Mart and put his presents in that.

He took the gift to Laura and handed it to her. "I hope you like it."

She pulled out the framed photo first. It was a picture of Sean and Kat, one of those posed photographs where someone had said, *Let's get a picture of the two of you together.*

Laura gazed up at Brady, her eyes shimmering. "Thank you. I needed a recent one to put on the mantel."

He didn't say anything. He knew that to her the photograph was worth ten digital cameras.

When she drew out the box with the camera, she seemed a little puzzled.

"Now you don't have to use Sean's," Brady explained. "Since he'll be taking it with him when he goes to college, I thought you might like to have one of your own."

Standing, she gave him a kiss and a hug. He held her for a few moments, appreciating the fragrance that usually surrounded her, missing the feel of her in his arms.

When she leaned away, she murmured, "Thank you. I can probably photograph the flower arrangements to feature in my brochures. Did Pat take you shopping?"

"No, Sean did. He's familiar with the camera's features."

Her gaze fell affectionately on her son. "Never expected to be chauffeur, did you?"

"Dad wasn't even a back-seat driver."

Brady could hear the surprise in Sean's voice. Apparently his son always expected criticism from him, although Brady tried to *not* criticize.

In some ways, he felt as if he'd been sleepwalking before heart surgery. Yet now, any step he took toward Sean or Laura was like foreign territory.

Looking a bit uncertain, Laura set the camera on the table. "Thank you all for the brunch and gifts. It was great. I'll have the charm attached tomorrow. And the camera—I'll be able to use that at Sean's graduation party. Which we have to discuss. I thought we'd have it next Sunday afternoon. I've already called the caterer. Should I invite your friends, our friends and family? Or would you rather have a separate party just for you and your classmates?"

Sean stared down at the floor, then back at them. "It's really great you want to give me a party and all. But I..."

He stopped for a moment and Brady sensed he was gathering his words. When he felt strongly about something, they wouldn't come to him. It was a symptom of dyslexia.

"I...I really don't expect any big explosion over this. Everybody graduates from high school. If you would like to invite Aunt Pat and Jack and Angie, that's okay, but not a lot more. As far as the kids at school, there are lots of parties. I don't need to add another one. A few of us are going up to Gary's cabin Memorial Day weekend."

"Will his parents be there?" Laura asked.

"His dad's coming up to stay overnight."

"Don't make light of graduating from high school, Sean. You've put in more work and effort than any kid I know," Brady said, quickly seizing the opportunity to give Sean a well-deserved pat on the back.

"It takes me hours sometimes to do what most kids can do in two," Sean said. "When I imagine writing papers and taking notes and organizing them and the hours of outside reading—" he shook his head "—I know you don't want to hear this, but I've been thinking about not going to Prescott. I've checked into an associate-degree program in graphic design at a school in Scranton."

"You *have* to go to college, Sean." Brady's voice was firm. His son had to realize how competitive the world was now, how more, not less, education was necessary. "You might want the easy way out now, but in the long run it won't be easy. Don't compromise your future."

All at once Sean's affability disappeared and his expression became defiant. "Getting an associate degree isn't the *easy* way out. It's what I believe I can handle. You want to be able to tell your friends I got a college degree. Well, I don't care about a B.S. or a B.A. I want to do something *I* want to do. For eighteen years I've followed your orders and your road map. Now I want to choose my own. If you won't pay for it, I'll get loans. Other kids do."

His chair scraped on the tile as he pushed it back, stood and went to the back door. "I'm going to spend the afternoon with Gary and Boyd. Tonight there's a party with kids from Red Lion. They don't know me and I don't know them. I won't have to worry…about hearing anything I don't want to hear. I won't have to worry about defending *you*."

His words were arrows, aimed straight at Brady. And they hit the bull's-eye in his soul.

Before he could even call Sean's name, his son was out the door.

Chapter 13

"You shouldn't be doing that," Brady said roughly the following Sunday afternoon as he came up behind Laura and settled his strong hands around her waist.

She'd been reattaching a light that had slipped from its clip on the patio awning. But she was standing on one of the lawn chairs, precariously perched. Today was Sean's graduation party and they were almost ready.

Her husband was looking so much more like himself, in charcoal slacks and an open-collared gray shirt. Her heart beat faster as she simply stared at him. "This one slipped."

"You could fall and break something. Then where would we be?"

Although his voice was heavy with criticism, she heard the concern there, too. At least that was something. His hands at her waist…that was something else. He hadn't really touched her in a sensual way since before his surgery. And even then there had been no tenderness in it—not the tenderness they'd once shared.

Gazing down into his blue eyes, she wished she knew what he was thinking and feeling. But not knowing had become the norm. She did suspect Sean's parting remark last Sunday had bothered Brady. But he wouldn't admit it.

He must have seen the remnants of sadness she was experiencing pass over her face, because he asked, "What?"

Lightly placing her hands on his shoulders, loving the solid feel of him under her fingers, she stepped down from the chair. She knew better than to start a discussion now, when guests were going to arrive any minute. "I was just thinking—you begin rehab tomorrow. Are you ready for it?"

He stepped away from her and that distance was there again. But so much more than physical distance.

"I'm more than ready, though I still tire too easily. I'm hoping getting in shape again will fix that."

"You'll have to go slow at first."

"I have common sense, Laura. I'm not going to do anything to set me back."

The impatience was in his voice again—an intangible quality that she now realized might go along with any resentment. How long had it been there? How long had she ignored it?

She'd always said she wanted to know what he was thinking and feeling, yet when he'd told her, how had she reacted? She'd looked at another man. She was disappointed in herself and worried that she and Brady might never find their way back to each other again.

She couldn't stop trying, though. She'd had an idea she

hoped he'd go along with. "Next weekend over Memorial Day, maybe we could do something…something fun. Just you and me. We could go to the movies or out to dinner. Kat's going to a sleepover at a friend's. Sean will be at the Laslows' cabin."

"Let's see what the week brings. I'll be starting rehab as well as going into the office."

"Full-time?"

"The doctor advises against that. But I've got to get back in there."

He was putting work before the two of them again. She'd held hope that would change after his heart attack…after his recuperation. But she'd been silly to think that. Still, he'd just take her words as criticism if she said anything about it.

I can never do enough or be enough for you.

Had she actually sent him that message with what she said and did? Or had his own regrets caused the resentment? It didn't matter. He felt it.

The sound of the sliding-glass doors from the dining room opening onto the patio interrupted them. Sean came out, looking like the young man he was becoming. He'd worn a suit for graduation and had seemed so adult. On graduation night, she and Brady had both gotten choked up. Afterward Brady had shaken Sean's hand and that uneasy truce had taken hold between them once more. Brady was still trying to convince Sean that he needed to go to a four-year college. She didn't know for sure what was best. No matter what curriculum Sean studied, there could be roadblocks with his dyslexia. She was inclined to believe that if his passion was really in graphic design, that could take him farther than any four-year degree.

Dressed in khaki slacks and an oversize striped shirt, Sean gave them a halfhearted smile. "There's lots of food on the table, and a car pulled up outside."

Laura started toward the house. "I should go see who it is."

"It's Jack," Sean informed her. "But, before you go..." He shifted from one foot to the other. "I hope you don't mind, but I invited someone else over today."

Laura looked to Brady, but he just shrugged.

"Who?"

"Her name is Valerie Johanssen. I went to a party at her place last weekend."

On Mother's Day night...after the blowup in the kitchen.

"She goes to Red Lion," Sean rushed on. "She's a junior. We talked for a bit, and I mentioned my graduation party today, and—"

"That's fine," Laura assured him. "We'd love to meet her."

Quickly reaching into the back pocket of his slacks, Sean pulled out a brochure folded in half. "And I wanted to give you this. Maybe you and Dad can look at it. It's about the school I want to go to. They sent me a whole packet of information, but this will lay it out. Their online address is there, too."

"We'll check it out." She hoped Brady could be open-minded about it, but he said nothing.

Hearing the doorbell chime, Laura slipped inside to welcome the first of her guests. She thought that maybe if she left Sean and Brady on the patio together they'd talk.

But when she glanced over her shoulder, she saw Sean had come inside, too, and Brady was moving the chair back where it belonged.

Soon the house began to fill.

Angie and Jack walked in with wide smiles, along with a present for Sean, and made themselves at home. When Pat arrived, she brought a date. The man had an easy smile and wrapped his arm around Brady's sister's shoulders as if they'd been together for more than a weekend. In a little while, he began talking to Brady about investments. Two more neighboring couples also came. Sean had helped them with yard work in the summers before he'd gotten a job at the Galleria in the sports-memorabilia store. He'd be starting back there after Memorial Day weekend. Kat flitted around from one group to another, and Laura knew she was going to miss her daughter when she went to summer camp for two weeks.

They were all filling plates from the dining-room table when the doorbell rang again. Sean rushed to get it. A few minutes later, a pretty, blond teenager followed him into the dining room.

After he introduced Valerie, Laura tried to make her feel comfortable. "We're glad you could join us. Just help yourself."

Valerie gave her a smile and Laura noticed when the girl looked at her son, there was interest there…the same interest she saw in Sean's eyes when he gazed at Valerie.

More than once she spotted Brady's attention on them, too. She wondered if he was thinking about young love, where it started and where it had to go.

But maybe not. He wasn't sentimental the way she was. In fact, she wondered if what they'd started with meant anything to him now. The basis of their love—who they'd been and where they'd come from—would always be with her.

As everyone talked and ate, Laura handed off her new camera to Kat, who'd agreed to take shots.

"I put the SD card in," Kat said. "So we can snap as many as you want."

"Get everybody. I want to make a scrapbook."

"You'll have them in a file on the computer."

"That's not the same thing as having an album to page through."

Kat cast her a questioning glance as if she didn't understand, and Laura supposed she probably didn't. She just wanted to sit on her sofa with the album on her lap so she could study each photograph long after the party. Sitting at the computer just wasn't the same thing.

After most of the guests had wandered outside, Jack put a hand on Laura's shoulder. "Brady's looking a lot better."

"I was scared to death for so long it's hard for me to believe he's finally recuperating. But he is...and he looks good, doesn't he?"

"Are you speaking from a health perspective or a wife perspective?"

Jack always had teased her and she didn't mind. They'd all been friends for a long time. "From both a health and a wife perspective."

Brady saw them talking and joined them. "What are you two plotting?"

"Wouldn't *you* like to know," Jack joked.

Brady's gaze fell on Laura. There was something indefinable there. Some of the old feeling?

Flustered for a moment, she searched for something to say. She asked Jack, "Did Brady tell you he's going back to work this week?"

Jack frowned. "Not ten hours a day, I hope."

"Those days are over," Brady replied with a grimace.

"You say that now, but once you get back in there again—I know you. You'll be designing or going after a contract and you won't even realize how long you're there."

When Laura swung her attention to Brady, their eyes locked and held.

Were their lives going to change? Was he really going to slow down?

Brady focused his attention once again on Jack. "Did I tell you about the new robot that..."

Within seconds the men were embroiled in a technical discussion about robots that mitigated improvised explosive devices. Over the years Jack had come to understand a lot of what Brady did, and was interested in it. To Laura, the mechanical aspects were still Greek. Instead of listening, she found herself journeying back about five years to a time when Brady's work had taken him away from her and the kids.

Although he'd worked long hours in the past building his company, they'd become even longer when Brady had won a surge of new contracts. In fact, he'd been away from home so much, spent nights in his office and called to say he was going to be late so many times, that she'd begun to wonder if he was having an affair. Wasn't that the first thing a woman thought when a man didn't make time to be with her?

She and Brady had planned a night out—to go to dinner

and a concert with Jack and Angie. Pat had agreed to stay with the kids. But at the last minute, Brady had called and told her he'd gotten tied up and he wouldn't be able to go. She should. She shouldn't miss the evening out with friends.

Miss the evening out with friends? She'd wanted an evening out with *him!* But she'd heard the fatigue in his voice and hadn't said anything when he'd phoned. She hadn't gone to the concert, hoping he'd return home at a reasonable time.

He hadn't.

By midnight, Laura had gone to bed, but she couldn't sleep.

When Brady came up to their bedroom, she hadn't known whether to pretend she was asleep or confess what she was thinking. If she put it into words…

He'd undressed, then slid into bed.

She'd turned toward him, hoping she was wrong… afraid she wasn't.

"I thought you were sleeping."

"I couldn't fall asleep. I didn't go to the concert. I've been thinking…" She swallowed hard, then let the question that had been plaguing her all night fly loose. "Are you having an affair?"

The sheet rustled as he shifted and turned onto his side. "What?"

"We've been together so little lately. Do you remember the last time we made love?"

"Last week…the week before…"

"It's been a month," she said softly.

He hiked up on his elbow. "That can't be."

"It was the night it snowed ten inches and our street

didn't get plowed. You came home for supper and couldn't get back out again. You went to the den to work and I came in and we had a little brandy. We made love. Then you worked until practically dawn."

Brady lifted her chin. Moonlight sifted into the room enough that she could see the set of his jaw. "I am *not* and have *never* considered having an affair."

Blinking back tears, filled with relief because he'd never lied to her and she believed him now, she admitted, "I miss you. The kids miss you. Do you really need to work as much as you do?"

"If we want Kat and Sean to go to a good college someday, if we want to give them advantages we didn't have, if we ever intend to retire, I have to go after contracts that will keep my company sound. I can't do that by going out to dinner and attending concerts with friends."

"I'd rather spend time with you, know you're making time for me and our kids, than worry about them going to expensive colleges someday. We already have some money invested for them. And as far as retirement goes, if you keep working like this, what will happen to our marriage?"

Dropping his hand, he seemed to move away from her, though physically he was still there. "Our marriage has already been through hell. A few late hours shouldn't affect it."

"It's been more than a few."

Obviously tired and frustrated, he ran his hand down over his face. "I don't know what else to say to you. *You* work. *You* do what you have to do to keep Blossoms in the black. I work to make our future secure, to make sure you and Sean and Kat have everything you need."

"We need *you*."

After a strained silence, he said, "Let's table this for tonight. We've got to get some sleep." Then he turned away from her, and Laura felt…alone.

Laura had wished for the days when they'd been so close nothing could tear them apart.

Apparently Brady had wished for the same thing. The following evening, he'd bought each of them a bicycle! Since Kat and Sean were outgrowing their bikes, he'd bought new ones for them, as well as more conservative models for himself and Laura.

"Tomorrow is Saturday," he'd said. "I'm taking off. We can drive to the Gettysburg battlefield and ride our bikes together. Maybe you can pack a picnic lunch."

After a Saturday morning of riding the battlefield, they'd eaten at a weathered picnic table. Brady had slid a box from his pocket and given her a bicycle charm for her bracelet. Then he'd kissed her and murmured into her ear, "Tonight we're going dancing. When we get home, we'll lock our bedroom door."

Brady had kept his promise. Brady always kept his promises.

They'd still been in love. They'd just had to remind themselves how good that love could be.

Jack waved his hand in front of Laura's eyes. "She's glazing over again. Why haven't you been able to get her interested in robots in the past thirty years?"

"I guess robots and flowers don't mix," Brady joked. "But then again, it's hard for me to tell a daisy from a marigold."

Bringing herself back to the present, focusing on what

Jack had said, Laura wondered if Brady also resented the fact she'd never understood his work. Had she made the effort? Or had she been so involved with their kids and Blossoms, she hadn't tried.

The silence grew long and awkward.

Jack gave Brady a curious look. Then he murmured, "I think I'll go get Angie. She wants to get a picnic together for next weekend at Caledonia. I'll find out the details."

"A picnic could be fun," Laura said lightly when Jack had gone outside. "We could wade in the stream the way we used to when we took the kids up there."

"When Sean caught crayfish in a foam cup?" Brady asked.

So he remembered, too.

"And we went on hikes on the nature trail."

"And Kat would squeak every time she saw a bug."

"Those were good times. We could have them again."

"Is that what you want?" His voice was husky.

Her throat tightened and she nodded.

Jack returned to them then with Angie in tow. "She said she wants to go up there on Sunday," he announced.

In those few moments, Laura had felt as if she and Brady were finally getting somewhere. Maybe past his surgery…past their argument…past regrets neither of them could do anything about.

What would it take to make their marriage whole again?

Chapter 14

The late-afternoon sun bounced off the windows of the toolshed the following Friday. Laura took a deep breath of the air, lifting her face to the sky. She *needed* to be in her garden. She was coiled up tight. Even yoga stretches hadn't helped. Time out here might.

Noting the grass was growing long, she remembered the gardener would be mowing and trimming tomorrow. Wes brought his mower and tools for the work he did. She kept implements of her own in the shed along with the extra patio chairs. Although she rarely had the time, once in a while she liked to plant a bed of flowers herself, weed the garden, feel the earth in her hands. She hadn't tended to her favorite flower bed, with its rosebushes and daisies, since the end of last summer.

When the lock on the shed released, Laura opened the

door and stepped inside. The heat within the small building brought warmth to her cheeks.

She selected a hoe and clippers, and was ready to carry them outside, when she decided to dig in the old chest for her mother-in-law's short gardening spade. It was an antique now, but she cherished it because she and Anna had shared the same love of flowers.

Laura raised the lid and was rummaging in the dark interior for the tool she wanted, when she felt a paper bag. At least, that was what she thought it was.

What was *that* doing in here?

Lifting out the parcel, she felt three hard bulges, like small bottles. Her heart raced as she set down the other tools, picked up the bag and unfolded the top. Inside she found a bottle of scotch, Jack Daniel's and one of vodka. She'd seen the tiny bottles in hotel minibars.

Setting them aside, she rummaged through the rest of the chest but didn't find anything else that shouldn't be there.

Could they be Wes's? Hardly. He could keep liquor stashed with his equipment on his trailer, in his pickup.... He'd never shown one symptom of being an alcoholic.

Sean, on the other hand...

She had to know if these were Sean's. Maybe his drinking *hadn't* stopped last summer. Maybe these bottles were evidence that something bigger was going on. It was possible in addition to these small bottles, he had a fifth stashed someplace else. This weekend she and Brady had planned to sit down with him to find out how serious he was about graphic design. But now another type of discussion was more important.

Not bothering to relock the shed, she hurried into the house. As she climbed the stairs to the second floor, she told herself not to panic. She told herself to respect Sean's privacy.

She told herself she had to tear up his room.

At the landing, she warned herself to calm down. If she searched Sean's room and found a bottle, what good would that do? Yes, she'd have proof. But at the end of the day, how much would that help? Instead of sorting through drawers and tearing apart her son's closet—which she could always do later if she had to—she hurried to Kat's room. Her daughter had been at the computer since she'd come home from school.

Kat's bedroom door was cracked open a couple of inches. Laura knocked.

"Come on in," Kat called.

When Laura pushed the door open, her gaze slid away from the huge Jesse McCartney poster on the wall and went to her daughter.

Kat didn't turn around but said over her shoulder, "If I had a new computer like Sean's, downloading music would be a lot faster."

Sean's graduation present had been a laptop for college. "Didn't Dad say he'd update your computer for you?"

Kat wrinkled her nose. "Yeah. But maybe I can get a new one next year?"

Instead of answering, Laura lifted shorts, jeans and T-shirt from the bedroom chair, laid them on the bed and pulled the chair closer to Kat. "I want to talk to you."

Kat swung away from the computer. "What about?"

Laura held up the bag. "Have you ever seen this?"

"No. What is it?" Her daughter sounded…wary.

Laura extracted the three bottles and laid them side by side on her lap. "Do you know what these are?"

Kat licked her lips, looked uncomfortable and replied, "Yeah. They're booze."

"Do you know anything about them?"

"No!" Kat seemed genuinely outraged. "I've never seen them before."

"Are they Sean's?" Laura asked softly, needing her daughter to confide in her if she knew anything.

Kat stared down at the floor and then shrugged. "Where did you find them?"

"In the shed."

"Maybe they belong to Wes. Maybe after he cuts the grass he swigs."

Laura kept her turmoil from showing. "I don't think so. If he wanted to drink, he could keep a bottle in his truck. And I've never seen any evidence that he's a drinker. He's a hard worker. He's always here when he says he's going to be and never shirks what has to be done."

Her daughter remained silent.

The less said, the less she'd incriminate anyone? "Do you know if Sean's drinking?" she prodded.

Kat looked up and away from her mother. "How should I know?"

"I think you might know things your dad and I don't."

"Well, you're wrong. I don't know anything."

"If Sean *is* drinking, he could be in trouble."

Kat faced her again. "What kind of trouble?"

"If he becomes dependent on alcohol to solve his problems, he'll never solve them."

Kat stared at the computer screen once more. "I don't know what Sean does when he's not here."

"What about when he *is* here?"

"Maybe you've got this all wrong, Mom. Maybe he's holding them for someone else and didn't know where to put them. Maybe someone gave them to him and he didn't want them in the house."

"There are garbage cans in the back."

Giving her a really elaborate shrug, Kat shook her head again. "I don't know anything, Mom."

Laura's maternal radar was on alert. Kat had seemed genuinely surprised to see the bottles of liquor, but Laura believed her daughter was holding something back. Was she protecting her brother?

If Laura searched Sean's room, there would be no going back. She really should discuss the situation with Brady first. Wait until tonight? She had an urgent feeling about this and didn't think it should wait.

"Will you be okay here for a little while? I need to talk to your dad about this."

"I'm old enough to stay here alone."

Although Laura felt pushed to talk with Brady, she had to take time for Kat. "You know, there's a reason I worry about you being here alone, other than a safety issue."

Her daughter's expression was curious.

"I don't ever want you to feel lonely or afraid." When she and Brady had adopted Kat, she'd been only two months old. Her mother had died in childbirth and her father had been in a fatal motorcycle accident a month later. Laura had vowed to give this child, like Sean, all the care and love she herself had missed when she'd lost her own parents.

Kat thought that over. "Were you lonely or afraid when you were my age?"

Her daughter was very perceptive sometimes. "Yes, I was. After I went to live with my aunt."

"I forget you didn't have your mom or dad when you were growing up. That had to be tough. If you and Dad weren't here, it would be so strange. I mean, I think about Tracey Davidson. She only has her mom now."

Kat knew the story of her adoption—that her birth parents had died. But they hadn't been real people to her. Her life had begun the day Laura and Brady had brought her home.

Leaning forward, Laura pushed Kat's curly hair behind her ear. "Your dad's going to take care of himself now. Hopefully we'll both be around for a long time."

"Dad's heart attack changed everything. He's different. You're different. Sean's different."

"We all got scared. And I'm worried that's why Sean might be drinking."

"When he goes to college, you won't be able to do anything about whether he drinks or not."

"No, I won't."

Kat chewed on her lower lip. "There's beer at the parties he goes to."

"I guessed that," Laura said mildly, waiting for her daughter to open up more.

She motioned to the bottles in Laura's lap. "Maybe he just wanted to celebrate graduating and all."

"Maybe he did."

Kat pushed her chair away from Laura's. "I'm going to see what's in the fridge."

Reading the signs, Laura realized this discussion with Kat was over. She gathered up the bottles and rose to her feet. "I'll be back in about an hour."

Brady had thirty seconds left on the treadmill when he saw Laura come into the rehab center. She was beautiful, even in a T-shirt and jeans. His body responded to the sight of her, and he suddenly wished he could shower and change before he talked to her.

He stepped down from the treadmill and took his pulse as he'd been trained to do, noticing the slight elevation from the number he'd gotten his last workout session. After he wiped his face with his towel, he flung it around his neck.

Abruptly he realized Laura shouldn't really be here. She'd told him she was going to spend the afternoon at home, puttering around the garden. Even though Wes Rossi did a superb job of gardening for them, she always liked to add her touches.

As she approached him, he asked, "Is something wrong?"

She opened her leather hobo bag and let him look inside. "I found these in the toolshed."

He recognized what the bottles held instantly. "Did you ask Sean about them?" There was no doubt in Brady's mind that they belonged to his son.

"He's at Boyd's." She glanced around at the recovering patients. "Maybe I shouldn't have come. Maybe I'm overreacting, but I thought we should tackle this…right away. I asked Kat if Sean's been drinking, but she wouldn't give me a straight answer."

"Did you check his room?"

"Should I? That's why I had to talk to you. I didn't want to interrupt your workout, but I knew you were stopping at your office afterward."

His wife was apologizing for interrupting him. When had *that* started? When had they become more like strangers living together than husband and wife? His heart attack had shone a light on the lives they were living and he couldn't and shouldn't turn it off. Not if he wanted his marriage to work again.

Suddenly Laura's gaze left his and fixed on something or someone over his shoulder. When Brady glanced around, he saw Dr. Gregano walking toward them. Brady had noticed him earlier, talking to one of the exercise physiologists.

As the cardiologist approached them, Brady saw Laura bite her lower lip. She did that when she was uncertain or uncomfortable or...nervous. Why would she be nervous?

The doctor smiled at both of them. "Brady...Laura. How are you doing today?"

The doctor had called Brady by his first name from the day Brady was coherent enough to appreciate his visit in the hospital. When had the physician begun calling *Laura* by her first name?

"Getting stronger every day," Brady assured him.

"Good. I looked over your progress report. You're right on target."

Laura was still silent and her cheeks were flushed. Brady was acutely aware of Gregano's gaze meeting hers...of their glances holding a few seconds too long...of Laura looking away. What in the hell was going on?

Jumping in finally, Laura asked the doctor, "Have you been back to the bagel shop?" To Brady she explained, "Dr. Gregano and I ran into each other when I bought those bagels last Saturday."

So they hadn't had a clandestine meeting, just a chance one? Brady didn't like the vibrations he was picking up. He didn't like the way the doctor's eyes gentled when he gazed at Laura. Gregano was at least ten years younger than she was, not that it mattered. Or maybe it did.

"Actually, I stopped in yesterday on my way home," Gregano replied.

Keeping his attention focused on the doctor, Brady asked, "Do you live in the east end?"

"I do. I'm in an apartment right now. I'm not home very much. But I'm considering buying a house closer to the hospital."

"Brady grew up in a house on Sleepy Hollow Road."

"I looked at a few properties back there. One on Highland. I'm going through it again tonight."

Brady listened carefully to the interchange. It sounded as though Laura hadn't known where the doctor lived. Maybe nothing *was* going on.

But when he saw Dr. Gregano's gaze fall on Laura again, there was definite interest there.

Whether it was ego or pride or simply male territorial behavior, Brady had the urge to claim his wife.

"I should be going," Laura said. "I told Kat I wouldn't be long."

Making an impulsive decision, Brady responded, "I'm almost finished here, then I'll be home."

"What about—"

"Work can wait. We should take care of that matter we were discussing." He wasn't going to let Laura go through searching Sean's room by herself. She'd had to do too many things by herself for the past six weeks and maybe even before that. When he got home, he'd find out exactly how well she knew Dr. Gregano. He'd find out whether the bagel shop had been a planned meeting or a chance one.

And if it *had* been planned?

Either way, he had to take a good hard look at that wall of resentment he'd put up between them. If he didn't, thirty-three years of marriage could just slip away.

Chapter 15

Brady held the small liquor bottles out to his son and waited for Sean's explanation.

Laura held her breath, wishing she'd never gone to the toolshed that afternoon. When she and Brady had searched Sean's room, they'd found…nothing. And they'd done a thorough search. She could tell Brady had been just as relieved as she'd been that they'd come up empty.

While Brady had driven Kat to Sandra's, Laura had mulled over the best way to deal with this with Sean. She'd finally realized there was no best way. They simply had to confront him.

Sean had come home from Boyd's with a grin on his face, his shirt damp over his swim trunks. Apparently Boyd's parents had readied the pool for Memorial Day weekend.

But now Sean glanced from his father to his mother,

his grin nowhere in evidence. "Yeah, they're mine," he said calmly.

To Laura's surprise, his voice was noncombative.

Sean went on. "They're nothing for you to get ripped up about. They've been in there since Christmas. One of the older guys got a bunch of them and handed them out. I knew if you saw them in my room you'd go berserk, so I stowed them out there. You can see they're not even open."

The seals were intact and Laura began to breathe a little easier.

But Brady was still wary. "How many of them were there to begin with?"

Sean hesitated only a moment. "That was it."

"If you weren't going to drink them, why didn't you just toss them?" Brady kept his tone conversational.

It was obvious that he was trying hard not to put Sean on the defensive. But of course the boy *was* defensive just by the nature of the conversation.

With one of those teenage shrugs that frustrate parents, Sean admitted, "I thought I'd take them along to college. You know. Thought I'd be cool."

Brady set the bottles on the counter, his expression worried. "Cool has nothing to do with drinking."

"Yeah, I know that."

"No, apparently you don't."

"They're *no* big deal," Sean repeated, getting a little heated now. "Certainly not as big a deal as me going to the school I want to go to. Did you look at that brochure I gave you?"

"Your mom and I both read it, but I want to check into the school's accreditation before you even consider it."

"You're always—" Sean clamped his lips together.

"Never mind." He pointed to the liquor bottles. "So can I go to Gary's cabin tonight, or are you going to ground me for something I picked up six months ago, stowed away and forgot I had?"

If he hadn't added the "forgot I had," Laura almost could have bought it. Still, she and Brady had no proof Sean was drinking. With Kat not confiding in them, either, they couldn't condemn him without any evidence.

Brady must have come to the same conclusion. "Are you sure Gary's father's going to be there?"

"He said he would."

"How many kids will be staying over?"

"Four…six. Not many. We're going fishing tomorrow morning, so I'll be back around noon."

"All right," Brady said finally, giving his permission.

Laura could see there were probably a thousand other things he wanted to say to Sean, too. But if he did, he'd be preaching. If he did, Sean would get defiant. If he did, they could lose their son before he left for school, no matter which college he chose.

"I just have to throw some gear in my duffel, then I'm out of here." After a last glance at the bottles on the counter, he loped toward the stairs.

When Sean was out of earshot, Laura asked, "What do you think?"

Creases furrowed Brady's brow. "I don't know what to think. It's possible these have been in the shed since Christmas. It's also possible there were more to begin with and this is all that's left."

"I just feel bad that we don't automatically believe him," Laura said.

"Last summer Sean gave us reason to worry. I can always call Gary Laslow's father tomorrow and ask him what went on."

"Sean would hate that if he found out."

"And probably hate me. But we have to figure out if he's telling the truth."

Heavy footsteps sounded on the stairs as Sean jogged down with his duffel. He called from the living room, "I'll see you tomorrow."

"Have fun. Drive safe," Laura called back.

The front door closing carried to the kitchen. When Laura's gaze met Brady's, he ruefully shook his head. "This doesn't get any easier."

He approached her then, and there was something different about the look in his eyes and the way he was studying her. Sex appeal had always emanated from Brady, had always drawn her to him, had always wrapped itself around him when they were together. It had been absent since his heart attack, as if he'd shut it down. But now it was there again and her stomach fluttered with excitement. He was standing close to her, very close.

While the late-spring breeze brought the scent of roses through the kitchen window, she examined her husband's face, hoping to catch a glimpse of what he was thinking. She never expected the question that he asked.

"Did you and Dr. Gregano plan to meet at the bagel shop?"

"No! Of course not. Why would you think such a thing?"

After a long pause, he replied, "Because you've had a lot to deal with and might have wanted to escape…us.

Because maybe you needed a man to give you attention I haven't. And I said some things I shouldn't have. I've been feeling raw and exposed and…powerless. After I got out of the service, I didn't want to feel powerless again. I've worked damn hard to control my life. Suddenly I was in the hospital with no control. That wasn't an easy place for me to be in."

Apparently Brady hadn't been immune to her feelings. Apparently he'd missed the loss of intimacy between them, too. "I know."

After debating with herself for a moment, she went on. "You've got to tell me the truth about something, Brady. You said my forgiveness was a burden. Have you resented me all these years? Have you *wanted* to be with me? Or was our marriage just like a lane in traffic you found yourself in and couldn't escape from?"

He stepped even closer. "Before I left for the army, I felt we were equals. When I came back, I never believed I was worthy of your love. I've always thought you got cheated because you fell in love with one man and ended up with another."

A deep womanly pulse inside her began fluttering and then racing with hope and the possibility of closeness with her husband again. "When I met you, you were a good man. When you came back from Vietnam, you were still a good man. Yes, you were different—more withdrawn, less open. Your joy and hope had left you. But it came back. On our wedding day, I was the happiest woman alive."

"And now?" His voice was husky.

"We've had a lot of bumps in the road and we've

managed to ride over them together. But this time, after your heart attack, we weren't working through the problems together. Since your surgery, you've closed me out. You wouldn't even touch me..." Her voice broke and she saw the turmoil in his eyes because he'd caused her this pain.

His arms came around her. "Let me tell you a secret, Laura Martinelli Malone. You have always radically turned me on. That didn't change after my heart attack."

"Brady—"

"I do *not* blame you for it. Or for my nightmares. I just hated having them again...putting you through this... being afraid I'd hurt you. On top of that, I also knew I had to shut down my libido. I was afraid to let my heart race. I couldn't even climb the stairs without getting short of breath, let alone think about making love to you. Can you imagine how absolutely frustrating that was?"

She pushed away from him and tilted her head up. "I didn't care about the sex. I just wanted to touch you and have you touch me."

He stroked her hair. "I couldn't. Not without wanting a hell of a lot more. And every time I was near you, I was afraid of my body's reaction."

Brady was a proud man. He never did anything halfway.

"I saw you and Gregano together today." His voice was tight. The nerve in his jaw worked. "I saw he was interested in you. I knew other men would be interested in you. You're a vital, beautiful woman. I realized if I didn't do something to bridge this gap growing between us, I could lose you. Tonight the planets must be lined up just right. I'm here, you're here, the kids aren't here. I think

Now Brady wondered if he didn't hold back who he was with everyone. Then again, maybe he didn't hold back. Maybe he'd lost part of himself and it was still back in that jungle. A man couldn't give what he no longer had.

"Dad, I really think this is the one." Sean pointed to a Kodak.

Brady looked at his son, really looked at him for the first time in a long time. He wanted to ask Sean if he hated him for all the things he should have done as a father and hadn't. He wanted to ask Sean if he despised him because of the things he'd read in that article. He needed to ask Sean if his son could ever respect him again.

But they were standing in Wal-Mart, a department clerk was headed their way and Brady couldn't ask those questions here.

Sometimes questions were better left unasked and unanswered. He should just be grateful that at this moment in time, he and Sean had found a little common ground.

After tugging a stepstool from a corner of her walk-in closet, Laura set it at the far end where her dressier garments hung. When she and Kat had returned home from church, Kat had found a note in her room.

Peeking out her door, Kat had called to Laura, "Sean and Dad ran an errand. They probably had to get eggs so we can make your brunch. They'll be back any time. Why don't you change. I'll call you when we're ready."

Laura wondered why both Brady *and* Sean had gone for eggs. That was unusual. But she was glad they had. Even if they talked sports the whole time, at least they'd be talking.

we need to get to know each other all over again and start a new phase in our lives."

"What phase is that?" she asked a little shakily, concerned having sex wasn't the fix-all he wanted it to be, yet hopeful because she felt the same way right now she'd felt when she'd first met Brady—excited, happy, desired.

"A phase where the two of us aren't too busy to have dinner, aren't too busy to sit and talk, aren't too busy to take a few days and go away together. Maybe your idea about a second honeymoon is just what we need."

Sliding his hands under her hair, he rubbed his thumbs along her neck. Then he bent his head to hers and kissed her.

Brady didn't waste time on a relaxed meander into passion. He dived right into it. His tongue boldly pushed into her mouth and she gasped from the pleasure of kissing him like this again. It had been too long since she'd wanted to feel his possession. He was obviously a man on a mission and that mission was to make her desire him…the mission was to make her remember what heated desire between them felt like. His mission was to take her back to a time and a place when everything was new and exciting and open to possibilities.

But then she remembered his heart attack and she became afraid for him.

Apparently sensing the change, he ended the kiss and pulled away from her. "What?"

"Are you ready for this? I mean—"

"I did two flights of stairs yesterday and didn't get short of breath. So I passed the test. I'm ready to take the chance that my body's healed enough. Are you?"

"You have to ask?" Her voice was wobbly, and then she was filled with so much anticipation and happiness she didn't know how to express it. "What do you want to do first?"

"You mean besides kiss you again?"

She felt heat rushing through her at the prospect of making love with him once more.

He grinned at her. "I love it when your cheeks get red. Why don't we go someplace for dinner—someplace quiet. Then we can come back, just take things slow and see where they go."

She wrapped her arms around him and laid her head against his chest, feeling almost young again, loved again, special again. If only tonight would last forever.

Maybe it would.

From the dock, Sean glanced up at the floodlight above him as it went on in the enveloping dusk. On the hill, music blared from the cabin's porch. There weren't any neighbors for at least a mile in all directions. Located north of York, the cabin sat wedged between pines and oaks that were scattered all over the property. With gray light turning denser, Gary's father was nowhere in sight.

Sitting on the rough boards near a pizza box, Sean picked up another slice. Two coolers with beer and ice Gary had provided sat haphazardly near the small dock. Tim and Boyd had arrived with three pizzas, hot wings and liters of Coke about an hour earlier. The six of them had devoured most of the pizza. James and Kent had taken one of the three canoes out onto the half-mile-long lake. The floodlight over the dock as well as the full moon illuminated their progress as they dipped their oars in and out, skimming the surface of the water.

Sean had swallowed swigs of a beer as he'd eaten pizza and wings, but he hadn't gone near the fifths of whiskey James had contributed to the party. Although Sean was trying his best to concentrate on the conversation Boyd and Tim were having about the players on the Orioles team this year, his mind skittered all over the place. Mostly he was thinking about Valerie Johanssen and her long blond hair, her green eyes and fantastic smile. She was so…real. After his party, out on the patio, he'd found the courage to kiss her. When he had, the most ridiculous feeling had come over him that no matter what happened, everything was going to be all right. Because of a girl with silky hair and a smile that made his insides melt?

He didn't know where they were going on their date tomorrow night. He'd much rather think about that than the scene with his parents in the kitchen. Daydreaming about Valerie was much more pleasant than admitting to himself that he'd lied again to his dad.

Hell, what was he supposed to say to him? *Yeah, I drank the other ten of those bottles I had. Booze makes me feel better when nothing else can?*

Wondering why Gary, who'd gone to the cabin to fetch a bag of chips, hadn't returned, Sean pushed himself to his feet and hiked up the incline to the screened-in porch. The door slapped against the frame as he went inside—and stopped short. The smell told Sean that Gary was smoking, but not a cigarette…a joint. His friend was lounging on the indoor-outdoor carpet next to one of the speakers.

Sean lowered the volume on the CD player and

crouched next to Gary. "What are you doing in here by yourself? The party's out there."

"I wasn't having any fun. We need girls to have fun." His friend's words were slurred. Sean had noticed Gary drink at least three beers since he'd arrived, and he was sure his friend had started *before* that. Along with the pot, he soon wouldn't remember his own name.

"Your dad said no girls allowed."

"You don't see him anywhere, do you? He called, said he got tied up, might be midnight till he gets here."

"He's in a meeting on a Friday night?" Gary's dad was a lawyer and Sean supposed it was possible.

"He's not in any meeting. He's with his girlfriend."

Sean was surprised by that news. As far as he knew, Gary's parents hadn't separated or anything. "What do you mean, he's with his girlfriend?"

"He thinks I don't know anything about it. I heard him talking to her on his cell phone one night. Mom was upstairs, so he wasn't talking to *her.* Her name is Sheila something-or-other. She's a paralegal in his office."

"You can't be sure."

"Yeah, I can. He was laughing, talking about meeting her at a motel. I'm not stupid." With a huge sigh, Gary levered himself to his feet. "I don't want to think about it anymore. Let's have some fun. If he's not going to be here, we might as well get hammered." He sucked another puff on the joint and offered it to Sean. "Want a drag?"

"Nah. I have a big date tomorrow night. I don't want that stuff to affect anything that does or doesn't happen." He'd heard guys couldn't get it up after they'd smoked weed. He wasn't taking any chances. He doubted if Valerie was the kind of girl who dropped her clothes easily, but who knew. Whatever happened, he didn't intend to dull any pleasure he might feel either by having the remnants of a hangover or anything else floating through him.

Gary gave him a lopsided grin. "It took you long enough to find a girl to your liking. Valerie *is* hot. I'm surprised she's not attached."

The screen door slapped behind them as they left the porch. Sean couldn't wait to find out more about Valerie. He just hoped she'd give him a chance.

The night was filled with the sound of a local band's demo CD, as Sean and Gary meandered toward the dock. Even in the encroaching darkness, Sean could sense Gary wasn't steady on his feet.

The sound of a car coming down the lane stopped Sean. "I guess your dad got here earlier than he expected."

"Nope. I called Paula Langston. I'm hoping she brought a couple of friends. This party's about to get better."

Sean wasn't so sure. He'd been to parties with Paula and her friends.

What was wrong with him tonight that he couldn't have a little fun? Or even a lot of fun? Was it the whole college thing? The confrontation with his parents? Jitteriness about his date with Valerie tomorrow night?

All of the above.

An hour later, Sean was back on the porch, sifting through the CDs and ignoring Kent and Nina Thompson, who were swapping saliva on a love seat in the corner. Not long after the girls had arrived, there had been a pairing off. That was always the way it was. He hadn't been interested in pairing off with one of them. He and Valerie had talked about stuff that mattered—college, for one thing—and he couldn't wait until he saw her again.

Boyd's voice sailed through the screen door. "Sean! Come out here and talk sense into Gary, will you?"

Gary was beyond hearing sense. He was both stoned and drunk.

Leaving the stack of CDs, he pushed open the screen door and stood on the top step. "I'm surprised Gary's still on his feet."

Boyd motioned for him to follow. "That's the problem. He's in a canoe and he's fooling around."

James and Paula were sitting on the hood of her car, looking as if they were having a heart-to-heart. Sean and Boyd jogged past them, down to the lake. "Where are Tim and Jeanetta?"

"Got me. They're probably in one of the bedrooms. Just look at that idiot." Boyd pointed to Gary.

Under the circle of the floodlight dappling the lake water, Sean could make out the canoe about twenty yards out. Gary stood in it, dancing to the beat of the CD that echoed across the water. He was backlit by moonlight, and the canoe was tipping from side to side.

"Gary!" Sean called. "Sit down and bring the canoe back in."

"Nah," Gary yelled back. "I'm having too much fun."

"How long has he been out there?" Sean asked Boyd.

"About fifteen minutes. He just paddled in circles for a while. But when that CD played, he stood up."

"Gary," Sean called again. But before he could repeat the command to bring the canoe in, the boat wobbled.

Gary lost his balance. Sean watched in horror as the canoe capsized and Gary sailed into the water.

After a stunned moment, Sean kicked off his shoes and took a running leap off the dock. The water was cold, though that barely registered. He saw Gary splash a few times and suck in air, but then his friend disappeared under the surface. He heard Boyd shout he was calling 911.

The floodlight reflected off the surface of the black water. The moonlight trickled under it. Sean dived, estimating how fast Gary might sink. Adrenaline shot through him. He couldn't see anything in the murkiness. He didn't know how long he searched until he either sensed or spotted movement…something. His hand closed on material—Gary's shirt?

Kicking wildly, he propelled them to the surface.

Sean's arms and legs felt numb. He remembered the rescue hold he'd learned in the summer safety class he'd taken last year but actually executing it was much harder than he ever imagined it would be. After he maneuvered Gary into the long grass on the shore, Boyd and James and Kent were there, all of them looking panicked.

Quickly Sean hefted Gary over and felt for a pulse. There wasn't one.

Boyd knelt beside their friend. "I can do chest compressions."

Gary wasn't breathing and Sean remembered his mother working on his dad. He began giving Gary mouth-to-mouth. Boyd did his part.

Over and over again, Sean puffed two times, mindful of Gary's chest rising and falling. Then he waited for Boyd, gave Gary his breath again, feeling light-headed, hearing buzzing in his ears. But he kept on, knowing he had to.

When Gary didn't start breathing, panic clamped a hold on Sean's chest. His eyes blurred. Tears ran down his cheeks as he heard the wail of a siren.

He was terrified help was too late.

The house was dark when Laura and Brady returned home from dinner. The giddy feeling in Laura's stomach had remained all evening. She almost felt as if she were on her first date with Brady. It was a *wonderful* feeling.

He unlocked the door and disengaged the security alarm. Then he gazed down at her with the crooked grin that had first curled her toes. "We could watch a movie…or we could go upstairs."

Was he as eager as she was to just hop into bed? To feel skin against skin, lips against lips and bodies against bodies?

"Let's go upstairs."

Depending on how this went, maybe they'd lie there all night, talking, holding, sharing. She told herself not to anticipate too much, but she was so hopeful, she couldn't wipe the smile off her face.

Brady made certain the green light was glowing on the security panel once again, then he took her hand and led her to the stairs.

In their bedroom, they glanced at each other like two newlyweds, uncertain of the protocol. Brady undid his tie and tugged it off. "I missed the chocolate cheesecake."

It was a habit of theirs to share a piece of chocolate cheesecake for dessert. That night, they'd both had fresh fruit. Sensing Brady wasn't just making idle conversation, she waited.

After he shrugged out of his suit jacket and hung it around the wooden valet, he crossed to her. "I don't know how this is going to go."

"Do you want to wait?"

Taking her face between his palms, he shook his head. "No. The first time is going to be an experiment no matter when we do it. I just don't want you to be disappointed."

"I won't be," she whispered.

With a smile and a tender look, he stroked her hair, then he wound her in an embrace and pulled her close to his chest. There was comfort and familiarity in being held in Brady's arms, yet a newness, too, and excitement and a yearning to be so much more than they'd ever been to each other.

When his lips covered hers, they were hungry, devouring, arousing. His tongue played with hers...explored...promised. The kiss seemed endless, and she wanted to drown in it...drown in him.

Reaching up, she wound her arms around his neck. "Make love to me, Brady Malone."

As he undressed her and she undressed him, they were eager to be rid of their clothes, but neither of them hurried. After Brady lifted her dress over her head, he placed slow tantalizing kisses along her temple. After she unbuttoned his shirt, she slid her hands across his broad shoulders, reveled in his male scent, then kissed his chest and his scar, running her hand down to his navel. His blue eyes darkened as he settled his hands on her waist, lowered his head and teased the nipple of one breast with his tongue. She gasped from the pleasure of it, and she realized exactly what they were doing—they were enjoying the journey. The main event might or might not happen, but getting there was going to be as pleasurable as both of them could make it.

"A chair might be the best place to do this," he growled into her neck.

The workshop they'd attended advised not putting pressure on his chest.

He took her hand and lifted it to his lips. His gaze found hers as he kissed down her index finger to the hollow at her thumb. As his tongue erotically tasted her, her knees felt weak.

"Come on," he suggested roughly and led her to the armless, high-backed, velvet-covered chair at her vanity. After he sat, he drew her to him.

"Are you sure this is okay?"

"Positive," he murmured as his hands played over her buttocks and she climbed onto his lap.

When she slid forward, his forehead tilted against hers. "I feel like I've waited forever for this."

"You'll tell me if…?"

"I'll tell you." His gaze raked over her. "You're as beautiful as you were the first night I made love to you."

Brady had never fed her a line and she believed he meant the compliment. She melted around him as she slid onto him.

Their arms went around each other and they kissed in that coming-home way lovers greet each other after a separation. Brady possessively devoured her mouth and she fervently responded, kissing him back just as fiercely, stroking her hands everywhere she could reach, wanting to be as close as she possibly could be. Her heart beat rapidly as desire built.

She couldn't help but wonder and worry about what Brady was feeling. Was he okay? Was his heart ready for this?

Breaking away, he gazed into her eyes. They were both breathing hard. She saw a wildness in his expression, maybe a recklessness. It was as if he was facing his mortality again but had decided making love with her was worth whatever happened. That scared her and thrilled her, until there was such love expanding in her heart she knew she'd never be able to express it all.

She took him in deeper, rocking with him. He didn't move inside her right away. As their gazes held, Laura felt the union between them that she hadn't experienced in years. When Brady began pushing in farther, she rocked with him, climaxing first into exhilarating and bone-melting ecstasy. As Brady groaned his release, she felt his heart pounding against her breast. She prayed it was whole and healthy and would last at *least* another thirty years.

He shuddered and she held on, wanting the moment never to end.

He was so still afterward that she began to worry. But then he passed his hand down her back and kissed her cheek.

"Are you okay?" she asked.

He ran his thumb over her bottom lip. "Just a little breathless, but that's probably normal."

Wrapping his arms around her, he buried his face in her hair. After a few moments, he leaned away slightly, his jaw tensed and he said, "It took a heart attack and seeing another man's interest in you to make me realize what I could lose. I told you there wasn't a bright light when I had the heart attack, but over the past weeks, I had this gut knowledge that I hadn't been grateful enough for what I'd been given. I just didn't know what to do about it."

"Do you know now?"

"No, but I'm going to figure it out. Selling my business might be one way to do that."

"You spent years putting all your energy into your designs, growing your company."

"I can still design. Maybe I'll consult."

When the phone rang, it startled them both.

"We can let the machine get it, but it might be one of the kids," Brady murmured.

Laura nodded. "Maybe Kat and Sandra had another tiff and she wants to come home."

After Laura slid off Brady, he went to the nightstand to answer the phone.

Laura headed for the bathroom, but when she glanced at Brady, she noticed his face had gone pale. His lips were a tight line. She stood immobile, watching him.

Finally he said, "I'll be there in ten minutes. Take a couple of deep breaths and just try to hold it together. Tell them the truth if they interview you before I get there."

With a stricken expression, he set the cordless phone on its base. "It's Sean."

"Is he hurt?"

"No, not physically. But he's at the police station. Something happened at Gary's cabin and Gary…drowned. The kids were taken in for questioning. Legally, since Sean's eighteen, I don't have a right to be there, but the investigating officer said if he wanted to call a parent, one of us could sit in."

Laura's body went cold. Her head swam. Gary…fun-loving Gary…dead. Dead.

Sean needed them. He shouldn't be there alone. She started for the bathroom. "I have to get dressed."

"No. You're *not* coming with me."

The vehemence in her husband's voice immobilized her. "Brady…"

"No, Laura. It will be easier for Sean if he has only one of us to deal with. Just grab some clothes for him while I get dressed. He went into the lake after Gary capsized the canoe and—"

Brady stopped abruptly, went to Laura and wrapped his arms around her. After a few moments, he released her, hurried to the closet and grabbed a pair of jeans. But he didn't say anymore.

She wanted him to tell her everything would be all right, but he couldn't. As she ran to Sean's room, her throat tightened against emotion. She prayed they'd all have the strength to deal with whatever happened next.

Laura sat at the kitchen table, nursing a cup of tea, waiting for Brady and Sean to walk through the door from the garage.

When they did so at 3:00 a.m., they both looked wrung out. Her husband was pale, with dark circles under his eyes. His face was almost gaunt. Worry lines etched the skin around his brows and mouth. Sean's hair was disheveled, his face was starkly pale, his eyes too bright, too dark, too desolate.

She stood, went to her son and wrapped her arms around him. "I'm so sorry, Sean. I know Gary was a good friend and he meant a lot to you."

Sean was stiff in her arms, unyielding, almost rigid. He was still holding his duffel and he didn't even drop it to the floor. He just stood there, clutching it.

She didn't want to let go of him. She wanted to somehow absorb his pain and erase tonight from his life history.

Although she didn't know the full story yet, from his face she saw he was changed, that he'd never see life the same way again. When she gazed up at him, she had a feeling he was still in shock and was in too much pain to let tears come.

"I can't talk about it now, Mom. I just can't." His voice was low and hoarse and hardly his.

Brady said, "I'll fill your mother in. Go on upstairs and try to get some sleep. We'll talk in the morning."

Sean shook his head. "There's nothing to talk about."

Laura was aching to understand exactly what had happened so she could comfort her son in some way, but she didn't want to ask questions he didn't want to answer. "Is there anything I can do for you?"

Numbly Sean met her eyes and shook his head. Without another word, he left her with Brady in the kitchen and went upstairs.

"Let's go into the living room," Brady said to her.

A few minutes later, on the sofa beside Brady, she watched him prop his elbows on his knees, drop his head into his hands, rub his face, then sit up straight. "What I wouldn't give for a cup of coffee laced with caffeine."

"I can make a pot of decaf," she offered.

He caught her wrist when she would have gotten up. "No. Just let me tell you what happened and then maybe we can get some sleep before we have to make decisions in the morning."

"What kind of decisions?"

"Whether we should hire a lawyer for Sean."

Panic gripped her. "A lawyer? Why?"

"He cooperated tonight. He told the detective everything that happened at least four times. I was there for three of them. But there will be an investigation."

"Into Gary's death?"

Brady nodded. "They're not accepting Sean's word for anything—or at least, that's the impression I got. Sean is scared out of his wits and I don't blame him. He saw his friend die." Brady stopped abruptly, and Laura knew what he was envisioning—his *own* buddies dying.

She moved nearer to him, laid her hand on his jean-clad thigh and waited for him to return to her.

When he did, his pain was shut off again. "Gary was gone when the medics arrived. So they called the coroner. I think Sean went on automatic at that point."

"How did Gary drown? I mean, what was going on? Was Sean in the canoe with him?"

Brady sighed. "No, Sean was on the dock. Apparently Gary was drunk, went out in a canoe, stood up and was acting foolish. The canoe capsized. Sean dived in after him, then brought him to shore. Boyd worked on him, too."

"So there was alcohol there?"

"Yeah, in plain view. All the kids got citations for possession and consumption of alcohol by a minor. The police treated the whole area like a crime scene, shot pictures, confiscated the canoe as evidence—I guess to check for any damage. I heard one of the kids say an officer asked over and over again if Sean was in the canoe with Gary. I guess they thought it was possible he pushed him overboard."

"Oh my God! You're not serious."

"They're just trying to get to the truth. Sean's story didn't waver. I talked to Boyd for a few minutes and he told them the same thing."

"I keep thinking about Gary's parents. His father wasn't there?"

"Nope. He'd called Gary to tell him he was going to be late. I overheard two officers and there's going to be an autopsy. I asked the detective how long the investigation would last and he said it could be a week or two. I'll tell you, when we were in that interview room, I wondered if I should just get a lawyer for Sean and he should keep quiet. But he wanted to tell what happened. He didn't seem to have anything to hide."

Laura raised a question that had been troubling her. "Besides the alcohol, were there drugs?"

"I don't think they found any."

"Did you ask Sean?"

"I asked. He wouldn't say. But after the autopsy's done, the police will know from the tox screen."

Brady was being so matter-of-fact. Every once in a while his voice went gruff and Laura knew he was more affected than he was letting on. "Are you okay?"

"I'm fine."

He wasn't, but as always, he was acting strong, not letting anything show, probably for her and definitely for

Sean. "I don't know the best way to help him through this," Laura admitted.

"All we can do is be here for him."

"I want to call Gary's parents."

"Did *you* want to talk to anyone after Jason died?"

She glimpsed the knowledge in Brady's eyes, the understanding and compassion and anguish parents suffer when they lose a child. All of it came rushing back, and Laura felt tears burning her eyes, felt the tightness in her throat, remembered too much of what she'd felt so many years ago.

Finally she whispered, "No, I didn't want to talk to anyone."

Although they rarely spoke about Jason, their first son was always there, a bond and a wound between them.

When Brady wrapped an arm around her shoulders, she leaned into him. They had to hold on to each other. They had to. If they didn't, they'd lose each other…and their marriage would break into pieces. She was sure of it.

Chapter 16

"You can't stay in your room *forever!*"

Brady climbed the stairs after spending Tuesday afternoon at his office and heard Kat's frustrated pronouncement to her brother. He agreed with her, but Sean wouldn't. Brady didn't know what to do to help his son. For the past three days, Sean had sat in his room and didn't want to see or talk to anyone. Brady understood how his son felt but didn't know how to assuage his grief. They'd heard nothing more from the detective in charge of the investigation. One of Sean's teachers had called them, explaining she'd been contacted by the police. They'd interviewed her, investigating what kind of kid Sean was. She'd felt Brady and Laura should know. She'd explained to the detective that Sean, Gary and Boyd were best friends and Sean was a good kid, who had to work extra hard in school.

Brady was afraid the police were trying to pin Gary's death on Sean somehow, or were searching for anything that would lead in that direction. Maybe he was just too cynical to believe when they heard the truth, they'd know it…that when they saw the truth, they'd believe it.

Standing at her brother's door, Kat had her hands planted on her hips. She was upset. Brady knew she was worried about Sean, too.

When he and Laura had explained to her what had happened, she'd cried and hung on to them.

Brady stepped into the doorway of his son's room. Sean was lying on the bed, staring at the ceiling.

"He won't come out," Kat complained. "He won't talk to me. He won't talk to anybody. Boyd called again a little bit ago and he said to tell him he was sleeping. I know he misses Gary and all, but he just can't stay in here the rest of his life!"

"It's been three days, Kat," Brady reminded her, attempting to cut through her exaggeration.

"Can you get her to leave me alone?" Sean asked his dad with a mixture of exasperation and anger.

Brady clasped his daughter's shoulder, "Why don't you go downstairs and help Mom fix supper."

"He's going to starve himself, too," Kat maintained, troubled. Then tears filled her eyes and she murmured, "If I had told Mom he was drinking, you would have grounded him. He wouldn't have been there Friday night and Gary wouldn't have died."

Dropping his arm around Kat, Brady pulled her away from Sean's door. "You aren't to blame for what happened. Even if Sean hadn't been at the cabin, this still might have happened. Gary acted foolishly and that wasn't because Sean was there."

When she gazed at him, he saw the logic might have gotten through. "I can't believe Gary's gone."

Brady gave her a hug. "I know you can't. Neither can I." He felt Sean's need pulling at him even more than Kat's. Releasing her, he patted her shoulder. "Go downstairs. I'll try to get Sean to come down for supper."

With a last sad look at him, she headed for the stairs.

Brady went into Sean's room, which Sean usually kept in decent shape. He was organized, maybe because his mind wasn't organized. He liked to keep things in order when he could. Doing it physically seemed to help him mentally. "She's worried about you and so are we."

Sean still didn't respond, just kept staring at the ceiling.

"Your mom wants to check on you every fifteen minutes, but I told her you need some time and a little space."

Sean's eyes met his. "I just want to be left alone. Did you know there were reporters here again today?" his son demanded, as if it was Brady's fault.

"Your mom told me."

"Why won't they just leave me alone?"

The morning after Gary's death, the news vans had driven up in front of the house once more. Brady had told them there would be no comment, that Sean had nothing to say. They'd gone after him then, since he was in the open, in their sight, and asked about the newspaper article. He'd simply said no comment to that, too.

"No one was here when I got home."

Sean let out a string of curse words. Brady saw and felt all the emotion behind them. He and Laura didn't abide that kind of talk, but he didn't say anything to Sean now. Sean was like a powder keg ready to explode, either at the world or at himself.

"I realize it's the last thing you feel like doing, but would you have supper with us? Your mother isn't eating, either. Maybe if you get a few bites down, she will, too."

Sean's dark eyes weren't angry now, only resigned. "I don't want to talk about anything, and you've got to make Kat stop bugging me."

"She just wants to know you're okay."

Now Sean kept his gaze on his sneakers. "She goes to summer camp soon for two weeks, doesn't she?"

"She leaves next week. Remember last year? She came home after a few days because she was homesick."

"Yeah, I guess she's really still a baby." Sean's words weren't pejorative, just matter-of-fact.

"Don't let her hear you say that." When his son didn't comment, Brady went to the door. "I'm going to change. I'll be down in a few minutes. It would mean a lot to all of us if you'd have supper with us."

Sean didn't say he would and he didn't say he wouldn't.

Ten minutes later, Brady entered the kitchen, glad to see Sean sitting at the table. He looked as if he didn't want to be there. He wasn't making eye contact. But at least he was there.

Laura's gaze met Brady's as she set a platter of chicken in the middle of the table. "I was just telling Sean that Valerie called again this afternoon."

"She's called every day," Brady agreed, checking his son's reaction. Sean had dated the past couple of years, but nothing serious. They'd been mostly specialty dates like the homecoming dance, the Christmas party, the prom. But he'd seen the way Sean had looked at Valerie at his graduation party.

Kat fidgeted with her fork. "I've been thinking. Maybe I shouldn't go to camp."

"Why not, honey?" Laura asked.

Kat glanced at Sean. "It's not that I don't want to go. I mean, I was looking forward to it this year, and I know I won't get homesick again. It's just—" This time her eyes landed on her brother and stayed.

He looked up from his plate. "Don't stay home because of me. Nothing you do or don't do will change what's going on. Gary's dead. Nothing will make that go away. If the police decide to arrest me, there's nothing you can do about that, either."

The silence around the table was deafening. The phone's ring cut the hollowness of it.

"I'm not here," Sean mumbled.

Laura was up and out of her chair before Brady could push his back. They were both hoping the police would call and tell them Sean was in the clear.

When Laura snatched the cordless phone from its base, she went a little paler and Brady thought it might be the police.

But then she said, "Just a minute, Mr. Laslow." She held out the phone to Sean. "It's Gary's father."

Sean didn't look surprised, just resigned. He took the phone and stepped into the dining room for more privacy. His conversation with Mr. Laslow was short, and Brady couldn't tell anything from what he heard.

"Yes, sir, I understand...I'm so sorry I couldn't—Right. Goodbye."

When Sean returned into the kitchen, he slammed the phone down on its base. "You want to know what that was all about? I'll tell you. Nothing's been in the paper about funeral arrangements. I wanted to know what was going on so I called Mr. Laslow this morning. The funeral is on Thursday, but he and Gary's mom don't want any of us there. They want to keep it private. In other words, they think we all killed him."

"No, Sean," Laura protested. "This is just a hard time for them. Losing a child is—" Her voice broke.

"Yeah, well, losing a best friend isn't much better." He headed for the door leading to the garage. "I'm going out."

"Where are you going?" Laura called after him.

"Someplace. I don't know. I'll be back when you see me." The door to the garage opened and shut with a slam.

Laura started to go after him, but Brady was up out of his chair and caught her arm. "No, let him go."

"He could be in an accident."

"We can't lock him in his room and we shouldn't want to. Maybe he's going to Boyd's or Valerie's. Let him go, Laura."

He could see she was near tears, but he was right about this. Sean had to start digging into the panic and grief and pain that was building inside him. If he didn't, it would smother him. Getting away from them and the house and the familiar was a necessity. Brady remembered needing the same kind of escape.

He remembered it too well.

★ ★ ★

That night when Sean got home, he was drunk. Brady could smell it on him. He'd waited up for him, sitting in the kitchen, drinking a diet soda. He'd told Laura to go to bed. She hadn't wanted to but she'd gone. Misery and worry and something like desperation hung between them because they didn't know how to help their son. They were just living through it the best they could.

Brady held out his hand, "Give me your keys. You're not going to drink and drive."

"I'm eighteen. You don't have any right—"

"I'm your father. You're living under my roof. I realize you're upset and depressed, but you're not going to get yourself killed while you're under my watch."

"Under your watch? Since when? Seems to me you've never wanted anything to do with me."

"That's not true, Sean. I've always wanted what was best for you."

"Yeah, well, that didn't turn out so great, did it?" He turned in a huff to walk away.

Brady grabbed his elbow and swung him around. "Don't let Gary's death destroy you."

"I might not have much choice about it. I could go to jail."

"No. Everybody knows what happened that night. Everybody's telling the same story."

"Maybe the police will think it's a conspiracy. Maybe they'll think everybody's protecting me. Don't you watch TV? Anything can happen."

"Sean, your mother and I love you. We believe in you."

"A lot of good that's doing me when Gary's dead."

Brady realized that absolutely nothing he said would get through to his son—not tonight, anyway. He released Sean's arm. "If I have to put you in rehab myself so you'll deal with this, I'll do it."

"You put me in rehab and I'll just start drinking again when I'm out. Don't waste your money, Dad." He tossed his car keys at Brady. "Keep the damn car. Boyd will pick me up tomorrow night."

Brady watched Sean walk away once again, feeling powerless to help him. Maybe once the investigation was completed, Sean would realize he had his whole life ahead of him. Maybe then he'd listen to what they had to say.

Going through the motions. That was all she was doing. Laura felt on the edge of tears most of the time, but she wouldn't let them fall. She didn't want either Brady or Sean to see her crying. Tears wouldn't help what was happening to them, not to each of them individually or all of them as a family. It was almost a relief Kat wasn't at home.

Two weeks had passed since Gary had died. Two weeks of watching over Sean whenever she could to make sure he didn't do something stupid or desperate. Two weeks of feeling the tension and distance grow between her and Brady again because neither of them knew how to help their son. Two weeks since she and Brady had spent a wonderful night together, reconnecting, rediscovering each other, only to have it blown to bits with Sean's phone call. Brady had held her since that night and she'd held on to him. But they hadn't made love again. They couldn't escape into that bliss when their lives were in such turmoil. Wasn't that the reason? They were just too worried about their son.

Whenever Sean went out with Boyd, she knew he was drinking. She was ready to drag him to a counselor. Yet as with Brady so long ago, counseling wouldn't help unless Sean was ready for it. Rehab wouldn't help unless he admitted he had a problem and wanted to do something about it.

The past few days, they'd all been like captains of ships sailing on the same ocean but too isolated, too involved in steering their own vessels to even wave at each other, let alone use their radios to communicate.

As Laura removed a casserole from the oven, she knew this would be another silent meal where all of them ate little, pushed food around their plates and went their separate ways again. Brady had come home from work about an hour ago. He was sitting in front of the TV, watching the news, yet he really wasn't watching. He was lost in his thoughts. Sean was upstairs in his bedroom, earbuds from the iPod in his ears blocking the outside world.

As she set the casserole on the hot plate on the table, the telephone rang. She picked it up, expecting to hear Pat's voice. Brady's sister had been calling every other day to check on Sean.

"Hello?"

Instead of Pat's acerbic cheeriness, a male voice asked, "Is this the Malone residence?"

"Yes, this is Laura Malone."

"Mrs. Malone, I'm calling for Sean. It's Detective Sergeant Deerdorf."

She recognized the name. Brady had told her he was the one in charge. Her heart began beating so fast she could hardly get her words out. "You've come to a decision?"

"I need to talk to Sean, Mrs. Malone."

Sean was eighteen, an adult in the eyes of the law. "I'll get him."

Instead of using the intercom to alert Sean to the call, she ran to the stairs and called to Brady. "It's Detective Deerdorf. He wants to talk to Sean." Then she ran up to the second floor, knocked on Sean's door and opened it. "Detective Deerdorf wants to speak to you."

As soon as her words sank in, Sean looked terrified, like a small child who was lost in a strange place and didn't know which way to turn. Almost in slow motion, he picked up the phone on his nightstand and put it to his ear. "Hello?"

It was only a few moments until Brady came into the room. He murmured to Laura, "It's a good sign he's calling instead of showing up at the door."

After Sean listened for a length of time, he nodded. "I understand. Thank you for calling." With sweat beading on his forehead, Sean swung his legs over the side of the bed and just sat there for a minute.

"Tell us," Brady prompted.

"Gary's death was ruled an accident. The investigation is closed."

"Oh, Sean." Laura went to him and hugged him. She could feel him trembling.

When Brady approached them, she felt Sean tense.

"It's over. You can put this behind you. I know you'll never forget what happened, but you can go to college and—"

Sean tore himself from her arms and stood. "Go to college? Jesus, Dad, you're acting as if this was an auto accident or something, a fender bender that can be repaired. Sure, Gary's death was ruled accidental, but it wasn't an accident. I mean, I could have prevented it. The autopsy showed high levels of THC in his blood. I could have taken the joints from him."

"If he was smoking it that night, it probably wasn't the first time that day," Brady reasoned.

"It wasn't just the pot. He didn't stop drinking from the moment he got there. I could have dumped all of it."

"Wouldn't he have sent one of you for more?" Brady was still playing devil's advocate and Sean didn't like it.

"You don't get it. I never should have left him alone. I shouldn't have let him go out on that damn canoe. I should have swum harder, gotten to him sooner, did CPR better."

Laura felt so much emotion rising inside her she was shaking. She felt gut-wrenching anguish for this boy who'd always been so close to her heart. She wanted to help him so badly. "His death was ruled an accident. That's what it was, Sean, a terrible, terrible accident. You were *not* to blame."

"Then why do I feel I was? Why do I feel I killed my best friend?"

When she reached out to touch him, Sean yanked away. "Just leave me alone, both of you. Get out of here. Just leave me alone."

When Brady stepped closer to Sean, their son almost jumped away.

"Don't you get it?" he screamed at them. "I just want to be left alone. Or should I call Boyd?"

"If you think another night of drinking will help this, you're wrong," Brady said quietly.

"You don't know," Sean yelled at him, tears falling down his cheeks. "You don't know."

Laura saw her son disintegrating before her eyes, but he wouldn't let her near. He wouldn't let her talk to him. He wouldn't let her try to make anything better. That was because he knew she couldn't. *She* knew she couldn't.

But she still had to try. "I'll leave you alone for now, but I'll be back. You're *not* alone, Sean, and I won't let you think you are." Then she left the room and went to her bedroom.

She heard Brady's voice, heard him still attempting to reason with Sean. But he obviously didn't get anywhere. He closed the door to Sean's room and came into theirs.

She couldn't keep the past two weeks of tension and grief and worry from pouring out. "I don't know what to do for him. What can we *do* for him?" Tears slid down her cheeks now and she didn't even try to hold them back.

"We have to give him some time."

"Time? Time didn't help *you*."

"Of course it did."

"No, it didn't. It's all still inside you. You've never let it out. You stopped counseling when you shouldn't have. You never went back. Don't you realize our marriage would have been so much different if you had?"

Brady's face was absolutely immobile. His blue eyes had gone dark with surprise. His shoulders were straight, his arms taut at his sides. "How much different do you think our marriage would have been?" His question was on the edge of terse.

"It would have been *very* different if you had accepted more help. You said you resented my forgiveness because it was too big a gift, a gift you couldn't accept. Maybe if you had gone to more counseling sessions, you could have accepted it. Maybe there wouldn't have been any resentment, just joy and relief. Maybe if after Jason died, if you'd come with me to that parents' group, you could have gotten over his death the way I did. Instead you let that sadness simmer inside you, so that when we adopted Sean, you couldn't love him."

"I do love Sean."

"Maybe *now*. But you didn't when we brought him home. After we adopted him, I thought maybe we'd made the worst mistake possible. I was so afraid you'd never feel for him…you'd never accept him for your son."

"But I did accept him for my son."

"When he was three or four or five? When you figured out he needed two parents to love him? When you realized we could help him overcome his learning disability and you could play a part in that?"

"Talk about resentment," Brady muttered. "Apparently yours has been building up, too."

She should stop. If she kept on letting out what had been buried for much too long, she'd tear them apart. But right now she needed complete honesty between them, no matter what it did, who it hurt or what it destroyed.

"Do you want to know what I resent most of all? I resent that you've always kept part of yourself hidden…that you've never given it to me or Sean or even to Kat. I thought that after your heart attack everything would change. The other night, it did for a few hours. We almost had back—"

A sob stopped her, but she swallowed it. "I have to

wonder if that night wasn't all about jealousy. You were jealous because Dr. Gregano might be interested in me. Your ego couldn't take it and you had to do something about it. It was about sex and male pride, not about us and our marriage and the bond I felt with you from the moment we met."

The silence that engulfed the room was claustrophobic in its intensity. She couldn't believe she'd put it all into words.

Brady looked shell-shocked from everything she'd said…how much she'd held back for far too long. Emotion darkened in his eyes, but he wasn't letting any of it loose. If only he would.

He raked his hand through his hair and just studied her for a few moments. "If holding you and making love to you again would make either of us feel better, I'd do it. But right now, I don't think you want me anywhere near you, and we all need a breather. I'm going for a walk."

He didn't move for a moment…as if he wanted her to tell him not to go, as if he wanted her to say, *Yes, hold me, make love to me, make it all better.* But she couldn't. She needed more than that and she couldn't even tell him what it was.

When he left the bedroom and closed the door, she sank onto the love seat, dropped her head into her hands, and cried.

On the patio at 3:00 a.m. Brady sat in a lawn chair, a flashlight beside his foot, and stared unseeingly into the black night. His shirt was damp from the sweat he'd worked up on his walk through the woods. The trail was groomed, the path unmistakable with the flashlight's beam. For some reason he'd needed to cut through the tress and brush…he'd needed to feel surrounded by night more primitively than he would have been on the street with gas postlamps lighting his way.

Propping his elbows on his knees, he dropped his head into his hands. He was going to lose Laura *and* Sean if he didn't do something.

Apparently for years Laura had bottled up her feelings. They'd eaten at her. Although she'd remained loyal and loving, the resentment had eroded the bond between them that had once been so durable.

He'd always attempted to look forward, not back. He'd always tried to be strong so she could lean on him. Yet somehow in that strength, there had been so much weakness. The breakdown of his family had been caused by the walls he'd erected to keep his pain and guilt contained.

The pain and guilt from his Nam memories had lain moldy, corruptive and decaying in the pit of his soul. They'd tainted everything he did, said and was, though he'd tried to deny it. When Jason died, his grief had added another layer to the quagmire.

That quagmire had kept him from loving Sean as he should. It had kept him from giving Laura what she needed most—a depth of love that could only find roots in revelation and vulnerability.

Through the years, he'd known that if he spoke again of his guilt and remorse after their session with John, he would be too vulnerable. The idea of going to the parents' group with Laura after Jason died had been anathema—because he'd known sharing *his* grief would lead him back to Nam. As he'd gotten older, he'd learned loss compounded loss and guilt compounded guilt.

As he lifted his head and looked up at the stars, he longed to find direction again. He longed to be connected—*really* connected—to Laura, to Sean and Kat, to his sister and brothers and friends…to himself.

One question echoed in his heart. *What do I have to do?*

Chapter 17

Before dawn the next morning, Brady sat on Laura's side of the bed, by her hip, and gently touched her shoulder.

She awakened instantly and he could tell she'd been crying. Her eyes were puffy, her cheeks splotchy. But she was beautiful, outside and in. She was his Laura. He *hoped* she was still his.

She sat up quickly. "What's wrong?"

"Pretty much everything, the way *I* see it. And that's what I want to remedy."

He must look as wrung out as he felt because she asked, "Did you get any sleep last night?"

"No. I walked, and thought, and sat on the patio and regretted everything I haven't done that I should have done."

Last night, through hours of soul-searching, he'd realized what he had to do—not only to keep Laura, not only to help Sean, but to make them a *real* family. He had to own what had happened in the past and what he'd done. He had to take it by the throat, shake it until he understood it and then tell those he loved what it meant. He had to puke it out like a poison so he could swallow their love and finally let it heal him.

In healing himself, maybe he could heal Sean and show him he *did* understand. Brady's memories, his pride, his guilt didn't matter anymore. His son mattered. His marriage mattered.

"I want to take Sean to D.C. to the Wall and I'd like you to come along. Will you? It's five-thirty. I'd like to be on the road by six and there by eight. Even this time of year it should be pretty quiet early in the morning."

Actually, every time he'd been to the Wall it had been quiet, like a church. And rightly so. He'd never been there with Laura or with anyone else. He'd always gone alone.

"I can be ready in fifteen minutes," she assured him. "I'll make a pot of coffee and put it in a thermos."

Right now Brady didn't know how to act with Laura. He didn't know how much resentment she might still be harboring. He didn't know if her love for him had withered away due to neglect...or due to his inability to be free from the past.

"Brady, about what I said last night—"

"Did you say anything you didn't feel?"

When she shook her head, her eyes became shiny with the turmoil and upheaval they were both going through.

"Then you don't have anything to apologize for. I do. I *have* kept everyone I love at a distance. I don't know if this pilgrimage will do any good for me *or* Sean, but I've got to start somewhere. I'm long past due. With him. And with you. I'm sorry for shutting you out. I'm sorry for not doing something to fix this a long time ago. I do love you, Laura. I always have and I always will. Will you give me a chance to start over? To make our marriage what it should be? Or is it too late?"

His heart pounded as he waited for her answer.

She slid closer to him. "It's not too late. I love you, too, Brady Malone. For always."

Her voice was full of emotion and her lower lip quivered. Leaning toward her, he took her chin into his palm. His kiss was long and soul-felt as he tried to express everything he couldn't put into words.

Finally when he broke the kiss, he saw love in her eyes—a love so much deeper and wider and higher than the love he'd found on the courthouse steps.

After he kissed her again, he stood. "I have to do this before *we* can be right together. I have to wake Sean."

She nodded and he knew she understood. He wiped a tear from the corner of her eye, and then he went to his son.

When he entered Sean's room, Brady realized Sean hadn't slept, either. He was sitting on the floor, the baseball scrapbook he kept, open on his legs. There was a newspaper clipping with a picture of his team. Brady realized his son's gaze was focused on Gary's face.

"Get dressed," Brady said gruffly. "We're going to take a drive."

"Are you going to lock me up in a detox unit? There's no point. I'm sober."

Brady could tell that he was. Sean's eyes were clear, full of defiance.

"No. We're going to D.C. There's something I want to show you."

Sean looked surprised, but then he frowned. "Now?"

"Do you have something better to do?"

Sean shrugged. "I guess not. Where are we going in D.C.?"

"You'll see when we get there. Be downstairs in fifteen minutes if you want to grab something to eat. We're leaving at six." Without giving Sean an opportunity to argue or to ask more questions, Brady left his room.

The drive to D.C. was quiet. Sean sat in the back, curled up, dozing.

Every once in a while Laura glanced at him, then at Brady. He had no way to know what she was thinking until she placed her hand on his thigh. The message was clear—whatever happened, she was there for him and for their son.

As they neared Washington and he took the Connecticut Avenue exit, his palms became a little sweaty. More than a little sweaty.

Checking in the rearview mirror, he saw that Sean was awake now. Alert. His eyes questioning as they met Brady's.

This early on a Saturday morning Brady found a parking spot on Twenty-second Street. Sean followed a few paces behind as they crossed Constitution Avenue. When they started down a path to the Mall, Sean finally spoke. "We're going to visit the Washington Monument?"

"No. We're going to the Vietnam memorial."

"Why?"

"Because I have something to show you. Something to tell you."

The path was tree-lined as they approached the chevron-shaped wall that sloped down both sides from its vertex, fitting into its surroundings with perfect harmony. The names began on the fifth of the smallest panels.

No one else was around. Lots of tourists hadn't arrived yet. There were wreaths, a bouquet of mums with a purple ribbon, a single red rose. Brady led as Laura, then Sean, followed in single file on the blocks of granite down the middle, not veering off on the tan cobblestones on either side of the path. Brady didn't have to consult one of the directories that listed all the names of the men and women killed…or missing in action. He didn't have to search for Mike's name or the panel or line numbers, because he'd never forgotten where it was.

The black granite wall was a work of art in many ways, not just in its symmetry and design but in the mirrored aspect of the black granite itself. As they stopped at a panel on the West Wall, the three of them were reflected behind the names. It was an odd feeling. A personal feeling. The reflection always pulled him right in…pulled him over those cobblestones toward the wall.

Laura's reflection became even clearer behind him. She stepped forward, put a hand on his shoulder and said, "I'll wait up by the Soldiers' Memorial."

There were benches up there. He nodded and let her go, knowing this was something he had to do with Sean. Knowing she couldn't help. Knowing he was at the end of the line if he couldn't get through to his son. Yet the tender squeeze of Laura's hand conveyed that she was with him in spirit.

"Why are we here?" Sean demanded, his voice low.

This memorial did that. In the midst of the hustle and bustle of the city it was an oasis, where voices lowered, where men and women grieved, where everyone remembered.

Brady dropped to one knee, ran his thumb over Michael Wolf's name and said to Sean, "Come here."

Sean hunkered down.

Brady pulled his wallet from his back pocket and slid out a thirty-eight-year-old Polaroid photograph that had peeled on one corner. He handed it to Sean. It was a picture of him and Mike outside their quarters.

"Mike was from Lancaster. We ended up in the same squad together. We talked about home a lot…how we'd grown up. He was engaged to be married when he got home. He knew I wished I had married your mom before I'd left. We talked about the kinds of lives we wanted to lead, the number of kids we'd like to have, the houses we wanted to buy. To keep us going through the tough days, we made plans for after we got back. After all, we didn't live that far apart. We swore we'd go to an Orioles game together. Double-date, so our girls could get to know each other. We had so many plans. We even shared letters from home. Each of those letters was like gold. They lifted our spirits, reminded us where we'd come from, where we'd find safety again. At least, that's what we thought."

He paused, then asked, "Do you know how many names are here, Sean? Do you know how many died over there?"

His son shook his head.

"Fifty-eight thousand, two hundred forty-five. The names of men and women are inscribed in the order of when they died or when they went missing. Fifty-eight thousand. If there's a diamond beside the name, death was confirmed. If there's a cross, they were either missing or prisoners at the end of the war."

Sean touched the diamond beside Michael Wolf's name.

Brady stared at his reflection and his son's shadowing the black granite. "I saw him get killed, Sean. I saw him get blown apart by a mortar round. So believe me when I tell you I understand what you feel about Gary and how he died."

When Sean lowered his gaze to the photo, tears began falling down his cheeks. The breeze swept his hair back, but he was unmindful of it as the sun glittered on the streaks down his face.

Brady stood again and laid his palm over lines of names. "There's another name on this wall of a friend I grew up with. Tom is missing in action." Taking in a deep breath, he turned to his son. "I want to tell you what happened over there, what that article in the paper was all about."

Sean stood, too, swiped his tears away with his wrist, but still held on to the picture of his dad and Mike. "You don't have to—"

"Yes, I do. I'm not going to have another heart attack, Sean. I know that's why you've been afraid to bring it up."

Sean looked down at his sneakers. "I guess I decided it wasn't any of my business."

"But I've come to realize it *is* your business. What happened over there has affected everything I've done, said and thought since I got back. Your mother's never talked about it, but we almost didn't get married."

Sean's gaze met his. "Why?"

"Because we'd been separated for two years and I'd seen

things I never thought I could tell her about. I had nightmares and flashbacks and I was afraid I'd hurt her if she woke me up suddenly. I hadn't left the war in Vietnam. I'd brought it home with me. She put up with me for almost two years and then gave me an ultimatum—either get help or live a life separate from her."

Sean's mouth opened a little in surprise. "You got help?"

"I thought I did. I went to seven sessions of counseling and I saw my guilt was eating at me, making me bitter, making me push your mother away. On the advice of the counselor, she came to an appointment with me and I told her everything that had happened. I was afraid she'd walk away. But she didn't. She told me she still loved me and wanted to make a life with me. That was the greatest gift I ever received. But I didn't always know how to accept it. Sometimes it just seemed too big and your mom seemed too good, too special. And I didn't feel I deserved her."

"Why?"

"Because of what I did." He hurried on. "I haven't always been the father I should be to you. I think I've always been afraid to let you get too close because you'd see I wasn't the man you thought I was. You wouldn't respect me. You definitely wouldn't look up to me."

"That's crazy, Dad. You've always done everything right."

"No, I haven't. I made a good living for us. But not being able to be close to you is my biggest failure. And it's *my* fault, not yours. After Jason died, I felt God took him from us as a punishment. When we adopted you, I was afraid to love you. I was afraid God would punish me again and take *you*."

Realizing thoughts were clicking through his son's

head, Brady wanted to know what they were. "Ask me whatever questions you have, Sean. I promise I'll give you the truth."

"Was that article right? Did you kill women and children?"

"Yes, I did. I was trained to be a soldier…to react first and think later. That never quite meshed with me, but I never understood just how well I'd learned it until that day—"

There was no easy way to say what he had to say. "We'd heard that the Viet Cong didn't have a uniform, that they used the local peasants and coerced them to fight the battles. During training we were told older men and little kids were just as dangerous as recognizable VC."

He stopped, dragged in a deep breath, then went on. "That day we learned the Viet Cong were seen moving cases of mortar rounds near a house in a hamlet. We were supposed to check it out. As we moved closer, our point man tripped a booby-trapped grenade. He went down and VC opened fire. I was leading the second squad. We maneuvered into a flanking position and rolled up the ambush."

As always when the memory flooded back, his adrenaline pumped and he was there all over again. Except this time he was aware of Sean and intended to let it all spill out for both their sakes.

Sean was staring at him…listening as he'd never listened.

Brady could feel the sweat trickling down his neck now, the cold clamminess invading his limbs. His words low and strained, he continued. "A VC broke for the nearest hooch. Carl and I fired as he turned the corner. Knowing he was armed, we approached cautiously. There was movement at the edge of the jungle. I opened fire. When we swept the area after the battle, we found—" He stopped. Complete silence seemed to almost smother them until he said, "I'd killed two women and two children—they looked to be ten or twelve. Both women had grenades at their waists."

His voice went even lower. "There was blood everywhere. And the smell… I just stood there in horror and couldn't look away. I felt such intense guilt I was sick."

He braced his hand against the Wall for support but kept his eyes on his son. "This was war. We'd witnessed buddies blown apart. We'd been taught how to respond. But all I could see were the two women and two kids. Women and kids. And I'd killed them. It was as if the world turned upside down that day."

"If you hadn't fired, you might have died! You probably would have."

"That's logical, Sean. That's reasonable. But I was only aware of my M16…of the dead bodies. And I was filled with the knowledge that I was capable of killing without much provocation."

"That's not true. You were fighting in a war."

"Yeah. I was. But if they hadn't had grenades on their belts, they still would have been dead. What if they'd merely been trying to seek cover? What if…what if…what if?"

He grasped Sean's shoulders. "That's what you're doing to yourself. What if you'd taken Gary's pot from him? What if you'd dumped out all the beer? What if you'd hog-tied him to a chair so he couldn't get in that canoe? What if he hadn't stood up? What if you'd gone with him? What if you'd *both* drowned?"

Brady shook his son a little. "Gary's actions were *Gary's*. You've got to see that. He smoked. He drank. He went out in that canoe without a life vest. You dived into water that could have given you hypothermia. You pulled him to shore. You did CPR. You prayed he wasn't dead. But he was, Sean. He was gone. And there was nothing you could have done about it."

Tears were cutting paths down both their faces. Sean's eyes were so full of anguish and pain and guilt.

Brady shook him slightly again. "Listen to me, Sean. Because of my guilt, I almost lost your mother. Because of my guilt, I kept from getting as close to her as I might have. I kept from getting close to *you*. Sure, there was a lot more to it. When Jason died, I felt responsible for that. It was an unexplained death, SIDS or not. What if Agent Orange put a defect in my sperm? What if *that* was the reason he died? Don't you see, Sean? I've always known how to accept blame and guilt, never known how to accept love and forgiveness. You have to forgive Gary—and yourself. You have to understand that life is short and all we can do is live it the best we can, with all of our heart involved in the process. I think I've only lived with half a heart. I realized that when I almost died."

Gazing into Sean's eyes, Brady felt an overwhelming surge of pure love for his son. Willing Sean to feel it, he insisted, "I don't want you to have to almost die to realize that you're important to us and you're *worth* loving. You can grieve over Gary, but don't you dare die with him. I love you. You *are* my son. And I'm going to be here for you, whether you want me here or not."

Then he took Sean into his arms, held him tight and let his tears fall on his son's hair.

Epilogue

"How do you think it went?" Laura asked Brady as they stood at the front door watching Bob Westcott back out of the driveway.

The August rain had stopped now, though it had pattered hard on the front windows as she'd sat with Brady and he'd talked with the reporter. For over an hour and a half he'd answered questions and related what had happened to him. He'd been honest about it all.

"I don't know. We'll see when the article's in print."

"You gave him everything, Brady. Absolutely everything. He'll honor it with a true representation of what you said. He's that kind of man."

"He was there. He understands."

Brady turned away from the front yard and nudged her around to face him. "But I didn't give him everything. I told him what happened to me. I told him how it affected us...and my family. But I *have* everything, Laura. I finally understand that."

Dressed in a light blue polo shirt and navy slacks, Brady was handsome, confident and more at peace than he'd ever been. She felt that her forever and Brady's had finally begun. That day at the Vietnam memorial, as she'd stood holding on to the stand where the directory of names was encased, she'd watched Brady and Sean truly become father and son. She hadn't heard what they'd said to each other, but she'd seen Brady drop onto one knee and run his thumb over Mike's name. She'd watched Sean hunker down beside him.

She'd been too far away to read their expressions as they'd exchanged words, as they'd risen, as Brady had shaken Sean's shoulders. Her heart had ached for both Brady and Sean because she'd known they were in pain. Yet she'd realized that at last they were getting to know each other. When they'd embraced, she hadn't been able to stay separate from them. She'd run toward them and Brady had drawn her into their circle.

Since that day Brady's nightmares had faded. He laughed more. He talked to her. And when they made love, there weren't any barriers between them. They reached for each other often and expressed physically what they felt in their hearts. Brady had talked to Kat, too, and let her ask all her questions. He kept himself available to Sean, and although their son still withdrew at times, was grieving and would be for a while, he'd talked more to Brady about Gary. Brady had finally forgiven himself and was an example to Sean that he needed to do the same. They'd even gone to church as a family again. Tomorrow their son would leave for college in Scranton, and after a few days or a week, Kat would miss him, though she'd never admit it.

Thunder grumbled outside the screen door, but it was farther away now. Laura gazed up into Brady's eyes, loving him so much her throat almost closed.

"What's wrong?" he asked.

"Nothing. I'm just so proud of you…and what you did today."

"It was a long time coming. I don't know how I'll feel when I see the interview in print, but I want to close the book. We have a lot of living ahead of us, and I'm ready for it."

"Are you going in to work this afternoon?" He was tying up loose ends this week and negotiating a deal for the sale of his company.

"Nope. I have other plans for this afternoon."

She caught the gleam in his eye and asked coyly. "Like…"

"Like…convincing you to spend the next hour or so in bed with me. And maybe after that we can drop in at the travel agency and make plans for our second honeymoon."

So much love for Brady filled Laura that her throat became thick and her eyes misty. She wrapped her arms around his neck, went up on tiptoe and kissed him. He made the most of the kiss, as she did, until they were hot, bothered, aroused and more than ready for an interlude in bed.

Brady broke away first, reached into his pocket and brought out a small gold box tied with a silver ribbon. "For you," he said, handing it to her.

"What's this?"

"Just something you might like. We're starting a new phase in our lives. I wanted to commemorate it somehow."

With shaky fingers she untied the bow and set it on the credenza. Then she lifted the lid. "Oh, Brady." It was a charm—three circles, one on top of the other, each mounted with a diamond.

Brady's voice was husky when he told her, "You know what they say. Diamonds are forever. It's a forever charm. A circle for yesterday. A circle for today. And a circle for tomorrow."

Wrapping her into his arms again and pulling her close, he said, "We've loved each other through a lot of yesterdays. We love each other today. I pledge my love to you for all our tomorrows."

Just then, with Brady's promise, the sun broke free of the clouds and shone brightly through the screen door. "It only seems fitting." He bent his head to kiss her again. Right before his lips found hers, he murmured, "'Let the sunshine in.'"

★ ★ ★ ★ ★

Welcome to cowboy country...

Turn the page for a sneak preview of
TEXAS BABY
by Kathleen O'Brien
An exciting new title from
Harlequin Superromance
for everyone who loves stories about the West.

CHAPTER ONE

CHASE TRANSFERRED his gaze to the road and identified a foreign spot on the horizon. A car. Almost half a mile away, where the straight, tree-lined drive met the public road. He could tell it was coming too fast, but judging the speed of a vehicle moving straight toward you was tricky.

It wasn't until it was about two hundred yards away that he realized the driver must be drunk...or crazy. Or both.

The guy was going maybe sixty. On a private drive, out here in ranch country, where kids or horses or tractors or stupid chickens might come darting out any minute, that was criminal. Chase straightened from his comfortable slouch and waved his hands.

"Slow down, you fool," he called out. He took the porch steps quickly and began walking fast down the driveway.

The car veered oddly, from one lane to another, then

up onto the slight rise of the thick green spring grass. It just barely missed the fence.

"Slow down, damn it!"

He couldn't see the driver, and he didn't recognize this automobile. It was small and old, and couldn't have cost much even when it was new. It was probably white, but now it needed either a wash or a new paint job or both.

"Damn it, what's wrong with you?"

At the last minute, he had to jump away, because the idiot behind the wheel clearly wasn't going to turn to avoid a collision. He couldn't believe it. The car kept coming, finally slowing a little, but it was too late.

Still going about thirty miles an hour, it slammed into the large, white-brick pillar that marked the front boundaries of the house. The pillar wasn't going to give an inch, so the car had to. The front end folded up like a paper fan.

It seemed to take forever for the car to settle, as if the trauma happened in slow motion, reverberating from the front to the back of the car in ripples of destruction. The front windshield suddenly seemed to ice over with lethal bits of glassy frost. Then the side windows exploded.

The front driver's door wrenched open, as if the car wanted to expel its contents. Metal buckled hideously. Small pieces, like hubcaps and mirrors, skipped and ricocheted insanely across the oyster-shell driveway.

Finally, everything was still. Into the silence, a plume of steam shot up like a geyser, smelling of rust and heat. Its snake-like hiss almost smothered the low, agonized moan of the driver.

Chase's anger had disappeared. He didn't feel anything but a dull sense of disbelief. Things like this didn't happen in real life. Not in his life. Maybe the sun had actually put him to sleep....

But he was already kneeling beside the car. The driver was a woman. The frosty glass-ice of the windshield was dotted with small flecks of blood. She must have hit it with her head, because just below her hairline a red liquid was seeping out. He touched it. He tried to wipe it away before it reached her eyebrow, though, of course that made no sense at all. Her eyes were shut.

Was she conscious? Did he dare move her? Her dress was covered in glass, and the metal of the car was sticking out lethally in all the wrong places.

Then he remembered, with an intense relief, that every good medical man in the county was here, just behind the house, drinking his champagne. He found his phone and paged Trent.

The woman moaned again.

Alive, then. Thank God for that.

He saw Trent coming toward him, starting out at a lope, but quickly switching to a full run.

"Get Dr. Marchant," Chase called. "Don't bother with 911."

Trent didn't take long to assess the situation. A fraction of a second, and he began pulling out his cell phone and running toward the house.

The yelling seemed to have roused the woman. She opened her eyes. They were blue and clouded with pain and confusion.

"Chase," she said.

His breath stalled. His head pulled back. "What?"

Her only answer was another moan, and he wondered

if he had imagined the word. He reached around her and put his arm behind her shoulders. She was tiny. Probably petite by nature, but surely way too thin. He could feel her shoulder blades pushing against her skin, as fragile as the wishbone in a turkey.

She seemed to have passed out, so he put his other arm under her knees and lifted her out. He tried to avoid the jagged metal, but her skirt caught on a piece and the tearing sound seemed to wake her again.

"No," she said. "Please."

"I'm just trying to help," he said. "It's going to be all right."

She seemed profoundly distressed. She wriggled in his arms, and she was so weak, like a broken bird. It made him feel too big and brutish. And intrusive. As if touching her this way, his bare hands against the warm skin behind her knees, were somehow a transgression.

He wished he could be more delicate. But he smelled gasoline, and he knew it wasn't safe to leave her here.

Finally he heard the sound of voices, as guests began to run around the side of the house, alerted by Trent. Dr. Marchant was at the front, racing toward them as if he were forty instead of seventy. Susannah was right behind him, her green dress floating around her trim legs.

"Please," the woman in his arms murmured again. She looked at him, the expression in her blue eyes lost and bewildered. He wondered if she might be on drugs. Hitting her head on the windshield might account for this unfocused, glazed look, but it couldn't explain the crazy driving.

"Please, put me down. Susannah... The wedding..."

Chase's arms tightened instinctively, and he froze in his

tracks. She whimpered, and he realized he might be hurting her. "Say that again?"

"The wedding. I have to stop it."

* * * * *

Be sure to look for TEXAS BABY,
available September 11, 2007,
as well as other fantastic Superromance titles
available in September.